THE MYSTERIOUS AND AMAZING BLUE BILLINGS

A BLACK & BLUE NOVEL

LILY MORTON

Warning

This book contains material that is intended for a mature, adult audience. It contains graphic language, explicit sexual content and adult situations.

For my dad who gave me my love of reading.
You taught me how to be funny and how to tell a story.
I love you

AUTHOR NOTE

Chapter Eleven features a few scenes that deal with grief and bereavement. If that is going to upset you, it's possible to skip that chapter and not miss a major plot development.

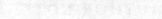

"'Tis the witching hour of night,
Orbed is the moon and bright,
And the stars they glisten, glisten,
Seeming with bright eyes to listen —
For what listen they?"
John Keats

CHAPTER 1

*L*evi

The massive golden expanse of the York Minster fills my eyesight as I drive up to it, keeping a wary eye out for the pedestrians around here who appear to be part lemming with their insistence on blithely sauntering out in front of cars.

"Take the next right," Brian Blessed growls. Well, not the real Brian Blessed. That would be epic. Unfortunately, this is the satnav version, and he's quirky.

"I can't take the next right," I mutter. "Not unless I fancy ploughing through a fucking house."

"Turn round at the next available opportunity," he booms, and I'm sure I'm not imagining the note of condemnation in his voice, but my attention is diverted when I spot the street sign I've been looking for.

"Yes," I say, punching the air. "Take that, Brian Blessed."

"You've taken the wrong turn, you steaming pillock," he growls again, and I stick my middle finger up at the dash. Then I think better of it and pat the dashboard.

"Sorry, Brian," I mutter before clicking on the indicator and taking the next left. The wheels of the Ford Focus bump over the cobbled lane, and I slow down, my eyes everywhere. I spot the man waiting on the narrow pavement immediately. He's wearing a three-piece suit and an irritated expression while checking his watch, so it's a safe bet that this is the person I'm meeting.

I pull up next to him and lower the window. "Mr Fenton?" I ask, and he nods, relief spreading over his face. "I'm so sorry I'm late. There was an accident on the motorway, and I got lost once I got into York."

"It's not a problem," he says in a smooth, posh voice. "There's a row of garages at the end of the cul-de-sac. The second one from the right is yours, so you can park in front of it for now."

I raise my fingers in a low salute and do as he suggests. The garages are neat and orderly, all of them freshly painted with shiny black doors. All of them except one. Mine. That's got peeling paint and looks like a poor relation at a wedding.

I turn off the engine and get out of the car, stretching up to my full height with a grateful sigh. The journey had been hellish with massive tailbacks. My mood hadn't been any better, being filled with a sense of excitement mixed with a very strong melancholy at what I was leaving behind.

I shake the thoughts clear of my head and turn back to the car before coming to a stop at the sight before me. The street is narrow and cobbled and the houses are, by and large, Georgian from the looks of them. But what strikes me most is the towering majesty of the Minster which is literally at the end of my street. I can see the huge arched windows and the massive entrance. If I squint, I can even see the intricately carved gargoyles.

It's been a cold April with no sign of any sunshine and the wind hits me now, cold and biting. I shiver and reach into the car to grab my jacket before moving towards the man waiting for me. He's examining the house in a slightly nervous fashion. Wondering if I've made him late for an appointment, I pick up my pace.

"Sorry," I say again as I get close. "Have you got the keys? I can do this myself."

He buttons his coat up and shakes his head. "Shall we get this done?" he says somewhat grimly.

I laugh. "Don't ever officiate at weddings."

He flushes. "Sorry," he mutters. "It's just that it's getting dark, and I can't be doing this then."

It sounds very much as if he's got a curfew, but since he's about sixty, I'd hope that isn't the case. "Okay," I say mildly. "Thank you for waiting. Have you got the key?"

He digs in the pocket of his overcoat and pulls out a set of keys on a blue plastic key fob. "I have to warn you that the house is in some disrepair. It's been empty for a long while."

"You said in your letter." I follow him to the house and look up at it with a sense of muted excitement. It's three storeys tall in a warm brick with the traditional Georgian barred windows giving it a neat and symmetrical appearance. "I'm afraid the letter wasn't very clear on the chain of events."

He pauses on the step. "It's been empty for rather a long while. The man who had it a few years ago did a fair amount of work to the house, particularly in the cellar as he was thinking of renting that out as a self-contained flat. The lady who bought it after him never ended up living here at all. She took against it for some reason, but she died before she could sell it. Her will was a bit of a mess, and so we set agents to finding any kin. Your mother was a second cousin of hers." I wince, and his gaze sharpens as he obviously goes through his memory banks. "Ah," he says suddenly, realisation dawning. "Can I just say how sorry I am for your loss?"

"Thank you," I say, my throat closing and tightening. Willing him to drop the subject, I gesture at the door. "Shall we?"

He jerks as if startled and darts another look at the house before visibly steeling himself and inserting the key into the lock. The click as it opens is almost anti-climactic, and I follow him in. A wave of dusty, cold air, liberally scented with damp wood and something unpleasant, hits me and makes me cough.

"Yes," Mr Fenton says dryly. "There is that. I think it might be because the house has been closed up for such a long time. Either that or a rodent has died or something. A builder talked to the previous owner about buying the house and turning it into flats, which has abruptly, and for a mad second, it feels like someone is waiting and listening.

I look over at the solicitor and do a double take at how pale and sweaty he is. "No, of course there isn't," he says quickly. "It's probably because it's such an old house. You'll find that they shift and make a lot of funny noises." My eyes narrow as I watch him dab his face with a handkerchief he takes from his pocket. He looks like if I said boo to him, he'd orbit the top of the building.

The floorboard creaks again, but this time it sounds like someone is deliberately standing on it with all their weight. Then comes the unmistakable sound of footsteps, heavy and solid as they move slowly overhead.

"There *is* someone up there," I cry and dart out of the lounge, taking the winding stairs up as fast as I can and hearing Mr Fenton's cry of protest from behind me.

Cobwebs fall around me and dust rises in a sparkling cloud as I pound up the stairs. I come out onto a small landing off which are four open doors and another staircase winding upwards and out of sight.

I pause there, aware of Mr Fenton's puffing gasps of breath in the hallway downstairs. The slow, deliberate creak comes again from one of the rooms, which a quick reckoning tells me is the one above the lounge where I heard the footsteps. Only this time I'm close enough to hear a rustle of clothing.

"If someone is here, you're trespassing," I say clearly and loudly.

The sound stops again, and for a second I'm sure I can hear someone chuckle. *What the fuck?* Rage fills me. This is my fucking house. I dart into the room only to come up short so quickly that I sway.

The room is completely empty. There isn't a stick of furniture anywhere, just the dim light filling the room that presages nightfall. Cobwebs hang from the ceiling, swaying in the breeze from the opened door. The floorboards are bare and covered in a thick layer of dust. I stare at them. Thick, undisturbed dust. No one has stood on them for a long time.

Flummoxed, I stand inside the doorway, hearing my breaths coming fast on the frigid air in here. Then I subside and laugh, hearing it echo around the room as Mr Fenton comes in.

"No one's here and I'm going mad," I say. "Please forget you ever heard me call out and warn an invisible trespasser." He stares at me. "I'm not used to old houses," I explain and then smile. "I suppose I'd better get used to this one quickly or I'll be on first-name terms with the police, thinking I'm being burgled every five minutes by the Invisible Man."

To my surprise, he doesn't laugh. Instead, he directs a haunted glance around the room. It's the same quick glance I used to give when I was little and my mum made me look under the bed to show me there were no monsters. At five years old, it didn't matter what my mum said. I still knew monsters weren't always visible.

"I need to go," he says so abruptly that he startles me.

"Okay," I say hesitantly. "I'm sure I'll be fine with looking over the rest myself."

Incredibly, he looks like he wants to question that, but instead he presses the keys forcibly into my hands along with a large file full of papers.

"The deeds to the house. Welcome to York," he mutters and goes to turn away, only to hesitate. "You have my number, Mr Black. Please call me if you need anything." He pauses. "*Anything*," he says with a funny sort of emphasis. "Carol's son can always call on me."

"Thank you." The words are said to his back as he turns and practically runs out of the room. I stare after him. "Weird," I say out loud and then shake myself. There's a tour of the house to do before the builder arrives.

The light gets dimmer as I poke my head into the empty bedrooms. Two are a good size, but the one I'll have as my own is the big room at the front of the house. I stand at the window, and smile in delight. I can see the Minster through the branches of a large tree that hovers over the lane like a drunk outside the pub at kicking-out time. There's a high old brick wall that runs alongside the lane, and beyond it is a large neat garden that obviously belongs to the big house set back from the road. The room is light and papered in a rosebud-patterned wallpaper, giving it an air of quiet femininity.

I wander into a bathroom before backing out just as quickly. "Nope, not looking at that in too much detail." Already I can feel the builder's quote getting bigger, and we haven't even met yet.

I hesitate at a set of stairs that must lead up to the attic rooms. Cobwebs festoon it, like the entrance to one of Indiana Jones's adventures. I put my foot on the steps, but for some reason I pause. *It looks so dark up there.* I shake my head and move to go up, but at that moment my phone rings startlingly loud in the absolute hush of the house.

I look down at the display and swear. Connecting the call, I say, "Mason?"

There's a pause and then my ex's voice. "Levi, you alright? Was the drive bad?"

His voice is so familiar to me. I've heard it in so many permutations. During rows when it's been raised, over the breakfast table sleepy and slurred, and at night in bed, hushed and intimate. It makes me wonder when I stopped listening out for it.

"I'm fine," I say. "The drive was on the motorway. When isn't it bad?"

He laughs. "Tell me about it." His voice lowers huskily. "Do you remember that traffic jam on the M4 going to Devon?"

"Did you want something?" I break in coolly.

There's a startled pause, and when he speaks next there's a regretful tone to his voice undercut with affront. I sigh. I've heard that a few times over the last year. "I didn't realise I had to want something to talk to you."

"Well, it's probably the only reason you should be calling me," I say in a matter-of-fact tone.

"Lovely," he sniffs.

"Mason." I elongate his name and sigh. "It's just the way it is."

"The way I made it, you mean?"

"Well, if you want me to put it bluntly, then yes, this is the way we are now, and you decided that," I say, irritated and unable to hide it.

"Why?" I ask, and my voice is amazed.

He shifts awkwardly. "No reason. Just take my advice and go and grab a hotel room. It's fairly quiet in York because it's a cold spring. Or as quiet as York ever gets. The hotel is called The Minster Quarters. Tell the manager I sent you and that you're going to be living here and he'll give you a good rate."

"Okay," I say doubtfully. "Well, thank you."

He shakes his head and without another word walks away down the road, his figure swallowed up quickly in the shadows.

I hesitate on the doorstep. I had intended to stay here even when the work was going on. I've brought all my camping gear, and I'm not afraid of roughing it. But now I reconsider. Shadows have gathered and the whole house seems cloaked in dark and stillness.

I shiver. *What the fuck is wrong with me?* It's a fucking house. Nothing to be wary of. I must be just tired from the drive and everything else that's gone on in the last year. I'll be clutching at my pearls next.

Nevertheless, I think slowly. *I have got the extra money from the sale of the flat now which didn't look like it was going to come through for a while.* I bite my lip and shift from foot to foot on the doorstep. A floorboard creaks loudly in the kitchen. That decides me. I'm not staying in a dark, cold house jumping at every noise because I'm too tired to be fucking rational. At least in a hotel I can get some work done and keep the money coming in.

The noise comes again, and I nod. That's what I'm telling myself, anyway. Mind made up, I dig the keys out of my pocket and pull the door closed, locking it and checking it a couple of times. I walk back to the car and grab my suitcase and the rucksack with my Mac in it.

Setting off down the cobbled road, I pause to look at the house and admire what is mine. *Mine.* I've never had something that is just my own. I lived with my mum before leaving for college and moved in with Mason straight after that. I smile. I think I'm going to enjoy this. It's just what I need.

A last shaft of light comes through the clouds, lighting the street and glittering on the windows of my house. I admire the view, and, that's when I see it. A figure, clearly defined in the shining light, standing at the window of the second floor.

I jump and drop my case to the cobbles. *What the fuck?*

Time stills for a long minute as I stare up at the dark figure. It's too dark for details, but I have a strong sense that he or she is watching me. Then the light dims and the first drops of rain start to fall around me, striking my face and stinging my hands. I blink, and, when I look again, the figure is gone.

I dig in my pocket for the keys, intending to run in and search the house. It's at that moment and as clear as day, I hear my mum say in my ear, *"No, Levi. Don't."*

I look around wildly, a small part of me hoping that none of the neighbours can see me behaving like a fucking nutcase. But there's no one here and the street is empty. A gust of wind blows down the lane, hurling the rain about wildly.

I look back at the house and hesitate. There's no one in there. I know it with an absolute certainty. We went through the house room by room. No one could have got in. *Do I want to go in there in the dark on my own and fumble through those empty, cold rooms where I know there's no one there?*

The answer coming through is immediate and atavistic. *Fuck no. No bloody way.*

Shaking my head, I grab my case and walk down the lane towards the light and life in the centre of York, leaving my house dark and still behind me.

CHAPTER 2

*S*ix Months Later

*L*evi

I push my plate away and sit back in my chair with a sigh.

Mary, the waitress at the hotel I'm currently staying in, comes over to clear the table. "Last breakfast, Levi," she says with a smile on her wrinkled face.

I grin up at her. "I know. I can't believe I'm moving in today."

"Well, we'll miss you, lad. You've been a pretty face to see in the mornings."

"You've looked after me very well. A home away from home."

"Well, you'll be in your own home tonight." She pauses in stacking the plates. "I remember your house," she muses. "I used to play there as a child with a little girl called Daisy MacIntosh."

"I remember seeing their names on the deeds. They lived there in the fifties, didn't they?"

She nods. "For a short while." A funny look crosses her face. "No one seemed to stay there for very long."

I open my mouth to ask why, but she shakes her head.

"Look at me gossiping. That'll never pay the bills." Giving me a harried smile without meeting my eyes, she pours me another cup of tea and bustles off.

I cradle the cup and look out the window at the street. On a weekday York is markedly quieter than at the madness of the weekends when you could do with a tank to get down The Shambles. At this point in the morning on High Petergate, there are only shop-keepers opening up for business and a few tourists ambling along. They're immediately identifiable by their slower gait and the way they look up rather than at what's in front of them.

A shaft of sunlight shines down, illuminating the church of St Michael le Belfry, and somewhere in the city, bells chime the hour. I hope it's a sign that the cold weather that's turned the city into Narnia for the last few weeks might be letting up.

I can't say I'm sad that I've stayed here for the last six months. The house took a lot more work than either the builder or I expected, and my original plan of camping in the house would never have worked. Besides, this is a lovely hotel, and, just as the builder promised, they gave me a good deal as a resident. There are places in my attic room where I can't stand up straight, but it has a view of the Minster and the sky, and there I've happily stayed through the summer and into the autumn.

My days have had an easy sort of uniformity to them. Every morning I've jogged along the wall, watching the mist wrap around York like a lover not wanting to rise and let the day begin. After breakfast, I've wandered round to the house to watch it coming together and then sauntered back, exchanging greetings with the shopkeepers who I'm coming to know. I've then retired to my room and worked away until lunch.

The late afternoons have been spent wandering York, exploring the little lanes and streets, and finding hidden jewels like the Snickel-ways, that give tiny glimpses of a largely unseen York.

But mainly I've worked, and this industriousness has resulted in me fulfilling a lot of my commissions early, which has thankfully reflated my bank balance to a healthy level. I can't deny I'm happy about that as the house has cost an absolute fortune to renovate. There were structural problems with it, and I'd had to have a new roof, not to mention the fact that I'd needed everything – new wiring, new boiler, and central heating installed throughout. And that was only the big purchases. But now it's mainly done. The only thing left is the cellar which the builders are having to leave for a few weeks to do another job.

A person with a head of blue hair moves past the window. He crosses the road, and I lean forwards, my interest sharpening.

It's him.

I'd first noticed him after having dinner at an Italian restaurant the other week. I'd been ambling along the Shambles, enjoying the quiet and peering into shop windows, when I'd heard a voice behind me. It was an interesting voice—slightly hoarse with an undercurrent of amusement cutting through it. I'd turned and found a party pushing past me, led by a bloke who looked to be in his twenties.

He was very eye-catching, not least because he had bright blue hair and was wearing a Victorian man's suit complete with top hat. A couple of inches shorter than me and thin, he appeared to be leading the group, and that was when I realised it was a ghost tour.

I'd learnt that York is supposed to be one of the most haunted cities in England, and to my amusement I'd seen ghost walks every-where – men and women in fancy dress leading groups of titillated people all over the city and telling tall stories.

This particular group had marched onwards, and his voice had faded away, but the impression he'd left on me hadn't.

I've seen him several times since. Queuing for a coffee in the market, wearing faded jeans and a big jumper, his cheeks flushed from the cold. Standing laughing with a busker in the square. And, just last night, he'd been part of a group of people in the pub near my house.

I'm oddly fascinated with him, and I watch him now as my tea gets cold. He's talking to a shopkeeper and smiling. The grin seems to take over his face, the lift of one eyebrow giving his expression a slightly wicked slant. The man claps him on the back and says something, and Blue, as I've christened him, moves onward down the street at a quick pace.

Every time I've seen him, he seems to be in motion. I keep my eyes on him until he disappears around the corner, and then I put my cup down. Time to pack my gear and finally move into my house.

An hour later I wander down the cobbled lane. It's bloody cold with the wind howling along and rattling the branches of the old copper beech tree that hangs over the road. I look up at my house and smile. The exposed brick has been cleaned up and the sash windows painted a light grey-green. The door has been painted the same colour, and the house seems to sit up straighter now that it's not the poor relation on the street. It looks serene.

Letting myself in, however, the first thing to greet me is some extremely inventive cursing coming from the cellar through the open door.

"Hello?" I shout.

"Oh, Mr Black." Kevin, the trainee builder, comes to the top of the stairs looking flustered. He's a thin, pale lad with black hair and acne blooming angrily over his cheeks. "I didn't realise you were here. Sorry about that."

"What? The swearing?" He nods, and I laugh. "I wouldn't apologise about that. I've heard far worse." I pause. "I've used far worse." He smiles, and I dump my case on the floor. "What's the problem?"

For a second he looks hesitant, but then indignation comes into his eyes. "Downstairs is a right mess," he mutters, jerking his head at the door as if I wasn't aware there was another level. My lip twitches, but I say nothing and follow him down the stairs. When we get to the bottom, I stop in amazement.

"What the *fuck?*" I breathe. "What happened in here?"

"*We* didn't leave it like this," he says slightly indignantly. "It was like this in the morning when I came in."

"Who the fuck did this, then?" I mutter.

Where yesterday there was a big empty space with bare brick walls is now chaos. The previously neatly stacked bags of cement have been ripped open and the dry cement thrown around liberally. The builder's tools have been similarly treated, although three or four lie in pieces as if someone has smashed them repeatedly into the concrete ground.

I look at Kevin. "Was it kids getting in?"

He shakes his head. "Kids didn't do this," he mutters. "If they'd got in, there'd be damage all over the house."

"Then who?" I breathe. He looks awkward and my attention sharpens as a sudden thought occurs to me. "Has something like this happened before?"

For a second he hesitates and then his obvious desire to tell the truth overcomes it. "There's been something weird happening down here every day."

"*What?*"

He nods solemnly. "Every day. Things going missing, tools damaged."

"But how?" I pause. "I mean, why?"

He shrugs. "This old house, I reckon. Mr Harrison, he was saying the other night it's a common happening. When he was clearing the house of stuff for the old lady, he'd regularly come in to find the boxes he'd packed the previous day had been emptied and the stuff thrown around."

"I'm not sure I understand," I say feebly.

He shoots me a look of almost pity as if I'm being extremely thick. "It'll be the ghost, of course."

"You've got to be *kidding* me." My instinctive laughter echoes around the empty cellar but unfortunately it has the effect of completely shutting him up. He bristles and clams up, and no matter how many questions I throw at him as he moves around the cellar collecting some of the gear they need for their new job, he refuses to say any more.

I give up and follow him to the door. "I'm sorry I laughed," I say, holding the door open for him. "It was really rude of me."

He thaws slightly, his young face taking on an earnest expression. "You can't help it, Mr Black. You don't know this place."

"This house, or York?"

He shrugs as he loads his gear into the van. "Either. We live here. We know York isn't like other places. It's different."

"Different, how?"

"Ah now, Mr Black, I reckon the only thing that'll make you believe me is to experience it yourself." He looks up at the house before he climbs into the van. "Reckon that'll happen soon enough, knowing this place."

"Wait. What do you mean *this place?*" I ask, but he slams the door of the van and with a wave he sets off jerkily down the lane.

Within seconds he's vanished and I'm left on the street, the wind blowing my hair around. Shivering, I look up the house and for a second it seems to tower over me, and I find myself searching the windows looking for something. *Someone.*

Then I shake my head. *What the fuck is wrong with me? Am I actually going to believe there's a fucking ghost in my house?*

The memory of that first night here stirs. It's faded into the background over the months, and the fear I'd felt then, that deep foreboding, I'd simply dismissed as being down to tiredness. I don't believe in spirits and things that go bump in the fucking night.

I shrug and make my way back into the house. I've had too many nights listening to the locals talk about the ghosts around the city, that's all.

I wander around the house with satisfaction. This is my place. Something that is just mine. Everything in it, every alteration, has been my choice, and I love the result.

The previously dark hallway is now painted white. The floorboards have been sanded and glossed and a huge blue and white oriental rug has been laid over them. The dining room walls are now a deep red, and when the new light-oak dining table and chairs arrive, it'll be a snug and cosy room.

One of the rooms I'm most pleased with is the kitchen. It took a couple of weeks of work but now the once-greasy-and-grim room is lovely. The builders stripped the walls back to the original brick and laid the floor with flagstones. New black cupboards gleam in the light, and an oak worksurface warms the room up. A black and gold roman blind has been fitted to the huge restored Georgian window. I look around the room. I just need to unpack all the boxes in here now.

My phone beeps with a message from the furniture company informing me that they're delivering the new sofa, bed, and other bits that I'd had to order.

When I walked away from Mason, I left him with everything. Whether it was petulance or a desire to never see anything connected with him again, I've started over from scratch. I've spent a small fortune, but I've reassured myself with the thought that I won't be moving for a while. Maybe not ever, I think as I look around, inhaling the scent of new wood, carpets, and fresh paint.

The doorbell rings and I spring into action. The next few hours are spent arranging and rearranging furniture until I'm happy with the results. The lounge now sports a huge grey sectional grouped around a low coffee table and set in front of the restored fireplace. Three of the walls have been painted a soft grey while the other one is a rich blue. I place a mustard velvet chaise lounge by the blue wall, and unroll a huge cream rug to bring everything together.

In my kitchen, I now have the choice of sitting at the small oak table and chairs set in front of the big window or at the barstools around the breakfast bar.

I can even sleep comfortably, I muse, attempting to shove the duvet into the new bed linen. I frown when the duvet seems to settle in the middle of the cover in a huge lump. Who the fuck manages to do this in one go? You'd need the intellect of fucking Einstein to get this massive fucking duvet into this cover.

It takes me fifteen minutes, but eventually it's done, and I look around happily at the room. A few months ago, the bedroom had been dark and cold and dusty. Now, it's painted a light grey, and the bed with its dark grey fabric headboard looks hotel-ready with its mixture of green and white bed linen. Big lamps sit on either side of the bed, so there'll be lots of light in here.

My mind supplies a memory of the footsteps and the chuckle I'd thought I'd heard in my first visit to this room. I shake my head. The solicitor must have thought I was on something.

Leaving the room, I bound up the steps to my favourite room in the entire house. My studio. I switch the light on and look around contentedly. My huge drafting table is drawn up under a skylight, and my desk and chair sit in front of one of the big windows. The room is painted a warm cream and the builders have sandblasted the beams. My artwork is framed and hung on the walls, and a massive oriental rug lies on the shiny wooden floors. The space is warm from the big radiator, but the atmosphere feels nice in a deeper way. Like a safe space, if that doesn't sound too ridiculous.

I spend a happy hour unpacking the boxes of my art equipment and shelving my books on the floor-to-ceiling bookcases on one side of the room. Then I sink onto the large red sofa and stare out the window, watching the rain beat against the panes of glass, blurring the outline of the Minster until it looks like an Impressionist painting.

I'm not sure how long it takes me to realise that there's a strong scent of lily of the valley in the room. By the time I do, it's incredibly strong. I look around for the source. There isn't one. Just the sweet scent that brings back memories of an old great-aunt who never wore any other scent. It drifts around me until it's almost choking, and I cough. Then as quickly as it came, it vanishes.

"What the hell?" I say out loud.

Did the builders put scent plug-ins in the rooms? Laughter bubbles up at the thought of Mr Harrison, the stoical builder, struggling to choose between warm vanilla and clean linen. My smile dies. Where *did* that smell come from, then? I stand up and pace around the room, but there's no sign of anything that could cause it.

The next second, there's an almighty bang from downstairs that practically makes me levitate off the fucking floor.

"What is it with this bloody place?" I groan and dash out of the room only to be brought up short on the stairs down to the first floor. It's fucking freezing down here, and it shouldn't be. When I went up to my studio, the whole house was toasty warm. Now it's so cold I can see my breath in the air. The banging comes again from downstairs. It sounds like someone is slamming a door over and over again.

I take the stairs at a run and stop dead at the bottom. The front door is open wide and swinging in the wind which is howling down the hallway. Shivering madly, I grab the door and slam it shut, looking down at the lock in consternation. *Is the catch faulty?* I'm sure I remember locking the door while I was working upstairs. Living in London all of my life means that habit is ingrained. I frown. Maybe I didn't. Maybe I forgot today, and the wind had caught it and blown it open.

It's still cold and there's a distinct draft coming from behind me, as well as a rattling noise coming from the kitchen. I go into the room and stop abruptly. The tall heavy sash window is raised to its highest level and the rattling I can hear is the wood rocking in the casement. A chill runs down my neck and back that has nothing to do with the cold. I might have forgotten to lock the front door, but I'm fucking damn sure I didn't forget opening this window.

Rain gusts through, and I curse. It's going to ruin the wooden worktops. It takes a few minutes of swearing and struggling, but eventually I get the heavy window down. I click the lock on it and make myself watch what I'm doing.

More banging erupts. This time I jump like a bloody child at a horror film. *What the hell is happening here?* Anger kindles as I move into the lounge. The new French doors are open, of course, and the wind is billowing the curtains back so fiercely they look like windsocks.

I shiver and stiffen my spine. Locking the doors, I make my way round the house in a grim silence. Every single window in the place is open apart from the attic where I'd been. For a brief minute I contemplate whether the builder did this. *Is he trying to scare me off?* He'd wanted to buy the house before. *Does he still?*

"Fuck me," I say out loud, the sound of my voice almost startling in the newly hushed stillness of my house. "You'll be writing fairy stories next, Levi Black."

The idea of the staid Mr Harrison creeping into the house and opening windows is faintly ridiculous. *Maybe someone else has keys*, I think suddenly. *Maybe this is vandalism.*

The words of Kevin the builder float through my mind, and I shake my head. "No bloody way, Levi. Get a fucking grip. There's no such thing as ghosts."

The whole house feels like the inside of a meat locker, and so I turn the heat up on the boiler. Then I stand staring out onto the lane outside my kitchen window, watching some tourists walk past clutching their maps of York, the wind blowing their clothing about. It looks such a normal scene. I frown. In the usual run of things, I don't make a habit of noticing what's normal, which should tell me how weird this whole situation is. I shake my head and switch the lights off. I've got boxes to unpack.

A few hours later, the last box for the lounge has been unpacked and the room is complete, apart from a few pictures that need to be put up. Barring my mysterious window opener striking again, I'm done for the night. My only plan for the evening is ordering a Chinese takeaway and having an early night. It's Friday night for everyone else.

I strip my clothes off and step into the shower. Blessing the fact that I bought a rainforest shower, I twist and let the hot spray pound down on my sore muscles. I soap up and fist my cock lazily, feeling it thicken in my hand. Searching my spank-bank images, I'm amazed to find myself thinking of Blue. And once he's in my head, I can't get him out. That sparky, defiant air about him, the slender body, and vivid face. I grunt as I fuck my fist harder and moan as I shoot against the wall, the water washing the spunk away down the drain as if it was never there.

For a second I rest against the wall and then shake my head. A person should really get out more if they're reduced to wanking over someone they've never met and likely never will.

I switch the shower off and stand drying myself with a large navy bath sheet and admiring my new bathroom. The floor is made of wide light-oak boards, and the room is white and light apart from the glass-encased shower which is tiled in vivid blue subway tiles. There's also a clawfoot bath which is about the only decent thing that was original to the house.

I pad back into the bedroom, which is thankfully warm again. I stand there, wondering where my fucking clothes are. Then I remember leaving my suitcase in the kitchen for some reason. All my other clothes are in a box somewhere that I haven't seen yet.

Running a hand through my hair, I wander downstairs as naked as the day I was born. I don't know why it's so freeing to walk around nude, but I've always enjoyed it. I wanted to go on one of those LGBTQ-friendly nudist beaches, but Mason would never agree.

I'm pondering this as I switch on the under-cupboard lighting in the kitchen. A woman shrieks, and I just about jump out of my skin, certain someone is in the house with me.

I spin around. A group of people is staring at me through my kitchen window, and as it's set low to the road outside, they are all, without exception, enjoying a close-up view of my dick.

"Fuck!" I choke.

I grab a tea towel and cover my cock with it. I then rather incongruously opt to cover my nipples with my arm. I'm really not sure why.

For a long second that stretches into eternity we all stare at each other, including, I discover, Blue. He's standing at the front of the group with a sardonic smile on his face and eyes that clearly express a desire to laugh. He's dressed in what I'm coming to recognise is his ghost-walk gear. Which means he's leading a ghost walk. And my house must be on the walk.

The two of us break the strange détente we're engaged in. Me, by reaching out and whacking the light switch off so the kitchen darkens, and him, by turning and gesturing theatrically at his followers to follow him as he moves off down the road.

"So, that's the Murder House," he says loudly, a thread of laughter running through his voice. "Very shocking, I guess you'd say."

"Was that a spirit?" an old lady asks him, her voice quivering with what I presume is excitement. Hopefully, it's not amusement. "I saw a ghost. Did you see it?"

"I did," he calls back. "As clear as day, but the ghost really needs to buy himself a bigger dish cloth."

I groan, throwing the tea towel on the counter. Why did it have to be him?

Then I still. *Did he just call my house the Murder House?*

I break my stasis and zip over to the window, but they're gone and the lane is empty once more. Just to make sure of no more flashing incidents, I lower the blind.

CHAPTER 3

$\mathcal{L}$evi

The next evening, I sit in my dark kitchen. I'm ready for when Blue brings the ghost tour by my house. I smile grimly. *Very* ready for some answers.

I woke up this morning to a wind blowing through my bedroom, which came from... You guessed it. All the fucking windows being open again.

The one in the small bedroom had been wrenched upwards with so much force that the catch had been bent out of shape.

When I got downstairs it was to find that the boiler in the kitchen had been switched off, as had the electricity. It's dark at seven in the morning in October, so I'd ended up stumbling all over the place looking for the fuse box. I'd found it in the cellar, along with a whole bag of cement that had been emptied down the stairs so it'd got all over my bare feet. The fact that I'd then had to shower in cold water had not helped my mood.

So, you could say that I've definitely got a few questions about the Murder House. I sigh and scrub my hands down my face and take another sip of my Jack Daniel's. What is happening that I, a sane person, am reduced to looking for answers about my own house from a man who leads ghost walks and dyes his hair in an apparent attempt to look like one of the Tweenies?

Voices suddenly sound outside the kitchen window, a few excited, one wry. *It's him.*

I sit stock-still as if they're going to see me, despite the fact that the blind is half closed and the room dark. I shift closer to the window to hear what they're saying, but at that point the phone rings. I hesitate as it rings again and then sigh and grab it, groaning at the sight of Mason's name on the display.

"*What?*" I whisper.

There's a startled pause. "Levi?"

"Yes, of course it is. You just rang me."

"Well, normally you don't talk in a voice that only mice could hear."

"What is it, Mason?" I sigh.

There's an offended pause. "Can't I ring you now?"

"No," I say patiently. "You can't. We're not together anymore." I pause. "And Sean might not like it."

"It's nothing to do with Sean," he says sharply.

"Like it or not, Mason, it is, and that's down to you. Now, what is it? I'm on my way out."

"Oh, you have plans."

"Of course I have," I say, stung because I really haven't unless you count stalking Blue.

"A man?"

Blue's voice speaks from outside.

"You could say that." The voice stops speaking, and I curse. "Shit! I've got to go. Bye."

I click End on the call and Mason's very irate voice, and dash to the door, but when I fling it open, the group is nowhere to be seen. There's a flash of blue at the top of the lane and then he's gone.

Shit! I hover for a second, undecided, but then a floorboard creaks overhead and that makes my mind up quickly. I pull the door closed and lock it before throwing my coat on against the cold. I pelt down the lane, my feet slipping slightly on the wet cobbles.

It's a cold and damp Saturday night but there are still a lot of people about in York. Couples stroll along dressed up and hand in hand, and I dodge around a group of women who are on a hen night, judging by the banner wrapped around one woman which proclaims her to be a learner. She's either the bride or an over-enthusiastic learner driver. She's also wearing a tiara. The women's shrill voices rise into the cold air as I look around frantically for the ghost-walk group.

I'm about to give up when the crowd clears and a blue head comes into view. He's moving along at a rapid pace, throwing remarks over his shoulder to the group as he crosses into the Minster Yard, the large paved space outside the Minster. I follow them over the ancient flagstones gleaming from the rain.

The Minster is the largest medieval Gothic cathedral in Northern Europe but at the beginning it was just a small wooden church. Kings came and went and that little church was destroyed and raised again, taking different forms until it reached its current glorious golden form. Although I've learnt that it takes constant maintenance to keep it looking so beautiful. If you spend any time in York, you'll find the air is always filled with the sounds of hammering from the stonemasons who seem to spend most of their lives up scaffolding.

It still amazes me that all this history is at the bottom of my lane. I've spent many happy hours wandering around here and marvelling at it, which makes me pretty sure that the ghost tour is heading towards the Treasurer's House, although some of the roads around that are gated off at night due to the private residences.

I follow them past the bronze statue of Constantine the Great who reclines in his chair as if he's at home and waiting for the wife to get dinner. Then it's a turn to the left past the Minster stonemasons' yard, and I finally catch up with the group on the corner of College Street where Blue stands outside a small house. It looks very old, and the group are looking up at it and whispering.

"Okay, we'll stop here, so gather around," he says, pitching his voice louder for the people at the back of the group. It's a rich voice with a hint of an Irish accent, and the group listen raptly. "In 1665 the plague came to York and brought with it fear and pain and paranoia. People were rightly terrified of catching the disease as it guaranteed a terrible end. However, they had no idea of how the plague was spread, and, as such, anyone who even appeared sick was considered dangerous. When the little girl who lived in this house became poorly, her parents and the locals got scared, and rather than nursing the poor child, they decided to take a horrible action. They locked her up in the house without any food or water. Of course she died, but it wasn't from the plague. Maybe it was heartbreak, because to this day, her small, tearstained face can be seen at that very window."

He gestures flamboyantly at a small window, and I wonder idly whether the owner of the house is an old hand at this, or if right at this moment, he's hiding behind the curtain so as not to be caught naked apart from a tea towel.

Then Blue tips his top hat back and the light from a nearby lamp plays over his features. My thoughts fly away, because he's stunning. His face is angular with very sharp cheekbones, a long nose, and full pink lips. A silver ring pierces the lower lip. His hair is shaggy and casts shadows on the clean line of his jaw.

It's a strangely timeless face. One I seem to have seen in many portraits over the years. He's wearing a Victorian outfit of black trousers, white shirt and cravat, an ornately embroidered waistcoat, and a long black velvet coat. He looks a little like a ghost on this cold night. I look at the hair and combat boots. Or a character from a steampunk gothic novel.

His audience are raptly hanging onto his every word, but attention is disrupted when a large group approaches. At its lead is a thin man with long black hair pulled back into a ponytail. He's handsome, but his expression is discontented and his mouth is sharp. He's dressed in similar clothes to Blue, and he carries a large wooden box.

The group moves past us, coming to a stop a few yards away. The man places his box on the ground with a rather dramatic precision. My mouth twitches as he climbs on with a great deal of dignity.

"I've brought you here," he says in a ghoulish tone, "to talk about plague and death and a terrible end in solitary confinement locked away in a small house."

"Excuse me." Blue's loud voice cuts straight through the man's dramatic spiel.

The man stops talking with an impatient sigh. "Can I help you?" he asks.

"I'll say you can," Blue says sharply. "This is my pitch for the next ten minutes. That's the agreement if I keep off the York Devil bit until last thing."

"Well, Frank changed the route. Sorry if you didn't get the memo," Box Boy says in a bored voice.

"You don't sound sorry," Blue says calmly. "You sound quite cross." He pauses. "Or constipated. I never could tell the difference." He looks him up and down. "Both ways were a build-up of shit."

The man seems to lose his grasp on his temper. "You don't own York," he says loudly.

"Obviously not," my guide says patiently. "Or I wouldn't be doing ghost tours." He clearly remembers his audience and turns back with a charming smile. "I would, of course, still be doing ghost tours for wonderful groups like this even if I owned the city of York, because I live to impart spectral knowledge." The other man snorts slightly, and Blue smiles at us kindly and winks. "You'll have to excuse us," he says. "We used to date. Can I just say there is no correlation at all between box size and penis size?"

I snort out a laugh despite myself and watch as the other man picks up his box and gestures to his group in a bad-tempered way. I watch him go, smiling. The grin drops away as I suddenly become aware that the group is staring at me and our guide is talking to me.

"Sorry," I say quickly. "I wasn't paying attention."

"Obviously," he says. "Because you missed the bit where I said I wasn't a resident charity."

"I think I've missed something," I say slowly.

The other members of the group shift slightly, obviously enjoying the entertainment, but not wanting to draw too much attention to themselves in case his laser gaze turns on them.

"You have missed something," he says. "You've missed the part where you pay for the tour."

"Oh fuck, sorry." I edge forwards and dig in my pocket for my wallet. "Of course I'll pay. How much is it?"

"Well, usually it's six pounds." I open my wallet, and he stares at me. "But that's for people who are on time. You, however, are late, so it's a tenner."

I'm about to argue with this logic when a big man stirs at the back of the group. "Can we get a move on? It's fucking freezing."

"Could you watch your language?" another man says crossly.

"I can. I just might not want to," the big man says.

My guide sighs and glares at me. "See what you've done now? This was a very well-behaved group before you turned up. You're like a human grenade."

I open my mouth to refute this unfair observation, but he shakes his head.

"Okay, people," he calls out to the group. "Let's be off to our next stop on the ghost tour led by the Mysterious and Amazing Blue Billings."

"Sounds like a circus act," I mutter. Then I pause. "Is your name really Blue?" I exclaim.

He stares at me. "Yes."

"You're *kidding*," I say far too loudly, making him and a couple of other members of the group jump. "Sorry," I say quickly. "It's just that it's what I called you in my head." I realise what I just said and flush.

"Okay," he says slowly. "And do you talk to the voices in your head?"

"Oh no, I'm not mad. Not that you'd have to be bonkers to hear voices," I say quickly to a lady who's staring at me and attempting to edge away. "I mean, who doesn't have a voice or two in their head?" I end slightly desperately.

A couple of people obviously don't as they move away from me too. Incredibly, Blue smiles. It's a real smile, not one of those sharp, toothy ones he seems to give everyone else, and I blink, struck by his quirky beauty. Then he turns, and I hasten after him as he sets off at a fast clip through the streets of York, his top hat set at a jaunty angle.

It seems to lose its jaunty air, however, as the tour progresses, and his ex turns up at three quarters of our stops, talking loudly over Blue, his larger group shifting us over.

Nevertheless, it's a testament to Blue's charisma that no one in our group gets fed up or demands their money back. Instead, a sort of solidarity grows up amongst us, and we start to boo the ex when he turns up at the last site. In the end he departs with his box under his arm, flustered, his group trailing after him.

We're on a shadowy cobbled back lane lit only by the desultory glow of a streetlamp. Around us are old Victorian warehouse build-ings. No doubt some of them are flats now, but it certainly looks spooky, as if we've travelled back in time led by our guide.

Blue paces back and forth in front of us. "We're standing on the site of a very famous murder," he says, his voice carrying on the stillness.

Some of our group don't appear to be breathing, and I'd lay odds on this site being the reason for their attendance on this tour. From the smile on his face, I'd say Blue knows it too.

"This is the scene of the fifth and final murder committed by the person we know as the Devil of York." He looks around at us solemnly. "Emily Harper was a prostitute. She lived not far from here in one of the little mazes of slum dwellings. In her early twenties, she had long red hair, and despite her occupation and poverty, she was known for her cheerful disposition which her neighbours said was made even cheerier by her love of gin." He winks. "But then whose mood isn't improved by gin?"

He sobers. "There wasn't a lot to smile about at that point in York, however. There had been four murders over the last two months. The women, who were all prostitutes, had been disemboweled after having their throats cut. There were whispers that Jack the Ripper himself had left London and set up business in York. How true that was, we'll never know, but the police took it seriously enough to send down the police officer in charge of the Ripper murders. He spent a few days here questioning the local force. There were also incidences of body parts turning up at tourist spots wrapped up in brown paper like presents."

Blue smiles faintly as some of the tour members gasp. "No one knew if the two things were connected, but it had an effect on customers, and on October the twenty-third, the streets of York were quiet. However, staying in would mean that she'd starve, so Emily, along with a few others, had been forced out onto the streets looking to make some money for rent. By eleven o'clock, Emily had in fact already made that money twice over during the evening, but a weakness for drink meant that she'd spent it and needed one more customer. She left the local pub and bid farewell to her friend with whom she'd been drinking. The last her friend saw of her was Emily's figure trotting down the road as the mist rolled in from the River Ouse."

Blue's eyes gleam as he lowers his voice slightly. "Her friend was the last known person to see Emily alive. An hour later, a man called out in a panic to a local copper that there was a body on the ground and that the Devil had struck again. The policeman hastened to investigate, and by the light of his torch saw a bundle of rags on the ground. Moving closer, he was shaken to see the body of a woman." He pauses dramatically and waves his hand lazily at the ground. "Right here, in fact."

Such is the power of his voice and the atmosphere that one of the women in the group squeals and moves back. He tips his hat at her. "Emily's throat had been slit from side to side, but the killer hadn't stopped there. They found bits of her scattered all around." He pauses. "The thing is, they never found her heart or her eyes. They also never found her killer. After this murder, he disappeared into the shadows and the murders stopped. However, Emily's spirit is supposed to remain here hovering over the site where her body lay. She's been seen many times."

It's difficult to take my eyes from Blue as he talks. His smile is wicked, the arching curve of his lips somehow devilish. He's very thin, but he's all wiry tensile strength. His face is vivid and engaging, with hollowed-out cheekbones and dark smudges beneath his eyes.

He looks up and catches my eye, and for a second he falters. Then he bows, removing his hat and flourishing it as if he was on the stage. I suppose he has been. The streets of York appear to be his stage.

"Well, that's all for tonight, folks," he says. "Try to have sweet dreams." The group stirs as if waking from a dream, and he grins at them. "If you've enjoyed tonight, please leave a review on TripAdvisor."

He's surrounded in seconds by people shaking his hand and asking questions about the York Devil. It's probably only me who sees the way his eyes keep straying to the street corner where a tree blows in the breeze, layering the spot in moving shadows.

I go still when a figure appears there, standing in the flickering light. In the next second, the breeze shifts the tree branches again, moving the shadows, and I want to laugh. I am actually seeing things now. Fucking York. A few months here and I'm seeing spirits. Give me another few months and I'll be fucking drinking them.

"You alright?"

I turn to find the rest of the group dispersing slowly with a lot of loud laughter and chatter. Blue is staring at me.

"Oh yes, I'm fine," I say quickly.

He looks at me quizzically and then buttons up his long overcoat, obviously about to walk away. "Well, goodnight," he says. "Try to join other ghost tours on time if you do it again. The other guides won't be as pleasant or as understanding as me."

"*That* was pleasant and understanding?" I say, amazed.

He grins. "Well, pleasant by my standards."

He winks and starts to walk away.

"Wait," I say, far louder than I need to judging by his jump. "Sorry," I say again. "But do you fancy going somewhere?"

A hard look appears on his face, and he shakes his head sharply. "Ah no, I don't do that."

"I meant do you want to go somewhere for a drink?" I jerk out. "Sorry, that was badly worded."

He stares at me, surprise and something else running over his face. "An actual drink? That's what you mean?"

"Yes," I say slowly. "That is what the words 'do you fancy a drink' usually mean."

He shrugs. "You'd be surprised." He studies me for a second. "You don't look the type to pick up strange men leading ghost tours."

"It's my first time. Be gentle," I say wryly and then pause. "Wait. What *do* men look like who pick up ghost-tour leaders?"

He looks me up and down very slowly. "Not you."

I rake my hand through my hair. "I don't think this is quite going the way I meant it to. Let me start again. I'd like very much to talk to you about my house, so would you like to go for a drink?"

Blue shakes his head. "This is the weirdest conversation I've ever had. Why would I want to talk about your house? Is it made of gold or gingerbread?"

I want to smile. "No, it's made of bricks, and it comes with the unfortunate nickname of the Murder House."

I say the last with dramatic relish and there's a startled pause. He looks at me closely before recognition dawns and he throws his head back, laughing loudly. It's an infectious laugh, and my own lips twitch in response. When he's finished, his eyes are watering.

"Shit, it's you."

I nod glumly which brings on more laughter.

"Fucking hell," he says, "that was priceless. I can still see you standing there with a dish cloth over your goolies and a hand over your nips. If you'd had pigtails, you'd have been a dead ringer for Babs Windsor in the *Carry On* films."

I shake my head. "Thank you so very much. York is proving very good for my self-confidence."

He laughs harder, his blue hair falling over his eyes for a second before he pushes it back. "One of the old ladies still believes you're a ghost. I saw her yesterday. She's christened you the Naked Little Sprite."

"That's not very complimentary," I sniff. "It was a cold night, and I wasn't expecting visitors."

He chokes and splutters while I stand patiently fighting a smile. When he sobers up, he stares at me. "I can't believe you're living there. What's it like?"

"Different," I say. I pause. "Do you have time for a drink?"

Something plays over his sharp face, and then he shrugs. "I suppose so."

"You're killing me with your enthusiasm."

He laughs. "Better that than with my pepper spray. Okay, let's go."

He leads me down a winding mess of side streets, setting a quick pace. He's obviously a local here despite the Irish in his accent, as he takes shortcuts without a second thought, moving as surely as a cat in the dim light. Finally, we end up on a busy main road, and we stop in front of a pub.

"The Golden Fleece," I read the sign out loud.

He nods. "It's jammed full of ghosts."

"Why didn't we see it on the tour, then?"

"Because Hugh, the arsehole, was very intent on fucking my tour up."

"He didn't succeed." I pause. "He seems very pissed off with you though. Were you together long?" I say tentatively, unable to believe I'm asking him that question.

Blue shrugs. "A couple of nights."

I stare at him for a long moment. "Oh, er well. That's nice," I say lamely before finishing slightly more robustly. "I'm afraid I just can't take a man on a box seriously."

He shakes his head and motions me into the pub, the quirk of his lips not quite covered. I look around as I follow him to the bar. It's wood paneled and narrow and very busy, and Blue is greeted left and right by people calling his name. He smiles at everyone, but that spark is somehow missing now. Like he's muted himself with his very own remote control. He looks even more tired than he did before, if that's possible.

When we pole up at the bar, the barman comes over immediately.

His hair is dyed green, and he's wearing a kilt with combat boots and a holey jumper. "Blue," he says. "Fay's looking for you."

A funny expression crosses Blue's face. "Well, she can carry on looking."

The barman shrugs. "Your funeral." He looks me up and down as I settle at the bar next to Blue. "He with you?" he asks, nodding at me.

Blue shakes his head. "Just having a drink." He looks at me. "What do you want?"

I order a pint of bitter and the Budweiser he requests. When the barman passes them over, I dig into my pocket. "My treat," I say and Blue shrugs, palming his drink and looking around.

"We'll go in the back," he shouts over the noise. "It's quieter in there."

I follow him into a narrow room at the back. It is quieter here, lacking the jukebox, and Blue unsmilingly indicates a table. His mood seems to have soured since the conversation with the barman.

I slide in and watch as he does the same, noting the way his eyes dwell on a corner of the room intently for a few seconds. I twist my head to look but there's nothing there.

When I look back, he's sipping his drink with a smile playing on his lips. "So, you mentioned it was different living in your house?"

I look cautiously at him. What I'm about to tell him would have me laughed out of the room in London with Mason. However, I have a feeling he'll understand.

"You could say that. It's got a bit of a funny atmosphere."

As I begin to explain, his open gaze and his calmness—the way it seems like there isn't anything that would shock him—I find myself telling him everything. The footsteps heard at all hours of the day and night, the way the cellar has been repeatedly trashed, the windows and doors opening of their own accord.

He listens, the only sign of disquiet a furrow above his nose. His eyes are a startlingly pale blue with a dark circle near the pupil. They remind me of wolf eyes—piercing and cold.

"Is that it?" he says when I draw to a fumbling close.

"Just about," I say, glumly waiting as he breaks into a fit of cough-ing. It racks his thin body and he shudders and swallows his drink quickly, motioning for me to continue. I consider asking if he's all right, but his closed expression deters me. "Apart from the smell of lily of the valley," I say slowly. "Like someone's upended a bottle of the stuff over the upstairs, mainly in my bedroom and the attic. Some days it's like walking past the fragrance counter in John Lewis." I run my finger carefully down the moisture coating my glass and look up at him.

He's playing with his lip ring almost as if he doesn't know he's doing it, his face deep in thought.

"You called it the Murder House," I say abruptly. "Why?"

He jumps and looks steadily at me. "It's quite a famous house. Didn't they tell you this when you bought it? I thought estate agents were legally obligated to tell you everything now."

I shrug. "I bypassed the estate agents. The house was left to my mum and therefore came to me as her next of kin." My voice, to my embarrassment, falters slightly.

His gaze sharpens, but when he speaks, it's gentle. "That'll do it, I suppose." He sighs and takes a sip of his drink, his full mouth closing around the bottle's lip.

A shiver erupts at the base of my spine, and I shift position awkwardly as he starts to talk. "It happened in 1895." His voice slips into the slightly dreamy tone he used so well on the ghost walk. It's husky and compelling, the Irish in it spinning a lilt to his words. "A brother and sister lived there from a wealthy family. Their parents died young, and as was the way, the man inherited the estate. His sister had been married, but she was widowed early and moved back in. From the stories I heard, she was really almost a prisoner there, dependent on his good graces."

"So were most women at that time," I venture.

He nods. "Hopefully, some of them were happy, but Rosalind Cooper obviously wasn't. Still, no one knew that until it was too late. Her brother Alfred was in banking and travelled up to London a lot.

She kept house and did a lot of charity work in the area. They were, by all accounts, liked in the community. Or at least that's what people said afterwards." He gives a slightly cynical smile. "I think people's opinions get better the deader a person is." I can't help my smile, and his gaze sharpens. "Anyway, there wasn't a drop of scandal about them until the morning of November the sixth when the maid came in to light the fires and get breakfast. Alfred had an early start planned, apparently, because he was catching the train to London. Rosalind was going to a meeting of one of her charities which tried to help fallen women." I raise my eyebrows, and he smiles. "Prostitutes. Not women with balance issues."

I grin. "What happened?"

"The maid, by her account, got the fires going downstairs and went upstairs with tea for her employers. She knocked at Alfred's door and, receiving no reply, she entered the room. The curtains were drawn and she thought he was still sleeping so she hesitated, but he'd asked to be awakened, so she opened the curtains. When she turned back to the bed, it was to find that he wasn't asleep."

"And?" I ask eagerly, and he smiles at me.

"He was lying in his bed with his throat slit. Blood was all over the floor and the bed and bloody footprints crisscrossed the room and led out of the door. She screamed and ran out of the room, following the grotesque prints into her mistress's room where she found her mistress hanging from the light fitting. Poor girl never recovered from the shock."

"Jesus," I say, sitting back. "What had happened?"

He shrugs. "The police investigated and deduced that Rosalind had quite calmly slit her brother's throat. She then walked back to her room where she removed her wedding ring and jewellery and hung herself."

"Why did she do it?"

"Who knows." He sips his drink. "The police never could work it out. The two of them obviously gave good face to the world. The only thing they could get out of the maid that cast any light was that she'd once heard her master talking to his sister in a very unkind voice and that she'd been crying. She was very indignant on her mistress's behalf but couldn't give any other instances. The police surgeon discovered in the autopsy that Rosalind was in the early stages of liver cancer and she'd been told that by her doctor the previous week. The police decided that she'd been driven mad by sorrow and grief from her husband's passing and then the illness, and the courts marked it murder and suicide while of unsound mind."

He sits back, and silence falls again. I notice vaguely that he looks at the corner of the room again but dismiss it as a thought occurs to me. "Which room did the brother sleep in?" I ask grimly.

He thinks hard. "I've been told that it was the room looking down on the garden, but other people say it's the one looking over the road."

"Shit, the one at the front is my room," I say glumly.

"Hope you washed the sheets."

I snort and shake my head. "I don't know …" I hesitate over how to put this, and he grimaces.

"Don't tell me. You don't believe in ghosts," he says in a glib, cool voice. "Must be another reason for this." I stare at him and he leans forward. "There are more ghosts around York than you can shake a stick at."

"Where?" I ask, stung. "I can't see them."

"Just because you can't see them doesn't mean they're not there." A bleak look comes into his eyes. "Like a lot of people around here." I stare at him and he shrugs, a cool expression sliding over his face. "So, that's the story. Did I earn my drink, Mister?"

It sounds dismissive, and by the way his face has closed up, I know I've overstretched his hospitality.

"Oh," I say. Then "Oh" again a bit louder. "Yes, thank you. I'm so sorry for keeping you," I say stiffly. I grab my coat and pull it on, standing up and offering my hand.

He shakes it with a bemused look on his face, and I try to conceal how affected I am by feeling those long fingers and his smooth palm slide against my own. My hand drops, and I stare down at him. He's running his finger through the wetness on the table making patterns. He's already dismissed me.

"Thank you for telling me," I say softly. "I'm very grateful. And thank you for the tour. I really enjoyed it."

I move out of the room towards the noise and bustle. At the last second, obeying my instincts, I glance back. He's staring once more at the corner of the room, his expression bleak and tired.

CHAPTER 4

*L*evi

I see him the next day when I'm queuing to buy a galette at the crepe stall in the market. He's sitting at a picnic table with another man. Dressed in skinny jeans, a white T-shirt, and a grey hoodie tucked under a coat, he's laughing at something the other man is saying. He's wearing the same combat boots from last night and his blue hair is tucked under a beanie. He looks cool and very eye-catching, and as I note how the other man is gazing at Blue and the lazy way that Blue is smiling back at him, I swallow hard.

The woman behind me makes a noise. I turn and note that she's staring Blue. She smiles happily at me. "Nice to have something pretty to look at when you're in a queue," she says cheerfully.

I chuckle. "They ought to employ him to just sit there."

She grins and edges closer. "He runs one of the ghost tours."

"Does he?"

She nods. "I've been on it four times now. I know the words better than he does."

I laugh, and the sound must cut through the crowd, because Blue looks up and catches my eye. For a second he doesn't seem to recognise me, and then an immediate wariness crosses over his face. I get the impression that he really doesn't want to talk to me which is understandable after my stumbling awkwardness on the ghost tour.

Stung, I nod coolly at him and turn back to face forwards in the queue, my face burning. This reminds me a bit of being at school, watching the cool kids and longing to be a part of them but being utterly dismissed as being below their notice.

Okay, that hurt a little, I say to myself. *But really, what do you expect? Look at the men he hangs around with. You're excessively boring compared to him. No piercings or tattoos and the only time you put colour in your hair was for a Comic Relief fundraiser.*

I gaze determinedly around at the multitude of people milling around the market. It's actually a nice market, unlike a lot of the ones you come across in England now which are filled with tat. This one has stalls of fresh produce and crafts and, I've come to realise, the best street food in York. There's an area to the side of the market which has picnic tables set under huge umbrellas. Tiny huts dot the edge of this area, selling everything from burritos to artisan hotdogs. The street food is gorgeous, and I've applied myself to trying something different every day, a lunchtime treat for getting my work done.

Suddenly, I catch the scent of peaches and something else that reminds me of damp wood. I turn to find Blue standing next to me looking at me quizzically.

"Blue!" the girl from behind me says. "How are you?"

He turns to her slowly. "Hey, Sandra," he says, a wide, charming smile lighting up his thin features. "How are you?"

"I'm booked on the ghost tour this Friday."

"Again," he says humorously. "You'll be leading it soon."

She laughs and nudges him, nearly propelling him into an elderly couple on his right. I grab his arm to right him at the last second, and he smiles up at me.

"Hello," he says. "Fancy seeing you here."

"Of all the gin joints in the world," I say wryly.

"Gin," Sandra says. "Are they serving gin here? I *love* gin."

Blue laughs. "Better than coffee any day." He smiles at me. "Didn't think you were going to say hello."

I shake my head. "I didn't think you wanted me to," I say steadily.

He looks nonplussed for a second, but I refuse to play games. I always have.

"Maybe I didn't want you to," he finally says, his face clearing. I stare at him, aware of Sandra watching us avidly. He raises an eyebrow. "What do you want?"

I shrug. "I'm not sure, to be honest. Maybe I want the truth about what's happening in my house. Maybe I'd like to talk to you about it and—"

"No," he interjects. "I mean what do you want to eat. The man's waiting."

Red stains my cheeks and I spin to face the man in charge of the food truck. "Sorry," I say hurriedly. "I'll have the goat cheese galette with some bacon on it, please."

"Anything else?" he asks in a bored voice. He spots Blue and smiles widely at him. "Alright, mate?" he says. "What you doing up so early?"

"Please, Rob, you'll give me such a reputation," Blue says, grinning and holding his hand to his head like he's going to faint.

"You've already got one of those," Rob says, guffawing loudly. I shift position, and he returns to his bored expression. "Anything else?"

I open my mouth, but Blue interjects. "Give us a couple of bottles of water, and I'll have an apple crepe, please." He smiles at me. "I've got a bit of a sweet tooth. It's got caramelised apples and almonds in it." He hands the man a twenty-pound note before I can even get my wallet out.

"Oh no," I protest. "You can't buy me food."

"Why not?" he asks interestedly.

"Well, because I don't know you," I mutter, watching the man pour batter onto a circular griddle.

"Goodness, this is just like one of those Jane Austen books. Do I have to put my name on your dance card before you can clutch your pearls?"

I shake my head, feeling a smile tug at my lips. "I don't mean it like that."

He shrugs his wide shoulders, accepting his food and nodding his thanks at Rob. "You bought me a drink last night, so I'm buying you lunch." He tilts his head. "Let's find a table."

I take my own food and smile a goodbye at Sandra, who's watching Blue move sinuously over to an empty table and therefore doesn't notice me.

I slide onto the seat opposite Blue. "So, you aren't normally up this early?"

He shakes his head. "According to Rob. Not sure why he thinks he knows me any better than anyone else." He seems to ponder that and then shrugs. "Who cares. I keep late hours with the ghost tour, and unless I'm working in the day, I dip about here and there."

I take a bite of my galette and groan. Inside the crispy pancake, it's a gooey mix of goat cheese and cheddar with pickled beetroot and tomatoes. "Shit, this is good." I look up and still. He's watching me with a very intent look. "You okay?" I ask, hoping I haven't got rocket in my teeth. "You'd better eat yours before it gets cold."

He smiles. "I've eaten worse." I open my mouth to ask more questions, but he forestalls me. "So, why the move from London? I can tell you're from down south."

"London born and bred." I watch as he takes a massive bite of his food. He chews quickly, his elbows out rather like a small child who's anticipating a bully taking the food off him. Before I'm even halfway through my lunch, he's finished. Looking up and catching me watching him, he flushes.

I burst into speech. "I was left the house, like I said. It came at a good time." I put my food down and take a sip of water. "I was ready for a change. A long-term relationship that I'd been in was ending, and I needed to get away."

He stares at me like I'm an animal at the zoo. Some exotic creature that he's never seen before. "How long?" he asks.

I frown, but then I realise what he's asking. "Oh, five years. Would you like to try a bit of mine?" I ask, catching his longing look at my food and offering him some of the galette.

He takes a bite, making an appreciative groan that goes straight to my dick. "Blimey, that's a long time. Why did you split up?"

I stare at him, slightly nonplussed. "Erm." I bite my lip.

"Is that too personal?" He shrugs, looking perplexed. "I never know what's polite or not, to be honest. I hate chit-chat. If I'm interested, I'll ask questions. It's the only way to get to know anything."

I blink. "Okay, I suppose that's right. Erm, we broke up because I found out he was cheating with someone from his work. He'd been sleeping with him for six months by the time I found out."

"That's shit," he says slowly. "Why?"

The incredulous note in his voice bewilders me. "Why not?" I shrug. "Not much surprises me anymore." I stare at his long fingers that are tapping on the table. "I once thought we'd be together forever. I was stupid. Relationships never last that long."

"It's not stupid to believe in forever."

"Do you?"

He looks startled and then shakes his head. "No, of course not, but don't hold me up as any example of brains, for fuck's sake."

I smile and then shrug. "Anyway, I probably should have seen it coming. I hadn't given him any time for a while. I was occupied with something much more important. He got bored of waiting."

He looks angry. "You were looking after your mum, weren't you?"

I jerk. "*What?* How do you know that?"

For a second he looks astonished and then he shifts awkwardly on the bench. "You said your mum had died recently," he says quickly. "I took two and two and made four."

For some reason that doesn't ring true. "Even so, that's quite a leap." I stare at him and then look blindly at my food before putting it down. I've completely lost my appetite now. "It was a very bad time," I finally say, unable to say any more.

"Of course," he says simply. "That bad time doesn't stop with someone dying, though." He pauses. "I'd say that he's not worth it if he didn't even care enough to help you."

I nod, unable to speak.

His hand comes down on mine, stopping the nervous pleats I'm making in the paper serviette. "I'm sorry."

The simple honesty in his voice floors me. He doesn't bother with platitudes or excessive words. Just an "I'm sorry" and the touch of his cold fingers.

I clear my throat. "It was a while ago now. We all move on."

"Do we," he says, staring past me at something behind me, his eyes intent and focused. "I'm not so sure."

Suddenly I can't talk about this anymore. I've avoided any discussion about my mum for months, so I'm not starting one in a market. "I have to go," I say, jumping up. "Thank you for lunch."

"Any time," he says lazily, sitting back and watching me ball up my rubbish.

I nod and walk away, blinking away the heat in the back of my eyes with the ease of long practice.

~

I'm so deep in my work the next day that the ring of the doorbell makes me jump, nearly ruining a whole morning's work. I curse under my breath and put my pencil down. The bell shrills again, and I contemplate ignoring it and hiding away up here. It's snug and warm and faintly scented with lily of the valley which for some reason seems comforting now.

I rub my eyes, feeling the grittiness. I'd hardly slept last night and had been up and down investigating the sound of footsteps which went on until about five in the morning. I'm not sure they finished then, but I did. I'd tumbled into bed and pulled the covers over my head and left my house to whoever was walking around in it. At that point I'd considered that they were welcome to it.

The doorbell rings again, the cheerful chime offsetting my dark mood. I sigh and shake my head. Then I wonder for a wild moment whether it's Blue. Before I know it, I'm on my feet and making my way downstairs, checking that I'm presentable in the hall mirror. I am presentable but only just, wearing old holey jeans and a navy jumper that matches the shadows under my eyes. It'll have to do.

I fling open the door and frown in disappointment when I see a woman on the doorstep. She looks to be my age and has a hard little face surrounded by lots of red hair. She's wearing a jumper with a long skirt and boots and has a half-smile on her face.

"Hello," I say quizzically. "Can I help you?"

"I think it's the other way round," she says in a broad Yorkshire accent. "I'm Fay. Blue sent me."

I look up and down the street. "*Blue* sent you?"

Her smile twists into something that, for a brief second, isn't quite nice. Then it widens into a friendly grin, and I wonder whether I imagined it. "He did. He said you'd been having some trouble here with spirits and asked me to help you."

For a second warmth stirs in me. It's nice to think that despite his cool demeanour towards me and my rudeness yesterday, he'd thought of me again. But then I mentally shake myself.

Flushing, I smile at her. "I'm not exactly sure that it *is* spirits. I've not seen anything."

"But you have experienced something?" she says sharply. At my nod, she moves past me. Before I know it, she's in my hallway handing me her coat rather regally as she looks around. Her stare is avid. "Amazing," she whispers. "To finally see in here."

I clear my throat and she jumps. "So, how can you help me, Fay?"

She rummages in her bag and comes out with a large object wrapped in a rainbow-coloured shawl.

I raise my eyebrows. "Thank you. It's just what I've always wanted."

She gives a high laugh that has no sense of amusement about it at all. "It might be," she says mysteriously. "Do you have a table?"

"In there." I gesture to the kitchen and follow her in, catching the scent of patchouli and a deeper smell like damp wood. It's what I smelt on Blue yesterday.

Once in the kitchen she unwraps the object with a flourish and lays it on the table. I lean closer and then just as quickly step back.

"A Ouija board? I don't think that'll be of any help at all."

"You don't believe in them?" she says slowly. I shake my head, but she carries on talking. "I don't think you believe in much, Mr—?"

"Mr Black. Levi Black. And no, I don't happen to believe in Ouija boards or anything like that." I think back to a Ouija session I'd done at college and how it spelt out *Fuck off, Mason*. I also think of how my roommate hated Mason with a passion and was steering the planchette at the time. I repress a smile.

She sits down at the table with a challenging look on her face. "Well, luckily you don't have to believe in it to see the results."

I remain standing. "Look, Fay, it's very nice of you but I really don't think—"

"But Blue sent me," she interrupts, her face twisted in an expression of confusion. "He said you needed help. Shall I tell him you said you don't need it?"

"No," I say quickly and instinctively. I don't want to piss Blue off and maybe cut off this line of communication between us. "Of course not."

She doesn't manage to conceal her smug expression quickly enough. I shrug. It's harmless enough, I suppose. I'll just get it over with. I pull out the chair and sit down.

"Okay, thank you for your help," I say.

She makes a moue of embarrassment. "That'll be fifty quid."

I stare blankly at her. "What will be fifty quid?"

"My help. That's how much I charge."

"You charge *that* for a Ouija board?"

She shrugs. "Blue said you wanted answers."

She obviously has no intention of leaving. The idea of throwing a woman out bothers me, so I sigh and grab my wallet from my back pocket, thankful that I went to the cash machine yesterday. I count out the money and hand it over, watching as it disappears quickly into her voluminous skirt.

She strokes her hand over the varnished surface of the board. It's a beautiful object and obviously very old. "Let's begin," she says solemnly.

"Now?" I ask, looking around. "It's not dark yet."

She gives a condescending sort of laugh. "I don't need darkness to do a session on a Ouija board."

I subside. After removing a notepad and pen from her bag, she brings out the planchette and places it carefully over the letter T.

"Are you ready?" she asks.

I nod, nervousness running through me suddenly and powerfully, making me want to get up and move away quickly. "Of course," I say instead.

"Put your index finger on the planchette," she instructs me. I obey and almost jerk my hand back when I do. The planchette is wooden and cold to the touch, but for just a second it almost seemed to be vibrating. She places her finger next to mine. A startled expression crosses her face along with something that looks very much like worry.

"Okay?" I ask, and she jumps.

"Yes, of course," she says haughtily. "Do not remove your finger from this, Levi. That's vitally important. Be careful what you ask the spirits. Do not ask the manner and time of your death."

"Damn, and I so wanted to make sure I'd be wearing clean under-wear. Is that it?" I joke. "How about the winning lottery numbers?"

"Do not mock the spirits," she says coldly. "It isn't wise."

Her words hang on the air for a second and then she moves her finger, and I follow with my own as she sets the planchette spinning in an idling movement.

"Are there any spirits present?" she suddenly asks, almost making me jump. "Please come forward and talk to us. We wish to speak to you."

I observe her from under my eyelashes and smile wryly. She's patently a con artist, and I mentally kiss goodbye to my fifty quid and the obvious loss of my common sense that has led me into this. All because I didn't want to piss off a boy called Blue.

Then I sit up straight as the planchette starts to move under our fingers and an expression of consternation crosses her face.

The planchette moves slowly from one end of the board to another in a lazy action that seems almost taunting. Her mouth drops open and she sneaks me a look, but when she catches my gaze, she shutters her expression.

"Spirit, we are pleased to meet you. Please spell out your name."

The planchette spins slowly before gliding to the word *NO*.

"Oh," she says. "Can you tell us your age?"

Again the planchette spells *NO* and continues to do so as she asks increasingly desperate questions about the spirit's place of birth, sex, and death.

There's almost a taunting quality to the interaction and I know she feels it too, and suddenly I'm sure that this is real and that she'd intended to trick me and now she has no idea what to do. It knocks me back for a few seconds. A large part of me is waiting for someone to leap out and proclaim that this is a silly joke. The other part knows there are strange things going on in my house and that the truth may lie in the little voice at the back of my brain that is getting louder every hour. It's telling me that the dark really does contain monsters and this world is stranger than anything I could ever have imagined. It's starting to insist that my house is actually fucking haunted.

"Do you actually want to talk to us?" I ask sharply, growing frustrated with the polite way Fay addresses whatever this is. I want some bloody answers. "Because if not, I have things to do. Give us a message or go."

Fay gasps and when I look up, I'm surprised to see how white and sweaty her face is. "You shouldn't," she says hoarsely.

"Shouldn't what?"

"You mustn't talk to the spirits like that," she whispers as if they can overhear us. "It angers them."

"And I suppose I wouldn't like them when they're angry," I ask, doing a Hulk impression and stopping as the planchette moves slowly over to the word *NO*.

It crosses the board again, edging to one letter after another. I call out the letters to Fay as she writes with her left hand. I look down at the pad and swallow.

HELLO, LEVI, it says.

Fay looks up at me, fear vivid in her face.

"Hello," I say steadily. "Did you want to give me a message?" Before I finish the question, the planchette moves again, no longer slow and taunting, but jerking with speed.

Fay holds up the pad. *LEAVE MY HOUSE.*

"Only it's not yours," I say slowly. "It's mine. Got the deeds and everything."

Again the movement. *IT WILL ALWAYS BE MINE.* Even before Fay finishes writing, it's off again, and I swallow hard at the message. *LEAVE OR DIE. IT IS YOUR CHOICE. MAKE IT SOON.*

Fay and I stare down at the board as the planchette starts to move again, whipping out of our fingers and performing a last figure of eight on the board.

"What is *happening?*" I ask hoarsely. The planchette spins slowly in the board's centre.

I jump and give an undignified shriek as the main light is switched on. An angry Blue appears in the doorway. His hair is ruffled, his face red, and he looks like he's been running.

"What the fuck are you doing?" he shouts. I open my mouth to answer, but then I realise that he's speaking to Fay. "What gave you the fucking right to do this?"

Fay sits back. "I did," she says coldly. "I don't need you telling me what to do, Blue. You may think you're the authority on this type of shit, but you're fucking wrong." Her expression is stony. "I warned you."

I look down at the table and swallow. The planchette is now moving down the alphabet from Z to Y to X to W. "Erm, you two…"

Blue jerks away from his stare-off with Fay to look where I'm pointing. When he sees the planchette, he blanches.

"Shit," he says. "Fay, Levi, put your fingers back on the planchette."

Fay looks like she's going to refuse, but he roars *Now!* at her, and she hastens to comply.

The planchette is positively vibrating now, moving faster down the letters.

"What is this?" Fay quivers, all spite gone from her voice and fear replacing it.

"This is what happens when a Ouija board goes bad," he says grimly. "You have a malevolent spirit in charge of the board." Fay goes to get up, and he shakes his head. "You have to stay, Fay. Take control, or it will."

"You do it," she shouts.

"I can't," he says. "I'm not part of this table. You two are."

"What shall I do?" I say steadily, watching the planchette move from M to L to K.

"Concentrate hard. Both of you move the planchette to 'GOOD-BYE' and dismiss it. Say goodbye politely."

I look at Fay, and she nods, sweat standing out on her face. A picture falls from the wall, and she shrieks. Blue turns to the doorway and winces. I follow his gaze instinctively but the doorway is empty.

"Now," he says harshly, dragging my attention back. "There isn't much time."

Fay and I bend, putting our fingers back onto the planchette. It wobbles violently, but, as we both focus on the board as if we're going to incinerate it with our eyes, we're able to direct the pointer to the word *GOODBYE*. It's as if we're pushing against some invisible force and I can feel sweat breaking out under my arms.

"Thank you for speaking," I say, amazed at the coolness in my voice. "We're going now, so you must say goodbye."

The planchette judders and spins and then slowly goes still. For a second, no one says anything. The atmosphere in the room abruptly lightens. Then Fay is up, collecting her coat and shoving the board into her bag.

"Wait," Blue says. She turns to him, poised to escape but held by the note of command in his voice. "You are not to come near Levi again. Do you understand me?" She opens her mouth as if to argue and he shakes his head, gesturing at something behind her. "She's disappointed in you today, Fay. Very disappointed."

Fay blanches and looks behind her. "Blue," she falters. "I didn't mean any harm."

"Yes, you did," he says coldly. "You meant to do this to spite me. You meant to use an innocent man to get back at me, and you were prepared to use the spirits to do it. They don't like that. You should be ashamed of yourself."

Abruptly, she rallies and flings her bag over her shoulder. "I'm not the one ashamed of myself," she says angrily. "You need to get over yourself, Blue, or the only way is fucking down."

Then she's gone, whirling out of the house in a flurry of patchouli and that damp wood smell, leaving us in silence.

I stare at Blue. He's dressed in skinny jeans, a black jumper that swamps him, and an ancient-looking denim jacket. If possible, he looks even more tired than before.

"What was all that about?" I ask.

He starts to speak, but a door slams loudly upstairs. We both flinch and look up at the ceiling as another door slams and then another and another.

He looks at the doorway again and his gaze sharpens. He nods as if answering something and turns to me. "Come on," he says urgently. "Grab your coat. We need to be out of here now."

Bewildered, but unable to ignore the urgency in his voice, I grab my jacket and follow him out of the kitchen. The lounge door opens and slams loudly as if in a fit of temper. As we step outside, I turn to shut the front door behind me. It's seized from my hands and slammed so hard that the house seems to shake.

For a long second, Blue and I stand there panting and looking at each other. The quiet of the street is almost shocking. *How can all that have happened in there and it be so quiet out here,* I wonder in a befuddled fashion.

He straightens, pulling his thin jacket closed as he shudders. "Come on," he says abruptly.

"Where? This is my house."

"Not at the moment," he mutters and gestures me down the lane, after stooping to pick up two large paper bags from the doorstep.

"Who was Fay?" I ask. "She said you'd sent her."

He shakes his head. "I didn't."

"Then why did she say that?"

He stops and looks at me, and I'm struck by how he seems both young and ancient. The wind blows his bright hair back from a clear, unlined forehead, but his eyes are shadowed by absolute weariness.

"Are you alright?" I ask, grabbing his arm gently as he goes to turn away. His arm is thin under my fingers, and a wave of sudden and disconcerting possessiveness sweeps over me, urging me to look after him. I don't obey. Instead I stand back. He grimaces as he notes my retreat.

"I'm fine," he says shortly and turns to walk up the lane. I notice that he seems to be moving stiffly as if he's hurt. "Come on," he calls back to me. "We'll find a spot in the park."

I follow him as he walks down to the Minster and passes left into the Dean's Park. I've sat here a lot over the last few months. It's a lovely, tranquil spot with ancient, gnarled trees bending solicitously over the stretch of grass, their branches swaying in the wind and giving glimpses of the Minster's honey-coloured stone.

Now it's deserted and left to us and the wind that tears around us. Finding a bench, he settles down and pats it. I consider staying standing but then give up and sit down next to him.

"How did you know she was at my house?" I ask.

He hands me one of the bags. I open it and find a galette which is a replica of what I ordered yesterday. I inhale the scent of cheese and look up.

"I was bringing you lunch," he says and shrugs. "I wasn't happy with myself, the way we finished our conversation yesterday. I was rude, and I upset you, so you didn't finish your food."

"Oh, there was no need," I protest. "You were being kind."

"Not kind enough," he says grimly. "And definitely not helpful. I could have told you a lot more than I have. I should have done that. Instead you were kind and polite, and I was a bit of an arsehole."

"Not really," I say. He looks at me sideways, and I smile. "Well, maybe a bit."

Incredibly he laughs, but it breaks off as he shivers. He pulls his coat sleeves down so they cover his fingers.

"You're cold," I say and strip off my coat. "Here, put this on."

"Oh no, I can't wear your coat. You'll be cold then."

I shrug. "I'm fine. I always run too warm. Here, take it."

He wraps it around himself and shudders as he absorbs the heat. "It's so warm," he says in a low voice. "Smells of you."

Feeling my cock twitch, I shift on the seat. His sharp features are shaded briefly by the shadows from the branches of a nearby tree. He looks wild and feral for a second and then his face clears.

He indicates the bag. "Eat up while it's still warm." He pauses. "Thank you for the coat, Levi," he says softly.

I nod and take a bite, groaning as the flavour hits my taste buds. I still as I find him studying me intently, his own lunch ignored. "It'll get cold," I say demurely, and he shakes his head and gives a deprecating laugh before falling on his food. And I do mean fall. He eats like a starving wolf would if someone was going to take his food away at any second.

He flushes as he catches me watching him and a strange shamed look crosses his face.

I can't bear it, so I race into speech. "Why has Fay got it in for you, and by extension now me too, apparently?"

He shrugs. "It's a long story. Fay pretends to be psychic. She's got a good con going on. She reads the tarot, or should I say bullshits the tarot, and claims to be able to see the dead. For a while both of us worked in a local occult shop for a total conman called Spud. We'd speak to people's loved ones and take their money hand over fist for passing on messages. There were waiting lists to see us, and we were rolling in money, although not quite as much as Spud." He must see the look of disgust on my face because his next words are spoken low and entreatingly. "I didn't question it at first, because I really needed the money desperately. I didn't want to—"

He stops talking suddenly, and I wait for a second before breaking in. "But why today? Where do I come into this?"

"Because Logan in the pub the other night must have called her and told her I was sitting drinking with you. I thought I saw her when I left the pub that night just after you, but I dismissed it. I shouldn't have because she must have followed you home and made four from two and two."

"But why does she dislike you?"

"Because I broke up the happy little group when I refused to do anything else for Spud. I realised it was wrong, and I didn't want to do it anymore."

Pride and determination are written all over his face for a moment, and my spirits lift that he did the right thing. "But surely that's no reason to hound someone. People are ten a penny who lie about being psychic. They could have found someone as quick as anything."

He shakes his head, staring ahead at the mass of the Minster. His eyes track something, and, as is becoming habit, I follow his gaze and find nothing there. It's unnerving. He shrugs helplessly before turning to me.

"I didn't need to lie about anything, Levi. The reason it worked was because it wasn't a con for me." He smiles at what must be the confusion on my face. "I am psychic," he says slowly, his wolf eyes steady and clear on mine. "I can see the dead." He huffs. "I can also occasionally hear the fuckers, and worst of all, they keep trying to bloody talk to me."

A startled silence falls. "You're not exactly Haley Joel Osment, are you?" I say faintly.

CHAPTER 5

*L*evi

He doesn't say anything for a long beat but then he snorts and breaks into laughter, and unable not to, I laugh too.

"It's true, isn't it?" I say after a few moments. Then suddenly I have to ask, "What were you looking at in the Golden Fleece the other night?"

He looks startled, as well he should, but he still answers. "The serving woman that always stands in that room."

"And I'm guessing she's not ..." I hesitate before whispering, "A person?"

He shakes his head. "Not anymore, no." He pauses. "Well, not unless she's got a major transparency problem."

Incredibly, I want to laugh, but more questions are forming in my brain. "And on the ghost tour at the last site you could see the Devil's last victim, couldn't you?"

A shadow crosses his face. "She's always there." He shudders slightly. "It's not pleasant." His gaze sharpens. "How do you know?" Then in a rush, he asks, "Did you see her too?"

Blue's voice is a mixture of cynicism and hope. It makes my stomach hurt. It must be so lonely being him. I shake my head and his expression falls slightly. "No, I'm sorry. I thought I did for a second, but when I looked again it was just the tree moving in the wind."

His mouth ticks up. "You'd be surprised. You know that flicker you sometimes get in the side of your eye?" I nod. "Well, that's a spirit." He pauses. "Usually, unless you've just got a really bad twitch."

"Really?" I ask, turning to him and propping my knee up on the bench in my eagerness. "So why can't I see anything?"

"Maybe because you turn too quickly to see." He shrugs. "I'm not sure, to be honest. I don't know how I do it. Maybe I move slower or my brain has a different wavelength than yours, but I see them."

"Them?"

Blue sighs. "All of them." He gestures to the Minster. "Like the two men on a scaffold over there who probably worked on the Minster hundreds of years ago, and the monk who crosses the park here, his hands in his sleeves, looking cold and cross."

I look at the empty view in front of us. "You can see all of that?" He nods. "You poor fucker," I mutter. "York must be a sodding nightmare for you."

A glimmer of humour crosses his face. "You have no idea."

"How long have you been...?" I hesitate, and he grins.

"You can say psychic, Levi. It's not the same as having the clap." I stare at him, and he relents. "Since I can remember. I've always seen spirits. Even when I was a child."

"What did your parents say?"

His expression closes. We've reached the end of that line of questioning. I try a different tack, not wanting him to leave. He fascinates me but not just because of the psychic business, which is making my head explode. I think if I hadn't experienced what happened in my house this week, I wouldn't have believed him. But I do. In some strange way, he seems like someone I've known for a long time.

"So, did you see anything in my house?" I ask.

He nods almost reluctantly. "Fay's mum was there, but then that's normal because she follows Fay everywhere trying to get her to be good. Poor woman must be knackered because that's a thankless bloody task."

"Anything connected to the house itself?"

"There was a woman in the doorway when I came into the kitchen," he says slowly. "She looked agitated."

"Could that be the lady with the lily of the valley perfume?"

He nods. "I think so. I smelled it strongly in the hall when I came in."

"So why is she doing all this?"

He shakes his head. "I don't know whether she is. It feels like there's something else in that house with her."

He pauses and despite the broad daylight, a shiver passes down my spine, and I suddenly feel like I'm five again and there's a monster under my bed.

"What?" I ask in a low voice.

He looks impatient and I draw back, stung. "I don't know, Levi," he finally says. "I couldn't see it. I could only feel a presence there, and it wasn't nice. In fact, it was fucking awful. Scary." He shoots me a sudden entreating look. "I'm not good at controlling this thing I have," he says in a hurried tone, the words skipping over each other like sticks on a busy stream. "I see ghosts when I don't want to, but I mostly can't hear what they're trying to say. I can get a sense of it, but I don't know whether I'm right or wrong. And sometimes I feel stuff but can't see it or say why."

I put out my hand on his arm to stay the words and still as a warm thrumming energy seems to coat my palm. He stares at me with surprise written on his face. I struggle to remember what I was going to say. "It doesn't matter, Blue," I say. "Just do your best."

He shakes his head. "It isn't good enough," he says angrily. "It never is. Why can I see a fucking grey lady in the Shambles and I can't tell a friend not to get in a car because they're going to die?"

"Because you're not in charge of the universe," I make myself say in a calm voice. I rub his arm. "At least not yet."

He subsides back on the bench, and a smile glimmers across his face. "Not yet, but I have big plans." He looks at me quizzically, and I realise that I'm now holding his hand.

"Sorry," I mutter and drop it quickly. For a second Blue stares at me and I rush into chatter. "So, you said earlier that you could have told me more about my house. Is there buried gold in the cellar, or a poltergeist in the parlour?"

A shadow crosses his face, and my smile drops away. He twists to face me. "You're not the first person to ask me questions about your house." He pauses. "Although you are the first person to gate crash a ghost tour." He sighs. "The man who had the house a few years ago came into the shop I was working at as a psychic. He wanted to know the house's history and about the supposed spirits."

"*What*? What did he say?"

"He seemed to be having the same problems as you. He said windows kept opening and he could hear footsteps and smell perfume."

"Oh my God, *really*?" I ask excitedly. "That's amazing. I remember Mr Fenton saying that he was the one who did all the work in the cellar. I'll ring the solicitors when I get back and see if he can forward this bloke my contact details. I need to talk to him."

He grimaces. "That's not exactly possible." He hesitates and then shrugs. "He died, Levi."

"*What*? When?"

"It was a couple of years ago." He looks at me uneasily. "He died in the house. They found him at the foot of the stairs with his neck broken."

"What the fuck?" I draw back in shock.

He grabs my hand. "I know. I couldn't tell you that on the ghost tour or in the pub." He shakes his head. "How could I have? You sat there all perfect looking and all I could see was the face of that other bloke and I felt…" He breaks off suddenly with a shocked look on his face.

"Felt what?" I ask, staring into the weary depths of his eyes.

"Nothing," he says. "It doesn't matter." I sag slightly. "I *promise* I'm going to help you, Levi," he says earnestly, his long cold fingers clutching mine. He sighs angrily. "Although what help I'll be, I don't know. I can't even control what I do." He squeezes my hand. "But I'll find someone who can help you. I promise."

I look helplessly at him. "I know you will," I say finally. "I believe you."

We stay like that for a long second until his phone rings. He jerks as he looks at the display. "Shit, I've got to go. Are you alright?"

I nod. "I'm fine, honestly," I say, resisting the urge to ask who he's meeting.

"I think that might be because you don't really believe all of this is happening."

I hesitate and opt for honesty. "Not really. But I will."

He nods. "It's inevitable." He pauses before speaking in a rush. "Listen, be careful. The other man's death was ruled an accident but…"

"But you don't believe that, do you, Blue?"

He shrugs off my coat and hands it to me. "No, I don't. There's something in that house. I'm not sure whether it's Rosalind, the Victorian murderess, or something else. I'll be in touch," he says with a world of weariness in his voice. The shadows under his eyes seem even more pronounced than they were earlier, and when he walks away he seems as ethereal as one of the spirits he claims to see.

Claims, or does see them? Am I actually sitting here believing the word of someone who has openly admitted being friends with con artists? Do I, who once didn't believe in ghosts at all, believe that Blue sees them? I think of his worn-thin appearance and nod. *Sees them and is tortured by it.*

I stare at the open expanse of grass and trees. There's nothing to see here at all but apparently it's teeming with spirit lifeforms.

"I do believe him," I say slowly.

I shiver as a gust of wind blows my hair about and penetrates the folds of my clothing like sharp fingers pinching. So, what now? My house is apparently haunted by the ghost of some random woman who may have pushed the previous occupant down the stairs. That's if some other spirit didn't get there first. I snort and shake my head. It's like *Poltergeist* but without the television.

I stand up. It's late afternoon, and it's gloomy and cold. Time to go home, much as I don't want to. That thought stops me in my tracks. *I don't want to go home.* What the fuck?

That place is my home. I've poured money and love into it. If there weren't any paranormal activities going on, it would be a real home. I stiffen my spine. It's not running me out of my home, whatever it is.

I take a step, and notice a wallet on the ground in front of the bench. I crouch down to pick it up. It's made of faded blue leather with a design of flowers cut into the material. It looks old and hand-made. I open it, hoping to find a driving license or contact details, but instead I find a twenty-pound note and a few business cards which have the details of Blue's ghost tours printed on them. That's it. Nothing else. No credit cards or store cards. No driving license or half a ton of crap like the stuff that bulges out my own wallet.

This wallet doesn't even look like something he'd own. I've already got the impression that he prefers starker things. I huff a laugh. Who am I kidding? I don't fucking know the man.

Nevertheless, he's now minus a wallet, and I race towards the gates to look around to see if I can spot him. No sign of him. I curse under my breath, because how can I return it to him if I don't know his address? I'm just reaching for the card to get his phone number when a crowd of tourists part, and I spot the blue of his hair as it bobs along before disappearing down a side street.

I start to run, dodging round tourists taking photos, and narrowly avoiding a collision with a shivering busker playing a lonely lament of "Purple Rain." When I get to the street Blue disappeared down, I look around wildly and spot him walking slowly down near the end.

He turns at that moment to look behind him, and I open my mouth to shout at him, but for some reason I hesitate. Thoughts fill my mind of his tiredness and the stiff way he held himself as if he was hurt today, and without thinking I jump into the nearest shop door-way. I wait there breathing noisily while an old lady looks at me in an affronted manner and manoeuvres round me with a put-upon sigh.

"Sorry," I mutter and poke my head round the entrance. Blue has turned back and is walking slowly again, his hand returning to his ribs occasionally as if supporting himself.

I ease out and start to follow him.

And that is what you're actually doing at the moment, I tell myself. *You*

started off with a kind gesture but now you are following this poor lad like
some sort of fucking stalker. Abort, abort. Stop doing this.

But I don't. I follow his slow pace, dodging around people on the
narrow cobbled lanes and occasionally hiding in doorways as he leads
me down street after street and the houses get progressively dodgier.
We're far from the touristy charm of the Shambles now, and I'm
having to go slowly because there aren't enough people around to
hide behind.

I look around curiously. This was obviously a wealthy street once.
The houses are big and gracious with bay windows and long front
gardens, but it's obviously fallen on hard times. A lot are boarded up.
Others have been made into flats, and saggy curtains hang across the
windows giving the houses a slovenly impression.

Blue's quite far ahead of me when he disappears. One minute he's
there, the next gone. I blink and look around, but the street is cold
and empty. I pick up my pace, still looking around cautiously. This
doesn't feel like the sort of place to be skipping about in. I breathe in,
considering for the first time whether Blue could have led me here
deliberately. I have the discretion of Inspector Clouseau, so maybe
he's been aware of me following him all along and led me here so his
mates could mug me. I slow down. I don't know him, after all.

But he brought me lunch. He confided in me. Surely that has to
mean something? There was that glimpse of a vulnerability under his
hard exterior that I'd witnessed for a moment before he shuttered it
away. I think of the way he's trying to help me, not because he should,
but because he wants to, and I walk quicker.

I trust my judgement. My mum always told me that. Trust what
your head and heart say if they speak together. Ignore society and
other people's opinions and do what you know to be right. I feel the
customary sharp pang in my chest at the thought of her and push it
away as I come to the spot where Blue just vanished into thin air.

I'm standing in front of a large old house. It must have been a
beauty at one time with its tall windows and graceful lines. Now, it
looks like it's on the way to the knackers' yard. Graffiti is scrawled
messily across its front, and the windows are boarded up so they look

like blind eyes staring down at me. Flyers and mail that have been stacked in front of the boarded-up front door twist and slide across the drive in the breeze.

There's no sign of life, but somehow it feels occupied. Like someone is watching me. I shove away that unpleasant thought and start to walk up the drive. In my head I can't help but wonder how the newspapers will report my murder and whether they'll use the words "criminally stupid," but my body forces my legs to keep moving anyway.

I look around. The front door is obviously out, so I make my way to the back of the house. Overgrown bushes rain water drops on me, so by the time I push into the garden I'm feeling damp and cross.

I look cautiously around, but there's nothing. The garden is wild, and the house forbidding. I shake my head. *Fuck this. I'll ring him on the ghost tour number, and he can get his wallet back then.*

It's as I move that my gaze catches on the board over the back door. At first sight it's nailed tight, but now I can see a gap through which a little light is filtering. The gap is the size of a human body. I'd have to contort a bit, but Blue would get in easily. I'm just contemplating it when someone comes up behind me.

"Can I help you?" a deep voice enquires.

I spin round. "Shit! You frightened me."

"Oh, I'm so sorry that I frightened the stalker. I do beg your pardon."

I look at the bloke standing in front of me. He's tall with tattoos spreading across his hands and up his neck. His hair is jet black with a steak of white running through it, and I have the highly inappropriate thought that he looks like a giant skunk.

I think of telling him that, but he doesn't look like he'd appreciate a shared piece of humour. "I'm looking for Blue," I say instead.

The intent look on his face deepens. "Blue? What do you want with Blue?"

"He left his wallet with me."

I don't know what the words mean to him because they seem fairly simple to me, but his face darkens with anger, and I back up a few healthy steps.

"Fucking idiot," he spits out. "I *told* him to stop doing that, but does he listen?"

I shake my head. "I don't know," I say cautiously. "Look, could I see him?"

"No, you fucking can't." He straightens up to his full height. "You can fuck off, mate. Right now." He shakes his head. "What the fuck is the world coming to when a john follows a bloke home to give him his wallet?" He holds out one massive hand. "Give it me and I'll see he gets it."

I stare at him. *A john? What the fuck is he talking about?* Then I look up at the abandoned house and think of Blue's thinness and tiredness, the way he was walking as if his ribs hurt today, and my heart sinks as I come to the obvious conclusion about him. Nevertheless, I stand up to my full height.

"No, I won't," I say sharply. "I'd like to see him, please. He looked like he was hurt this afternoon and—"

With eerie speed, he backs me against the wall. "What the fuck did you do to him?"

"I didn't do anything." I'm trying for indignation but it's a bit wheezy. "I fucking swear. We ate in the park and talked, and that's it." He stares at me. "I *promise*," I say, investing all my sincerity into the words. After a long pause, he steps back, and I draw a breath. "I want to see Blue," I say again, wondering where this suicidal stubbornness is coming from. A normal person would have run off by now.

He stares at me and then shrugs, his shoulders moving like a mountain under an avalanche. "Okay. Come on in." He pauses as he peels the board back and gestures me through. "But no wandering off. This isn't *Through the Keyhole,* so don't poke your nose into anything."

"Okay," I say quickly, squeezing through the gap, aware of him following me. We step into a kitchen, and after one careless inhale, I try to breathe through my mouth.

It's lit by a candle that's casting off a patchouli scent that can't overlay the stink of old damp wood and mould and other even more disgusting scents. The kitchen is cobwebbed and full of rubbish piled high. I shiver at the freezing temperature, and turn to face my assailant, looking at his face curiously in the flickering light.

It's a surprisingly gentle face on the top of such a man mountain, with a soft mouth and very bright blue eyes, and I relax a little. Someone with that mouth can't be a coldblooded killer. I think of the imaginary newspaper article again and amend it so that it definitely says genius level of stupid.

"Come on," he says after examining me in the same way. He jerks his head towards a set of stairs that lead up and out of the kitchen. "Blue will be in his room."

"His room?" I echo, wishing I could take the startled sound of my voice back.

A flicker of humour crosses his face. "Yes, he's got the royal suite. Always stays there when he's in town."

"Well, it's a home away from home," I say faintly and turn in amazement as he breaks into a clap of booming laughter.

When he recovers, he slaps me on the shoulder so hard I nearly headbutt a cupboard. "I think I might like you," he muses.

"Well, if that's how you like people, I'd hate to get on your bad side," I mutter, peeling myself off the cupboard and following him up the stairs. They're covered in a threadbare carpet and dangerously rackety. I pick my way past a couple that are nothing but a hole and find myself in a long, narrow hall that looks like something from a horror story. More graffiti spreads across the walls, covering the patches left by the wallpaper peeling away. It's dark and lit by the flickering glow of more candles that are guttering in the ruins of old ones and set alongside the bare boards.

My companion picks his way delicately across to the end door where he bangs loudly on the door. "Blue, you in there?"

My heart inexplicably picks up speed. It's only at this point that I stop to consider the fact that Blue is going to be very angry with me for following him and intruding into his personal business. I look back longingly at the hall behind me, contemplating throwing the wallet on the floor and making a run for it, but at that point the giant opens the door and looks round it.

"You've got a visitor," he says.

I hear Blue's voice say, "What," and the giant gestures for me to move forward and ushers me through.

I edge past him into the room. It's small and freezing cold and smells of damp and mould overlaid with the faint fragrance of deodorant. There's no furniture apart from a side table on which is a pile of paperbacks and a candle in a saucer. Blue's ghost-tour suit hangs from a nail on the back of the door and Blue is…

My gaze snags on him lying on an old mattress covered by a bright blue sleeping bag. He has a blanket wrapped around his shoulders which is no wonder, because when he gasps "Levi," his breath shows in the air.

"Surprise," I say faintly as he surges to his feet. I cringe, waiting for the angry words, but I'm blindsided when he steps quickly towards me.

"Are you alright?" he asks urgently.

"Why wouldn't I be?" I say slowly.

He hesitates. "Has something happened at the house? I didn't like leaving you." I gape at him. Realisation replaces his worried expression. "How did you know where to find me?" he says sharply, embarrassment showing as he shoots a quick glance around the room.

I wince. "I followed you." Anger crosses his face and I quickly hold my hand up, aware of the giant observing us silently. "I'm sorry. Before you justifiably shout at me, I didn't know I was going to do it before it happened. You dropped your wallet, and I ran after you, but then I just kept following you, and I know it's no excuse, but I was worried about you because you were moving like you'd hurt yourself, and you looked so tired." I force myself to stop the incredible vomiting of words and drop the wallet into his hand. "So anyway, here's your wallet. Ta-da!" I say faintly. "You're very welcome."

Blue stares at me open-mouthed. The shocked silence is broken by the giant behind me breaking into that hoarse thunderclap of a laugh.

"Will," Blue says in a warning voice.

The giant shakes his head, detaching himself from the wall so abruptly that I take a wary step back.

"I was worried," he says, grabbing Blue's shoulder gently. "He had your wallet, and I thought you'd been…"

Blue shakes his head, resignation and a horrible shame crossing his face. He shoots me a hopeless sort of look that stops my heart. "For fuck's sake, Will. I don't do that anymore." He sneaks another glance at me, and, although he looks back at Will, the next sentence seems meant for me. "I haven't done that in a *long while.*"

"I don't care about that," I say into the silence. "I mean, that's your business." I pause and then back comes the word deluge. "Do you have to stay here? I don't mean to be rude about the place, but it's damp and that won't do your cough any good. You're pale and tired and look like crap, and not warmed-up crap either because you couldn't warm a fucking gnat up in here." I pause. "Not that it's any of my business," I say primly and nod vigorously to emphasise my point.

Humour and irritation vie for prominence in Blue's face, but irritation wins. "Yes, I do have to stay here unfortunately, Little Lord Fauntleroy. You see, unlike yourself who's been gifted a massive fucking house in the nicest area of York, some of us have to settle for this bag of shit because it's either this or the street. Have you ever faced that choice?" I shake my head, and a scornful expression crosses his face. "No, of fucking course you haven't. I might have guessed that by your posh voice and nice stuff. Well, you won't be surprised that I have, and I never want to do it again. Along with my career as the crappiest rentboy in Yorkshire, I was one of those people covered in a blanket in a shop doorway, and let me tell you, the candle shop does not take kindly to people warming their entrance up and that perfume smell gave me a right headache."

He pauses for breath and breaks into a fit of coughing.

"I'm sorry," I say, and without thinking, I step into him and rub his back. "Take little breaths," I advise, looking around. "Have you got any water?"

"Council cut it off," Will says laconically. "They're quite unhelpful towards squatters. I'm thinking of lodging a complaint. I certainly won't vote for them again."

Blue holds his side.

"How did you hurt your ribs?" I ask.

He shakes his head and then directs a fulminating glance at Will as the big man says, "Got into a fight with Fay's bloke last night when he found him in here looking through his stuff."

"Fay? Ouija board Fay?"

Blue reluctantly nods and I whistle. "No wonder she had it in for you." I skate my fingers down his ribs and look up anxiously as he shudders deeply. "Shit, sorry. Did I hurt you?"

He shakes his head, and Will chuckles. I look at him in consternation, but he just grins at Blue. "You okay now?" he asks.

"No, he's not," I say hotly.

Blue groans. "Fuck's sake, Levi."

"Well, you're not alright," I protest. "This place is …" I pause. "Not really very comfortable," I say earnestly. Will and Blue give me synchronised smirks. "It's damp and freezing. No wonder you're ill. You can't keep living here."

"And what do you suggest, Levi?" he says, angrily pulling away from me. My hands automatically miss the warmth of his body. "Shall I buy the house down the road from you? We can be neighbours and have tea parties with tea and scones where we lift up our little fingers when we drink. Or maybe I should contact Prince Harry and take him up on his invitation of a room in his palace."

"Or you could come and stay with me," I say. The words burst out unplanned.

It's like a silence grenade has gone off as they stare at me open-mouthed.

CHAPTER 6

*B*lue
 "I'm sorry," I say. "Did you just ask me to come and stay with you, Levi?"

I expect him to laugh but instead he nods earnestly. "Yes. Come and stay with me. I know it's spooky and the ghosts are probably homicidal, but at least you'll be able to lie in a bed and have a bath before they gruesomely murder you in your sleep."

I suppress a groan at the thought of clean sheets and hot water. "Did he hit his head coming into the house?" I ask, looking at Will for confirmation.

He shakes his head, a wondering smile crossing his face. "No, he's sane." He looks at Levi. "Well, as sane as you can get for someone who's asking you to be their roommate."

"Oh, shut up," I mutter as he grins.

I turn back to Levi and swallow at the sight he makes in this shit-hole of a room. Dressed in jeans with a navy jumper and a heavy navy peacoat over it, his wavy brown hair gleams in the candlelight. His open, expressive face, with full lips and a sharp nose, looks earnest and full of purpose.

He's pretty, for sure. I'd noticed that the very first moment I'd looked through his window and saw him naked. Well, I'd noticed his large cock first. *Then* I'd noticed the prettiness.

It wasn't the first time I'd seen him though. I'd caught sight of him in a pub a few days before then. I'd been with some mates after a ghost walk and couldn't take my eyes off him as he stood leaning on the bar sipping his pint with a faraway look in his eyes. Sad eyes.

I knew he'd lost his mum before he even told me. I hadn't been trying to read him. I don't try to read people at all—it's how I keep myself safe.

Despite my efforts, people's thoughts and emotions pour into my head all the fucking time without stopping, but I tried to hold back with him, closed my brain off so he could have some privacy. It's difficult because he's so honest and transparent. His loss leaked through loud and clear.

And now this pretty man with the sad brown eyes knows that I once hooked for my doss money, that I was a party to lying and cheating desperate people, and that I live in a total shithole. I think of his lovely house and feel heat on my cheeks. He needs to go far away from here and back to his real life. I really am no good for him.

"You need to go," I say abruptly and sigh at the hurt look on his face. "You can't be here." I can hear the desperation in my voice and look at Will for help. He shakes his head in silent refusal and leans back against the wall. *Wanker.* I turn back to Levi. "Look, this is none of your business. Where and how I live has got fuck all to do with you."

He folds his arms, and a stubborn look comes over that kind face. I almost want to laugh because he looks like a billy goat who's tried to eat the washing. "I said I'll help you," I say quickly. "And I will. But my personal life has nothing to do with you. I don't need your charity. So you can go back to your own house."

Levi shakes his head immediately and predictably. "It's not charity." He unfolds his arms, and for a second I think he's going to put those hands with their beautiful long fingers on me. Earlier his touch had felt like he'd seared me. "It's not charity," he says again insistently. I raise one eyebrow, and he sighs heavily. "It's *not*. Listen, you're the first friendly face I've met here, and you've been very kind to me."

I'm about to suggest that he needs to get out more when Will shakes his head fiercely at me. I glare at him and then turn back to Levi as he carries on talking. "I know I'm probably a bit boring." My mouth drops open. "Because I work from home and don't get out much. But it can get lonely, and I really like your company." He pauses. "So, you'd be doing me a favour, really."

For a second I actually believe him, and then I catch a glint in his eyes that makes me want to laugh. "Bullshit," I scoff.

He sags slightly before rallying. "Well, how about the fact that you can tell me more about what's going on in the house?"

"Did you miss the part where I told you I can't control it?"

Will jerks and looks startled. "You *told* him?"

Levi looks at Will curiously, and I hope the dim light is covering my red cheeks. "Yes," I mutter. "Doesn't matter."

"Oh no," Will agrees mildly. I scowl at him and turn back to Levi to find him looking curiously between me and Will. I open my mouth to send him packing.

"Please," Levi says quietly. "Let me do this for you."

And my words die away. No one has ever wanted to do something just for me. Will is my best mate, but it's survival of the fittest around here. No one has ever wanted to do something for me simply because they can.

I stare at Levi for a long moment. The thing is I like him and that doesn't happen often. He's kind, funny, and a bit shy, and something else that I can't put my finger on. And I want to be with him. The idea of staying in his house with him makes my stomach clench. I like talking to him. He doesn't talk down to me, or he didn't. My heart sinks as I wonder whether he'll start now that he knows my history. I look at that handsome face and those earnest eyes, and I know he won't. He isn't that type of person.

Finally, I sigh. "Are you sure?"

He grins happily like he's just allowed Jude Law to lodge in his house, not a semi-literate ex-prostitute.

"Really?" he says.

"Yes." I hold my hand up. "But I will pay you rent." He starts to argue but I shake my head. "That's a deal breaker. I'll pay you rent and the second you decide I'm overstaying my welcome, you'll tell me." He looks unsure, his kind eyes worried. "That's an unbreakable condition," I say firmly. "I overstay my welcome everywhere. I'd hate to be doing it at your house most of all."

"Okay," he says softly. "It's a deal."

"And you won't argue when I leave, Levi?" I add. "I always leave."

For a long second he stares at me and then nods, putting out one big hand for me to shake. I swallow and let his hand swallow mine, feeling the heat and the flutter of his pulse against my fingertips. "Deal," he says happily. "Shall we pack you up?"

I shake my head. "What am I doing?"

Will nudges me. "The right thing for once."

"He's not a mark," I whisper as Levi walks over to grab a bin liner from the table.

"I know," he says. "And more importantly, so do you."

"What are we taking?" Levi calls.

I turn to him. "You won't need a binbag for my stuff. Will can take my sleeping bag and keep it for safekeeping." *For when I come back* is the unspoken message and Levi's face falls for a second before he looks down at the horrible mattress and round at the room. I flush, wondering if he's judging me, but he smiles.

"Well, what about this?" he asks, lifting up the pale blue blanket on the mattress.

"Yes," I say quickly. "I need to take that." He looks down at the soft knitted blanket, and when he sees the word 'Blue' embroidered by my mum, his eyes soften and he folds it up as gently as if he's handling the coronation robes.

I unhook my suit from the wall and hand it to him and grab my backpack with my clothes in it. There's never been any point in unpacking as the roof leaks, and the clothes would have been as wet as the woodwork within a few hours. "That's it," I say.

He glances around the room and his eyes light on the pile of charity-shop paperbacks on the rickety table. "What about those?"

I shake my head dismissively. "No room for them. I can't keep books."

I wonder whether he caught the note of sadness in my voice, because he immediately switches the suit to one hand and gathers the books up under his other arm. "There's plenty of room in my house for books," he says briskly and nods as if to emphasise his point. "There's a couple of titles here that I fancy reading myself."

Moisture pricks the back of my eyes. *Who is this man?*

Not giving me a chance to speak or muster an argument, he smiles at Will and then at me. "Ready?"

"As I'll ever be," I mutter.

Will waves Levi to walk in front of him. "Watch the stairs," he says, and Levi nods, walking down the corridor. Muscles play down his back, drawing my gaze to slender hips and a small, tight arse. I swallow hard.

"Well, if you'd read your own tea leaves, I bet you'd never have seen this coming," Will remarks companionably, keeping an eagle eye on where Levi is putting his feet.

"I do not read the fucking tea leaves," I say waspishly. "You make me sound like I should have a fucking crystal ball and a stall on Blackpool Pier."

"The sea air is very bracing," he says solemnly.

"So is in here." I stay him with a hand to his forearm. "You going to be okay? I hate leaving you."

"Why?"

"Because you're my friend."

He smiles almost pityingly at me. "Blue, if this happened to me, I'd be off without a look back. It's just the way we are."

I ponder his words and then shove him. "Oh, fuck off. No, it isn't."

He shrugs. "I'll be fine. I get on better with everyone in the house than you anyway."

"That's certainly true," I say sourly, still feeling the pull and burn of my ribs after last night. "Don't lose touch," I instruct him.

He tips his fingers to his head. "I won't," he says serenely. "You're still in York, not moving to Australia. I'll meet you in the week for breakfast at Sals."

I nod. "It's a date."

"Perish the thought."

I laugh. "I want to say men would pay to date this, but only half of that statement would be true."

He shakes his head. "I don't need the tea leaves to see that things are changing for you, Blue. I know it the same way I know when the wind changes."

"You should have worked at the Met Office, then."

We pause at the kitchen door, and I'm so relieved that we haven't seen anyone else. I don't like my business being known, and I fucking definitely won't have Levi's connection with me spread around.

I hold out my arms to Will, and he lowers from his massive height so we can hug. "Take care," I say fiercely. "You won't have me to watch your back."

"Considering you only reach halfway up it, that's a lot less useful than you think."

Levi laughs, the sound merry and warm in the dim kitchen. He offers Will his hand.

"Look after him," Will says.

Levi nods calmly. "I will."

"We're not eloping," I say, peeling the board back a bit and wriggling through. "But if my father does come after Levi with a shotgun, please don't tell him where we went."

Will's laughter follows us out until it's cut off by the board being pulled closed. I shiver. It's like the stone to a tomb being rolled over.

"Do you want him to come and stay too?" Levi asks.

"He wouldn't come. He hates feeling obligated to anyone," I say and then shake my head in disbelief. "Are you set on moving the whole squat in?"

He shrugs. "Just the one you care about."

"Why?"

The question is bald, but he considers it seriously. "I'm not sure," he finally admits.

I laugh quietly. "You're as mad as I am."

"What a scary thought." He looks at me until I break the gaze and stare up at the house.

"Alright?" Levi asks quietly.

I turn to him, analysing that question as if he'd asked me something important. "As I ever am," I say slowly and follow his wide-shouldered shadow out of the garden.

~

When we get to the house, I stop dead, feeling a cold chill run down my back. The building is dark and seems to stoop over me.

Levi comes to a stop next to me. "Everything okay?" he asks.

I search the windows one by one, but there's no one there. Levi shifts position, and I look at him. "No, it's fine," I say slowly. "Just felt for a second like someone was watching me."

He glances up at the house, his eyes wild.

I thread my arm through his. "I can't see anything." I glance around at the damp night. "Let's go in," I say on a shudder.

His expression immediately shifts into concern, and within seconds, he's whisked me into the house and is in the kitchen shouting about turning the heating up.

I look around warily. There's no sign of the woman I saw earlier. In fact, there's no sign of anything. The house is as quiet as the—

I stop that thought straightaway.

Levi comes out of the kitchen. "You alright?" he asks again. I wonder fleetingly how bad I must look for him to be so concerned. I nod, and he smiles. "Do you fancy a shower?"

"Oh my God," I groan. "I would like that more than I'd like to shag Josh Hartnett."

He laughs. "That much, eh?"

Ten minutes later finds me standing under the hard spray of the shower in the bathroom, hot water beating down on my shoulders as the steam eases my chest. As someone who's lived in a place with no running water for a year and had to wash in pub bathrooms, I've never appreciated a shower more.

Eventually, I switch it off before I use up all of his hot water and possibly the whole street's too. His towels are as soft as silk and smell of fabric softener and not mould, and I swallow when I see the blue mark on the towel from my hair. *Shit.*

I dress quickly in the pair of boxer shorts and T-shirt that Levi had lent me. He'd put my entire wardrobe in the washer saying he needed to make a load up. I'd waited to feel shame, but somehow it didn't come. Levi's kind, warm smile doesn't allow embarrassment. It's the sort of smile that says, *I think you might be my friend and you'd do the same for me.*

And the funny thing is I would do the same. And that's *never* been said about me before.

When did that happen? I gaze at my reflection in the mirror.

I don't help people. Taking on extra weight is the quickest way to slow yourself down. Apart from Will, I don't make ties, and I'm ready to move at a minute's notice. So why do I feel this connection with someone who is a virtual stranger to me?

I take a breath, inhaling the woodsy scent of Levi that lies under the fabric softener on his T-shirt. I force away unfamiliar feelings and start to clean my teeth meticulously. No matter my circumstances, I've always looked after my teeth. Probably because I couldn't afford to have any of them taken out.

Eventually done, I gather up the stained towel and go looking for my landlord.

I find him in the second bedroom at the back of the house. He's putting sheets onto the bed, and I watch for a second.

"Thank you," I say.

He jumps, turning around. "Fuck!" he says. "You startled me."

"Bit jumpy."

"You will be too." He looks suddenly worried. "Probably more. I didn't really think this through. Are you going to be okay here with your gifts?"

"*Gifts?*" I query, astounded.

He nods seriously. "Yes, gifts. Might not seem like they are at times, but there's always a reason for things, Blue."

"I'll take your word for it. I'm not sure these gifts will get me on *Britain's Got Talent.*" I fidget in his clothes. "Thank you for doing my washing too," I say awkwardly.

He smiles at me as he pushes a pillow into the case. "I put your blanket on a delicate wash, or it might have shrunk."

My chest gets tight at the thought of him carefully handling my mum's blanket. "That's so good of you," I say hoarsely.

He shrugs and goes back to making the bed.

"Erm, while you've been doing all those nice things for me, I sort of fucked your towel up," I say gruffly, showing him the offending item. "It's my hair dye. It gets on everything like towels and…" I pause, watching him. "And bed linen."

He grins. "It's a bit like a dog peeing on things to mark territory."

"Oh, so I'm a dog now."

He starts to laugh. "A skinny, scrappy one."

His chuckle is infectious. I manage not to laugh but can't stop my smile.

"Doesn't matter," he says, nodding at the towel. "Everything washes clean in the end."

"Does it?"

He nods serenely. "Oh, yes. Some things just take more effort."

I pull my gaze from his and pace around the room as he finishes the bed. "So, this is the brother's bedroom?" I finally say.

He joins me at the window that looks down onto the garden. "I'd put you somewhere else, but the small bedroom at the front hasn't got a bed, and it's full of boxes." He pauses. "You could always sleep in my studio upstairs. That's got a nice feeling to it, and the sofa's really comfortable."

"It's got a nice feeling because it was hers. Her sewing room," I say dreamily, and then start.

"How did you know that?" he asks, looking unnerved.

"I don't know how," I say apologetically. "I just know things some-times." I pause. "But mostly when I don't need to know them. I'm also not sure I'm right with that, anyway. Why would a murderess's room be cosy and safe? It doesn't make sense." I look around. "The house is very quiet at the moment," I say slowly.

"Isn't that good?"

"Sometimes." This doesn't feel like one of those times though. The house actually feels like it's waiting, gearing up for something. But I don't say that. Instead, I shrug and pat his arm. "I'll be fine in here. Don't worry. I know he died violently, but he was blameless, so hope-fully he's moved on."

He looks undecided, but finally he nods and leaves me, shutting the door with a quiet click. The bed beckons, and I slide under the heavy duvet, pulling the sheets over me, inhaling the scent of lavender and feeling the softness settle over me, burying me in a sweet-smelling cavern.

I can't resist the groan of happiness and stretch out, feeling the sheets warm around my body. Sleep tugs at me with the promise that I can fully go under now that he's nearby and will watch out for me. I open my eyes sleepily and that's when I see it.

A small bookcase stands at the side of the bed with my books neatly lined up in it. A note is pinned to it and I reach over and grab it. He's written in an elegant slashing script, "Plenty of room here for some more," and underneath he's drawn a tiny cartoon figure of me curled up in a big chair and reading. I smile widely, feeling my cheeks hurt as I run my finger down the figure with wild blue hair and a frown of concentration on its small face. It's rough and has obviously been drawn in a hurry, but his talent is obvious, as is his humour.

I set the note on the bedside table and turn on my side to look at it. I blink slowly and then again even slower, and the last thing I see before I slide into sleep is that drawing. I think I'm smiling as I go under.

CHAPTER 7

*B*lue
  I come awake with a horrible jerk when the covers are
pulled off me.

"What the fuck?" I mumble, sitting up and rubbing my eyes. "If this
is your idea of a joke, Levi, then..." I switch on the light.

I'm on my own in the room. On my own with the covers thrown
on the floor.

"Okay," I say slowly. I look around. It's freezing in here. So cold
that I can see my breaths in front of my face. "Where are you?" I
whisper.

I climb out of bed, stand up cautiously and inhale, catching the
burning scent that signals spirits are near. The atmosphere is ener-
gized with anticipation, like when a storm is about to break. My hair
raises with the static.

I jump as the door opens so forcefully it slams into the wall. I look
wildly at it, prepared for anything, but there's nothing there. Just an
empty doorway with darkness beyond it and the door swaying gently
with the force of movement.

I breathe out slowly. Even before she appears, I know it's going to happen. I can't describe the feeling. It's like I've watched this scene before, and I'm anticipating the actions.

She looks the same as when I saw her outside the kitchen while Levi and Fay were at the Ouija board. A stout woman with her brown hair piled up in a bun. Dressed in a violet-patterned long dress, she has a sweet-looking face. Spirits usually appear to me as they died, but this one shows no signs of injury. But she does show signs of agitation again.

She disappears and suddenly reappears closer to me. And then closer again, flickering like frames of a movie. That creepy shit never fails to freak me out. It's like watching a shark preparing to attack you.

"What do you want?" I whisper.

She startles, like a glitch in a tape, and I wonder whether she can hear me. I brace, preparing for her answer, but as usual, I get nothing. Instead, she moves her hands in an agitated shooing motion, gesturing at me and then the door.

"What's your name?" I ask.

I jerk as in my head I hear a soft, cultured voice say, *"Rosalind."*

So, it is the sister. I want to marvel at the fact that I actually heard a spirit speak, but the increasingly urgent feel to this encounter, plus the fact that she slit someone's throat, recalls me to the present. However, it doesn't stop me trying again. "Rosalind, do you need my help?"

What can only be described as a *what the fuck* look crosses her face, and at that point the light goes out and a door somewhere downstairs slams. I whirl to face the doorway, aware in my peripheral vision of Rosalind still gesturing. She's a faint glimmer in the moonlight. Then comes the sound of slow, heavy footsteps coming up the stairs. There's something about the deliberateness that chills my blood and makes the hair on the back of my neck stand up.

I look wildly at Rosalind, and for some reason she appears almost worried. At that point she flickers like someone is draining her battery. She makes a last ferocious gesture and half winks out. Still the footsteps come.

Suddenly, I've had enough. I've seen shit and done shit that would turn most people's hair white, but I don't think I've ever been so terrified as tonight in this bedroom.

I dash to the door, the scent of lily of the valley almost choking.

I hesitate at the entrance. The darkness in the hallway is like a sentient being, the shadows seeming to boil and roil. For a wild second I consider slamming the door and going back to bed and hiding under the covers, if only so I don't have to go into this darkness.

Then there's a sound like the rustle of clothing and everything goes quiet. A waiting quiet. My slow, panting breaths echo on the air, and then suddenly a deep chuckle sounds from nearby.

"Fuck!" I shout, almost levitating off the ground.

It's the motivation I needed to run through the darkness. I expect something to grab me and drag me back, but within seconds I'm bursting into Levi's room and slamming the door shut.

For a long second all I can hear are my breaths sawing in and out. I yelp loudly when there's a sudden heavy bang on the door. The sound seems almost petulant.

The lamp switches on, and I want to cry with the happiness of having light. Levi sits up, the covers falling to his waist. I'm about to have a heart attack, but I can't help appreciating his body. He's all wide shoulders and smooth chest, glowing in the lamplight like golden syrup. His hair has a ruffle like a cockatoo. His bleary eyes quickly clear.

"What is it?" he says hoarsely. "What's happening?"

"Erm." There's another bang on the door, and I'm ashamed to say that I squawk like a chicken. "Fuck!" I gasp.

He jumps out of bed and comes to me. "Who is that? What's making that noise?"

"Ah, that would be the ten-million-pound question."

Levi stares at me, and I conjure the strength to explain. "Well, I woke up when the lady of the house, who incidentally is a murderess, ripped the covers off me and basically herded me like a sheep over to this room to get out of the way of whoever was coming up the stairs.

Someone or something that she was scared of. Someone or some-thing, and I need to repeat this quite strongly, that a known cold-blooded murderess is frightened of."

"Who was coming up the stairs?"

"Is this my specialist subject?" I ask waspishly.

The door creaks slightly as if someone is applying pressure from outside. We exchange wide-eyed glances, and then, without saying anything, we press our backs to the door.

The door handle turns questioningly. It's a small movement, but it sends chills down my spine.

"Has this happened to you before?" he asks.

He locks the door, which probably won't make much difference to a ghost, but it does make me feel a tiny bit better.

"No, I mainly see people milling around with various wounds." I pause to consider. "There's a lot of weeping and wailing and wringing of hands but not so much attempting of physical harm and intimida-tion. A bit like Parliament but without the security."

"Well, I'm so glad that I'm giving you new experiences."

"I'll make sure that I put it on my TripAdvisor review," I mutter, smiling as he laughs.

Silence falls outside and we both listen intently. "Is that it, do you think?" Levi whispers.

I shake my head. "I don't think so," I say cautiously. "There's a really bad atmosphere in the house tonight."

"I don't—" He breaks off as a huge, heavy slam comes from down-stairs. "What the fuck?" he mutters. "That's the front door." He unlocks the door, and I grab his arm.

"Where are you *going?*" I hiss.

He looks askance. "I'm going downstairs. I don't need the front door being left open. It's hardly the message I want to send to burglars. I might as well issue an invitation to please come in and help yourself to my TV."

"You *can't* go out there," I whisper, intense fear battering at me. "Anything could happen."

"Yes, like my TV going walkabout."

"There are worse things that can happen to a person."

"Like what?" Levi scoffs.

"I don't know," I whisper furiously. "But I pay attention to my instincts and you should too because they're more developed than yours. You should also try remembering that the last person who asked questions was found dead at the bottom of your bloody stairs."

I want to grab him and shake him because I'm truly frightened tonight. Not of the ghost so much, but oh God, yes, I am shit scared of that. But it's more that Levi's pigheadedness might get him hurt and I can't bear the thought of him hurt like that other man. It's kept me awake the last few nights. I don't want to think about why I'm so fucking concerned about him of all men, so I push it to one side.

Something about my expression must convince him, because he leans back against the door, the fight draining out of him. I quickly flick the lock again in case he changes his mind.

"So you're actually saying, Blue, that there are apparently two ghosts here of whom we know next to nothing, and that one of them woke you up to make you come in here out of the way of the other one."

"*Yes.*" He looks incredulous, and I shake his arm. "You *know* there's something going on out there. It's just that you refuse to acknowledge it properly, because if you do, then you have to admit that your previous world view might have a few teeny tiny holes in it."

Rational arguments form in his eyes, but he never gets the chance to deliver them. A dragging noise sounds from downstairs along with smaller thuds and bangs.

"What in the name of *fuck* is happening now?" he breathes.

I bite my lip, listening intently as the erratic dragging continues, sending urgency and muted rage through the house. "I don't know," I finally admit. "But it feels fucking bad."

We lean against the door as the noises continue. I'm scared shitless but relax slightly as I feel his warmth against me. It's a lot less scary to see and hear things when someone else is close.

Relaxing allows me to appreciate certain things. Like the heat his tall body gives off along with the scent of washing powder and the faint woodsy scent of his aftershave. Or the way his boxers hang from his narrow hips and how wide his shoulders are and the fact that his nipples are a pearly pink.

Eventually, I stir as the house falls silent again. I turn my head, searching as if I'm scenting the air. "It's finished for the time being," I finally say, breathing out in relief.

"How do you know it won't happen again?"

I shrug. "I can't describe it properly. The atmosphere's changed. When a spirit is around, the air feels charged and full of something. Now, it's calm again." I pause. "Well, not calm exactly but it doesn't feel quite so bad." I reach down to unlock the door and pull it open, only to come up short. "What the fuck?"

"Is the lock sticking?" he asks.

I pull it again. "No, it's unlocked but I just can't open the door."

"Here, let me have a go." Levi pulls me gently out of the way but the door refuses to budge no matter how hard he pulls it.

I cough as the air is suddenly filled with the scent of perfume.

He looks around. "It might be just me, but I think the lady's trying to keep you in my bedroom, Blue."

I snort. "I could do with her when I'm out trying to pull."

He laughs wildly. "Oh my God, is this my life now? When did she turn into a bloody pimp?"

The scent churns and intensifies. "I don't think Rosalind likes the word pimp," I observe from my position leaning against the door.

His abashed expression is fucking adorable. "Sorry, Rosalind," he whispers. "*Can* I call her Rosalind?" he asks, looking at me. "Should I call her 'ma'am'?"

I shrug, trying not to laugh. "What's the worst that could happen?"

He blinks. "Erm, she could murder me in my sleep."

"Oh *that*," I say.

His laughter turns into a huge yawn. It's contagious, and I echo it.

"Stay," he says sleepily.

I gape at him. "Are you serious?"

He nods. "I am." His eyes go suddenly intent. "I didn't like you being in that bedroom, anyway. It feels wrong to me. Probably because the poor bugger was killed in his bed. I set one foot in there the first day and knew I wouldn't be sleeping in there. God knows what it feels like to you."

"It was fine up until half an hour ago. Then it was definitely wrong times a hundred thousand million," I say slowly.

He shrugs. "Well, then. Look, we've got a couple of hours before we've got to be up. Let's go to sleep and talk about this in the morning." He smiles kindly. "Just sleep. I promise."

I consider his earnest face for a long second. "Okay, if you're sure," I finally say softly.

Levi smiles. It's potent this close to him. His warm brown eyes are flecked with green around the pupil and fringed with thick lashes. When he walks to the bed, I tag along, watching the way the muscles in his torso twist sinuously under the skin. He's the same golden brown all over, which I can actually say with authority as he's only wearing a pair of blue and white striped boxers. He's very fit looking for an artist.

He slides into the bed and holds up the covers for me and I sigh happily as I flatten myself onto the comfiest mattress I've ever felt. Not that there's been a huge amount of competition. He pulls the covers over me, and I inhale the woodsy scent of him on the cotton.

"Alright?" he asks. "Do you think we're okay to sleep now?"

I snort. "I just want you to know I appreciate how difficult it was for you to say that sentence."

He grins but then sobers. "*Is* it okay? If not, I'll stay awake so you can sleep. You look knackered, Blue, and at least that way you'd feel safe enough to sleep."

I swallow, astonished and not a little touched. "You'd do that for me?"

He looks startled. "Of course. We're friends, aren't we?"

The notion doesn't seem as absurd as it would have done a few weeks ago. Somehow this man is more my friend than some of the people I've known for years.

"We are," I whisper. "But it's okay. The house is quiet now."

"You said that before."

"That wasn't a normal quiet. This is. This is quiet without being silent. It's abnormal to be in an environment where it's totally silent. If that happens, you should get out very quickly."

He yawns. "You remind me of a gerbil preparing to run away from the cat."

"What a lovely comparison," I sniff.

He laughs sleepily. Silence falls for a second and then Levi shifts onto his side, his eyes drowsy but still alert in the moonlight.

"Do you mind me asking why you're living in a squat?" he asks.

I stiffen, but he grabs my hand.

"Sorry," he says. "Oh my *God*, that was so rude. Don't answer."

Ironically, I feel the need to answer with more than my standard fuck off. "No, it's fine," I say softly, moving to my side so I can watch him as I talk. It's extraordinarily intimate in the moonlight. "I've been on the streets since I was thirteen."

"*Thirteen!*" he bursts out.

I shush him, but I don't know why. The only other occupants of this house don't exactly need to get their beauty sleep. "My mum died when I was that age." I sigh. "That's where I get it from."

"What?"

"The gift." I raise my fingers in a quote sign. "Only it's not," I say fervently. "It drove my mother mad. Literally." I bite my lip, thinking of her blonde hair and the bright blue eyes that always seemed to be looking a million miles away from me. "She couldn't control it. She saw them everywhere and it sent her bonkers. She couldn't cope with it, and while I know enough not to acknowledge ghosts when I'm in public, she didn't think that way. She'd shout and scream at them and have mumbled conversations. It's no wonder she couldn't keep a job."

I pause, and then admit, "I think there was something else wrong with her as well. She had really extreme mood swings. One minute she was ecstatic, swinging-on-the-ceiling happy, and the next day she'd be so low she couldn't get out of bed. Possibly if they could have medicated her properly, she'd have been able to deal with being psychic better."

"How long had she been like that?"

"She was always like that," I say, hearing the incredulity in my voice.

"Did she try to get help?"

"She tried. Unfortunately, telling doctors that she could see people who weren't there got her sectioned a couple of times and me slung into foster care. After that she wouldn't trust doctors or anyone in authority. We slipped further and further down and out of the reach of the system. She'd meet blokes and move us in straightaway. We'd be there a few days or maybe a couple of weeks, and then they'd have had enough and on we'd go again."

"I'm sorry," he says softly. "That must have been so difficult."

"It wasn't easy," I admit, feeling my eyes burn at the simple truth in his voice and the sympathy. I've never told anyone this apart from Will. I don't know why it's all spooling out of me now. "Particularly as I could see them too. I spent a horrible few years thinking I was going to go mad like her." I still think that, but I'm not going to tell him.

"So what happened?"

I swallow hard. "We were staying in a squat in London. She slashed her wrists. I found her in the morning." I think of the blood pooling rustily in the folds of her sleeping bag, the empty eyes and gaping mouth, and I shudder. I inhale as he slides closer and pulls me tight, hugging me to him.

"That's fucking awful," he mutters. "I'm so sorry."

"It is as it is," I say, trying for coolness and probably hitting inappropriate flippancy. "I ran away that day."

"Why?"

"Because I'd already been in care and it wasn't the pleasantest of experiences. I took the cash she had, my blanket and some photos, and I hitched to York."

"Why York?"

I shrug, feeling the hair in his armpit tickle the skin on my shoulder. "I couldn't go back to Ireland because I hadn't got the money. York seemed as far away from London and anyone I'd know as I could get."

"But you were thirteen," he bursts out. "How did you even cope?"

"You know how I coped," I whisper and he stiffens. I go to withdraw myself from his arms, feeling shame lash me, but his grip tightens.

"I'm so sorry you had to do that," he says. "But I'm not sorry at the same time because you're here and whole. The past is what we do to get to where we are."

"How philosophical," I say tartly. "You should write that on a tea towel. You'd sell a shedload."

"Only if it was hundred percent cotton. I cannot have man-made fibres near my skin," he says pompously, making me laugh. "So, how did you go from that to ghost walks and squats?"

I snuggle in closer, feeling the warmth of his body seep into mine. I'm always so fucking cold, and he's so toasty it's like sleeping next to a fire. "One of my johns, Spud, had a shop. He was a repeat customer and he wasn't a total wanker like some of them." I pause. "Well, not at first, anyway. He always wanted me to come when he fucked me and he'd buy me breakfast afterwards, which to me made him Mr Fucking Darcy. I trusted him and told him about being psychic. He introduced me to Fay and said he'd pay me to work in his shop." I shake my head. "I was ecstatic," I say slowly, feeling sleep pulling at me. "I have no qualifications at all, and I'm thick."

"Not judging from the titles of those books I carried back here. They weighed more than your other stuff."

"I like reading. But it doesn't mean much in a world where I don't exist. No NI number, no qualifications, nothing. I'm nobody. With the money Spud was paying me, I was able to get a room in a house that a friend of his owned. I loved that place," I say nostalgically. "It was small, but it was all mine. I bought my own bed linen and I used to lie in bed in the morning watching the oak tree tap its branches against the window."

"What happened?"

I shrug. "The usual. It didn't last. I told you. I said I didn't want to do the psychic stuff for him anymore. He wanted me to say stuff, lead people to buy stuff, or get them to give me personal details. When I realised he and a mate of his were then burgling these people, I walked out. I couldn't afford my room anymore, so I was chucked out and back to the next squat I went." His arm tightens, but he doesn't say anything, which I'm glad of. I don't need false platitudes. I never have. "An old hook-up was working the ghost tours."

He snorts. "Small Box Boy."

I laugh. "That's him. Wanker," I say with feeling. "Anyway, I signed on to work for the same company and then realised I'd make more money if I went on my own, so I did. Then one day I happened to look through a window and lo and behold, I saw my prince, naked apart from a dish cloth."

"Tea towel," he corrects me.

"And he swept me off my feet and made me set up home with him. My head is fairly twirling," I say in a funny voice, and he laughs.

Silence falls, and I'm just dropping off to sleep when his hand squeezes mine.

"Thank you for telling me that," he whispers. "I don't think it was easy."

"Nothing worthwhile ever is," I say softly. He mulls that over and I nudge him. "You can tell me more of your story next. I only know about the wanker boyfriend."

"It's a date," he says sleepily and I nestle in closer to him, feeling his arm tighten.

In some strange way, he's already my friend. I don't have enough of them, and Levi is different from those who came before. He's special in some way. But he's not my prince. He's not my boyfriend or even a hook-up. I need to remember that because, knowing life as I do, this will end before it ever begins.

It doesn't stop me curling into him and pretending for a little minute that he's my bloke and this is our house, and we're just a couple lying curled together warm and safe. Then tomorrow we'll get up and go to work and argue about who did the laundry and whose turn it is to cook dinner, and then we'll go to bed again. Together.

It's a surprisingly sweet thought, and it stays with me until I slide into a dreamless sleep.

CHAPTER 8

*L*evi

    I come awake slowly the next morning, the covers piled around me warm and softly scented with peaches. I open one eye cautiously. Why does my bed linen smell of peaches and why is my pillowcase stained blue? Then memory dawns and I groan.

"Fuck me," I grunt, throwing myself on my back and rubbing my eyes.

A warm chuckle sounds from the door, and I open my eyes to see Blue standing there watching me. Dressed in his big black jumper and skinny jeans, he looks the same but somehow different.

I narrow my eyes. Same hair. Same clothes. Same attitude. *Or not.* He grins at me and that's when I see it. He's lost a tiny bit of his cocky demeanour. He looks scrubbed clean and softer somehow. Like he washed a layer of that suspicious attitude off in the shower.

I feel a wave of warmth wash through me and swallow it down. "How do you feel this morning?"

"Fine," he says happily, forcing a mug into my hand. "This is for you."

"Oh God, I need this," I say fervently and take a sip. "That's lovely. What did you do to it?" I ask and can't help the surprise in my voice.

"Oh, that'll be the Rohypnol."

"What?" I gape at him.

Blue breaks into laughter. "I added cinnamon. Nothing else." He shrugs, looking gratified as he watches me drink. "I used to do casual work in a coffee shop. Got paid under the counter."

"Did you enjoy it?"

He shrugs. "It was alright until the fact that I was paid under the counter left the owner with the impression that I'd thrown my arse-hole into the deal as well."

I gape at him, feeling anger rush through me. "What the fuck?" I sit up straight. "Give me the wanker's name."

"Okay," he says obligingly, and I subside, looking at him. He smiles innocently. "It was King Richard the Third before he rode off to Bosworth." I shake my head, and he breaks into laughter. "Of course I'm not going to tell you."

"Why?"

"Because you look perfectly capable of going down there and giving him a piece of your very poshly spoken mind. He'll argue. You'll brawl. I'll try to split you up and die tragically with you both weeping over me. Then you'll spend the rest of your life mourning for me. Like that dog statue in Scotland."

I blink. "You're very colourful for …" I look at the clock. "Nine in the morning."

He laughs and settles down on the bed next to me, sipping his own coffee. His feet are bare and for some reason are completely fasci-nating to me. They look elegant and high arched. "I'm very colourful at any time of the day or night," he says happily.

"I'll take your word for it." I watch him laugh with pleasure. He should always be happy. "You're cheerful," I observe. "Considering we were locked in a room by a murderous ghost to get us out of the way of something even worse."

He shrugs. "I have to say it's not the strangest evening I've ever spent." I laugh, and he winks at me. "I have had a good idea, though."

"Is that slightly ominous, or is that just me?"

He cocks his head to one side. "What do you think?"

"Ominous," I offer judiciously.

"Normally, that would be the case, but not today. Today, Levi, we're going to a book shop."

"That is not what I thought you'd say."

"I don't want to know what you thought. With your imagination, you were probably thinking we'd start the day by resurrecting Van Helsing and staking a few vampires."

"That's not too far from the truth," I say slowly and Blue laughs and nudges me.

"I was just thinking that we need to know more about what we're dealing with here. We know now that the ghost is Rosalind, but there's something else here too. Maybe more than one something."

I mull that over. "I know it's an old house, but there's only been one murder and suicide here."

"That you know of. York's like that. Houses built on top of old sites. Half the time you're walking on someone's gravesite. Who knows what else happened on this site? That's why we need to do some research."

I pause. "Oh my God, what if there are more spirits? It's like *Rentaghost*."

"What's that?"

I shrug. "A really old children's programme that my mum loved about these ghosts who worked in an agency that hired them out. She had it on DVD and used to watch it with me. I loved it." I swallow hard, and when I look up it's to find him observing me gently. I tense, expecting him to ask questions I can't answer, but he just nods.

"Sounds good. Maybe we could watch it together?"

"Won't that be a bit of a busman's holiday?"

Blue laughs. "Back to business. I've only heard one story about this house, but I'm not an authority. So I thought we'd go to a bookshop I know on Minster Gates. It's an old house stacked full of books and they've got a huge occult and local history section." He shrugs. "We can do some research so we know what our plan of action should be."

I consider it. "That's a really good idea, but can we have breakfast as well?"

He smiles and gets off the bed, taking my cup with him. "Sounds reasonable. Have a shower and we'll get breakfast out."

"There's food here. We don't have to eat out, Blue."

He bites his lip. "I think it might be best."

"Why?"

"Because the house is quiet at the moment, like its battery has run down. But I don't think it'd take much to recharge it, and my presence might be enough to do it. I've noticed that spirits can get quite strong-willed around me."

"Really?" I ask, startled and anxious. "This isn't good. What if something happens to you?"

He shakes his head. "I've dealt with worse than this."

"I don't want you to, though. Maybe it would be best to leave the house."

His face falls before he immediately assumes a stoical expression. "You want me to leave?" he says in a cool voice. "That's fine. I'll get out of your hair."

"Not you, silly. *Us.*" I get out of bed and stretch. "We could take a bed and breakfast while we work out what to do next. *Oof!*" I look down in amazement as my arms are suddenly full of Blue. "You alright?" I ask, giving in to all my impulses and hugging him tight, loving the softness of his bright hair against my face and the wiry strength of his body in my arms.

He nods. "Thank you," he says, and it's choked up.

"Hey," I say, pulling back. "Blue, what's the matter?"

He shakes his head and steps back. "For being so good." He looks at me, his eyes extraordinarily bright. "You're such a fucking good person, Levi," he says passionately.

I smile at him. "I'm really not, but thank you."

We stand there for a second staring at each other. His eyes are clear and almost colourless in this light like shadowed snow, and I realise again with the same sudden shock that always happens how very beautiful he is. I realise that I'm staring and make an awkward gesture. "So, I should really get a shower."

He jerks as if waking up. "Oh, of course. I'll wait downstairs."

A board creaks outside the bedroom door, and we stand stock-still. There's a gentle shushing noise as if someone is passing by us wearing long skirts.

"Don't be too long," he says with wide eyes.

I nod forcefully. "I really won't be."

Fifteen minutes later I pound down the stairs wearing jeans and an old denim shirt. Blue is waiting for me, pacing up and down. He's wearing fingerless gloves, a military jacket, and combat boots. He darts glances towards the back of the house, where there's a knocking noise. I shoot a look at him, and he sighs and shakes his head as if telling me not to ask.

"You'll need a hat," he says. "It's snowing."

I reach into the cupboard and grab my parka and a beanie and one for him too.

"Come here," I say.

Blue moves forward obediently. "Why? What are you doing?" The last bit is slightly higher and muffled as I push the hat onto his head and tuck his blue hair underneath.

"You need one too unless this dye makes your head waterproof."

"Not that I know of," he mutters as I step back.

"There, you look lovely and warm."

He actually looks cute, that angular face framed by the beanie and strands of bright hair escaping from the sides.

He shakes his head. "You've got all the ingredients to make a successful daddy. All you're lacking is age and chest hair."

"That makes me very happy. Come on, boy."

I dodge him laughingly and suddenly we're engulfed in a flood of lily of the valley. Blue coughs and I shake my head.

"My uncle used to overdo the aftershave like that. You practically ate the stuff if he was nearby," I say cheerfully.

"And did your uncle also slit his brother's throat?"

"Oh no," I say, startled. He nods meaningfully, and I jerk into action. "Come on," I say quickly. "Let's get going."

The air outside is ice cold. There's a thin coating of snow on the ground already and tiny flakes of snow fly about in front of us like confetti at a wedding. The heavy sky is that peculiar yellow-grey that promises a lot more snow. The narrow lane looks almost magical and the sounds of the city are muted.

As if by mutual consent, we put our heads down and make our way down the cobbles. The slippery cobbles.

"Watch your step," I mutter as Blue skids. "Oh shit!" I windmill my arms as his weight hits me, and we slip and slide about before I fall against my neighbour's house. "*Oof!*" I say as he hits me. I open my arms to hold him upright, starting to laugh helplessly because he looks like he's auditioning for *Dancing on Ice*.

My laughter dies away as he rests against me, his front pressed to mine and his face lifted up, laughing and so bloody pretty. His smile fades as he stares up at me and silence seems to stretch like hot toffee. Without saying another word, we move as if in a dream, and our lips touch. They rest softly for a second in an almost innocent fashion as if we're both stunned by the change in our dynamic. Then his lips part, and I send my tongue inside, tasting toothpaste and coffee.

For a second Blue's still and then he groans low under his breath and tangles his hands in my hair. My hat falls to the ground and he gives a sigh of satisfaction, rifling his fingers through my hair.

It's at this point that I think we both lose our minds because I would never in a million years stand snogging on a street in broad daylight. That's asking for a punch from an idiot. We should move away from each other and laugh and make polite conversation. We should do that straightaway.

Instead, Blue presses into me so I can feel his dick hard against mine, and I groan under my breath as it gives my own cock some much needed friction. I reach down and grab his narrow hips, directing him to grind harder, and he moans, sucking on my tongue before plunging his tongue in to twine against mine.

I'm not exactly sure what would have happened next if the Minster bells hadn't started to ring loudly to announce a service. Luckily for us, they stop our drive towards indecent exposure, and we pull back. His face is flushed, his eyes bleary and sexy, and I'm pretty sure my face shares his own expression of incredulity.

I look up and down the street quickly, but luckily we're alone and this house is rented out to holidaymakers.

He shakes his head in disbelief. "Well," he says and clears his throat. "Well ..."

I bend to pick up my hat. I cram it down over my head and for the want of anything better to do, I nod with emphasis. "Well, there's that then," I say.

We stare at each other. A slow smile spreads across his face, and I feel an answering one dawn on mine.

"Okay," I say heartily. "Onwards."

"And upwards," Blue mutters sotto voice, a cheeky smile on his face as he readjusts his dick in his jeans.

I shake my head but can't stop the smile. "Ever upwards."

His laughter drifts around us like the snowflakes as we resume walking, but it makes me feel as warm as if we were sitting in front of a fire.

*B*lue
I shoot glances at him as we walk down the Shambles eating our croissants and sipping at coffee. The lanes are quiet this morning, as all the tourists are probably still tucked up in their hotels eating toast and marmalade. As such, there's a stillness about the narrow cobbled streets that is almost timeless as the snow billows down around us. We could be in any time gone past.

We crunch through the snow, and I marvel at the fact that this time last week I'd have been fretting at how cold the squat would be and wondering if the police would leave us alone long enough for us to get through the winter before we became homeless again.

That's the thing about living like I've been doing. You're so close to the abyss that one wrong step and you'll tumble over and spiral downwards. I shudder at the thought and the memory of sleeping in these doorways, being spat at and rough handled.

"You okay?" Levi immediately asks. "Are you cold? That coat's not very warm." He looks like he's about to whip his parka off for me.

"I'm fine. My coat's warm."

It isn't, but Levi's knightly impulses are really going to get him into trouble one day. He's so kind and generous. It still makes me angry to think of walking into the house and seeing Fay's hard little face watching him to see how much money she could take him for.

I shake my head. Not on my watch. I sneak another glance at him as he walks beside me. He's bundled up in his coat and his high, flat cheekbones are dusted with colour. His lips are full and red, and I think back to that kiss. He'd tasted of peppermint and something that was just him.

The kiss made me feel wobbly in the worst way. I've traded my body in the past easily for somewhere to sleep or shower or money for food. I didn't enjoy it, but it was so necessary I couldn't afford to have finer feelings. Sex therefore for me has always been a commercial enterprise. Something I've occasionally enjoyed, but more often something to be endured with a smile on my face.

That kiss was totally outside my comfort zone. There was no room for calculating my angles and how to please him so he'd pay up. Instead, I'd gone under, and my only thought had been *my* pleasure. *My* wants.

That way lies danger. Levi will help me for a while, but I can't allow myself to settle because in a few days or weeks or months he'll meet someone else who will be a more fitting match for him, and I'll have to move on. I'd far rather do that heart whole than broken. I nibble on my lip, turning my lip ring over and confirming my plan. I'll stay with him for a bit until the house is safe again.

"What are you thinking?" he asks curiously.

I shoot him a glance. "The house," I finally say. "I don't like it, Levi. There's something going on almost constantly. You said it wasn't doing that before, which means that the spirits are gaining energy and revving up for something. As someone has already died in there, I don't trust that they're gearing up to throw you a nice welcoming party."

"How are they getting the energy?"

"From people, I think." I dodge around a slow-moving old couple in front of us who are picking their way carefully over the cobbles. "I've noticed before that ghosts seem to draw energy from people's emotions."

"Good or bad?"

"Powerful ones. Hatred, love …" I falter slightly. "Desire."

He shakes his head. "Oh, lovely. So, I'm never to get laid in my house again because of cockblocking ghosts."

"Not unless you fancy dying horribly." I savour his laughter. It's so rich and warm on the cold air. But then I remember the man who died, and my stomach twists at the thought of it happening to Levi. "Seriously though, I also wonder whether it's because of you." I hesitate. "You have a very strong presence about you, Levi," I finally say, cringing at the possible laughter coming my way.

Instead, he looks startled. "Have I really?"

I nod. "You do. You're very strong and centred emotionally." I hesitate. "But there's a lot of pain underneath and that's like fucking catnip to ghosts." Something flashes across his face that I don't like. Hurt and sorrow. I hate that he feels them. "I'm probably way off base," I say quickly. "Like I said, I really don't know how it works or what I should do." I sigh angrily. "I need to know. I can't have anything happening to you."

"Hey." Levi draws me to a stop by grabbing my arm gently. "This is *not* your responsibility. I'm so grateful you're helping, but it isn't your problem."

"It's yours, isn't it?" I say acerbically. "Therefore, I need to solve it."

"Why?"

The question is stark and falls between us like a rock in a pond. "I don't know," I finally admit. "I just know I want to help you, and you should really accept that because my desire to help people only comes around every new millennium."

"I'll endeavour to appropriately appreciate this miracle," he says solemnly, and we grin at each other and begin walking again.

"That's where we need to go," I say, nudging him towards a street on the right. "This was once called Bookbinders Alley, because it was where the book sellers and printing presses were." I point to the statue that sits on the side of a building. It's high up and unnoticed by most of the tourists. "That's Minerva. She's giving you a clue about your location by leaning on a pile of books."

He stares up at the brightly coloured statue. "She looks a bit drunk," he observes dryly. "Those books are totally propping her up."

I laugh and guide him down the street. "There it is." I gesture at the narrow four-storey house tucked neatly between a chocolate shop and a cafe. The Minster stands solidly in front of us. Normally, the stone steps up to the shop are cluttered with baskets containing books of all shapes and sizes, and there's a table in front displaying local artists' work. Today, however, with the snow thickening, the only sign that the shop is open is the sign on the door.

"Come on," I say, leading the way up the steps. I pause, making him stop as well. "Be careful with your elbows in here," I say, looking at his tall, wide-shouldered body dubiously. "There are books everywhere, and you're so tall, you're likely to knock shit over."

"I'm not the BFG," he mutters.

I ignore him. "The old bloke who owns this place is a really grumpy git, so don't damage anything."

"Have you been in here before, then?" he asks as we enter the shop.

We're instantly greeted with warmth and the smell of leather and old papers. I inhale happily. "Yep. I love it in here. I used to come in a lot when I first got to York because it was warm, and I could curl up in a corner and read."

"So, the grumpy old man used to let you sit and read all day?"

"Yes." I hesitate. "Oh, I see what you're doing here." He smiles. "Okay, he wasn't that bad. But he's very cutting if you mishandle the books, and he doesn't like people very much."

"Oh, what a terrible person."

I reach over and pinch him and his startled "Ouch!" is loud in the confines of the shop. The old man looks up from his perch behind the counter where he's reading and smoking a pipe. He has wild grey hair and a bushy beard. His faded blue eyes still feel like they have the power to shake loose all my secrets.

"Ah, Blue Boy. Come to read some more of my stock without paying for it? I really must set up a library someday when my old bones are turfed out of my shop because customers stopped paying for shit."

I wink at him. "Don't EU regulations prohibit the smoking of pipes in enclosed spaces?"

"And your point is?" he says blankly.

I grin at him. "It's bad for your health."

"I'm far more likely to die being crushed by a stack of books than I am of a smoking-related disease."

I look at the teetering piles of books on his counter. "You should really shelve them."

He sniffs. "My old bones aren't happy with the stairs. Someone will want something from the pile at some point, so they can just stay here."

I shake my head. "We're just going to look at the local history section," I say, pointing to the stairs.

"Can I just express my sincere appreciation for you bringing me *another* book shop lodger? It's such good company for me in my old age."

I grin again. "This one's a payer," I stage whisper, pointing at Levi who immediately looks like he wants to vanish on the spot.

The old man opens his mouth in a startled fashion. "You mean this one won't read and put back on the shelves?"

"Nope. This one will *buy* before reading."

"Best get him up there then, lad. He can pay a bit towards the cost of keeping you entertained over the years."

I laugh and push Levi towards the stairs. "Age before beauty," I say demurely.

"Shit," he whispers as his foot catches a stack of books, causing them to topple over.

"Now I see the truth," the old man shouts. "This one's going to destroy them *before* reading."

"It's okay," I shout back. "Just putting them back properly."

"Good luck with that, lad."

I restack the books on the stairs, where more stacks lie higgledy-piggledy on the steps and on open shelves in the stairwell. Free wall space is crammed with paintings and drawings of the local area.

We round the steps without any more incidents, and I steer Levi over to the local history section. "You have a look here," I instruct. "I'll do the occult section."

He nods and begins to peruse the shelves. I step over to the occult section which is a cosy corner by a sashed window looking out onto the lane below. I used to spend hours in here, not just to get warm, but to try and find any information about my peculiar talents.

I smile as I see the battered beanbag on the floor which had suddenly appeared a few weeks after I started coming in here. I'm also remembering how the old man had always had plates of food on the counter that he claimed he was trialling for a local café and could I taste test for him. He accompanied the offer with tart observations about youth and hair dye, but it's a sure fact that some days that was the only food I'd eat.

I know the old bloke's cutting and everyone runs scared of him, but somehow I've always felt safe with him, and after a while the remarks became a sort of banter between us. I wonder how much he saw. Probably everything. Teenagers tend to think of themselves as mysterious, when really they're as see-through as a window.

I start to look along the shelves for local ghost legends. Sitting here and reading these books gave me the information I needed to run my ghost tour, but I'd never really focused on Levi's house beyond the knowledge of a Victorian murderess killing her brother in there.

I wonder again at her actions from last night. Why do I get the feeling that she was trying to protect me? This woman slit her brother's throat in cold blood and then calmly went back to her room and took off her wedding ring before she hung herself without any words of regret. What could she possibly fear so badly in that house?

I remember that chuckle in the dark and a chill runs down my back. There had been something in those shadows, something malevolent. Was it a spirit older than Rosalind? Maybe it was responsible for what she did. Maybe she was haunted by it too.

I turn back to the shelves with renewed interest, grabbing two slim books and a huge leather-bound tome entitled *York's Spirits and Monsters*. "Sounds promising," I say.

I make my way over to where Levi is sitting on the floor, leaning against a bookcase. He's absorbed in a book, long legs stretched out and his brown hair falling over that starkly beautiful face.

I kick his foot gently. "Found anything?"

Startled, he looks up. His grin does strange things to my heart rate. It's so wide I can see the snaggle tooth on the right side, giving his expression a crooked edge that's oddly charming.

"There's a whole book written about the house," he says, showing me a cover with a picture of the house on the front.

"It looks like something an old professor would write and accidently bore himself into death while he was doing it."

He blinks. "It's quite interesting, actually. It traces the house occupancy right back to when it was built, but get this, it was constructed on the site of a much older house that was around at the time the first brick on the Minster was laid."

"That's York for you," I say, lowering myself to sit next to him.

I lean into him, relaxing against his body and inhaling his woodsy scent. He hums and turns another page, his face intent. I sigh and look at the shelves before pulling down a book on the York Devil and other murders in York. It was good when I read it a few years ago and I could do with reading up some more for my tour. I need to add a bit of new detail.

The light outside grows dim as the yellowish sky ladles out more snow. The flakes tumble down outside the window, but inside we're sitting together in a cosy nest surrounded by towering stacks of books. A safe and warm den—that's how it used to feel to me. This was my safe place.

My book lies forgotten on my lap as I lean further into him, his body heating my side. I watch a lady walk past us dressed in the outfit of a Victorian maid. I incline my head respectfully and look up to find Levi watching me. "What?"

"What do you see?" he asks, shutting the book and adding it to the stack next to him.

"A maid." She walks past me and disappears into a bookcase. "She's gone now, but she'll be back. She shows up every hour during the daytime."

He shakes his head. "It's amazing what you can see."

I shrug. "Not sure about that."

"Are you ever scared?"

I turn to him. His face is closer than I'd thought. I breathe in sharply and focus on his question.

"When I was younger, yes. I was scared shitless most of the time because they came to me and tried to talk, and I didn't know what to do. It was no use asking my mum, either, because she was more scared of them than me. But not in this shop," I say slowly. "This place was safe."

"When's the last time you were scared?"

I stare at him. "Last night," I finally whisper. "I was fucking petrified."

"Of the lady?" Levi asks, looking troubled.

"Strangely, no. I know she murdered someone, but I was more scared of what was waiting in the dark. Maybe it's like predators," I muse as he watches me with his kind eyes. "She's the tiger shark, but there's a Great White circling in the dark."

I shudder, and he flings his arm around me. "Cold?"

I shake my head. "No."

His face comes closer and closer. My eyes close and my head falls gently against the bookcase as he kisses me. It's a soft kiss with none of the passion from the street. He rubs his lips over mine, playing with my lip ring, sending his tongue to glide over my lower lip and tracing the fullness before pulling back to blow on it. It electrifies me, my spine arching and my cock hard.

He pulls back, breathing heavily. "This isn't the time or the place."

"Not sure about that," I say, tugging his head back towards me. His lips have just touched mine when a voice shouts from downstairs.

"You two okay up there? Shall I ring the butler and ask him to prepare a tray of tea?"

I groan and rest my head against him, panting gently. "Shit," I whisper, and he laughs. "We're just coming down," I shout. I look at Levi, noting the huge pupils and the slight swollenness of his lips. "You got everything?"

"Everything I need," he says solemnly.

I shake my head, jumping up and extending a hand to help him up. "You can't say things like that," I instruct. "It's just not done."

"Those are other people's rules," he says steadily, cupping my face in one of his big hands. "I play by my own rules."

I smile. "Is that actually true?"

He laughs loudly. "No, but it sounded good. A bit anarchic."

I pull back. "Come on then, Johnny Rotten."

He lets me lead him towards the stairs, pausing to bend and pick up the book I was looking at and adding it to his pile.

"No," I protest. "There's no need for that. I was just looking up some juicy stuff for the ghost walk."

He shrugs carelessly. "Okay." But the book stays on the pile, and I follow him downstairs, standing to one side as the old man starts to total the purchases. "Thank you," I mutter to Levi.

He grins at me. "You're welcome."

I shrug awkwardly and turn to study the cramped room which was the front room of the original house. As per usual, the ghost of an old lady is sitting on the orange velvet armchair sleeping peacefully.

"It's rude to stare," the old man at the counter says suddenly.

"*What?*" I jerk my head towards him.

"It's rude to stare at the dead."

Levi stares at me in astonishment.

"Oh my God." I take two steps towards the counter. "Fucking hell, you can see her. And you know that I can see her too. *Fuck!*"

Levi looks from the old man to me like he's at a tennis match.

The old man shrugs. "Of course you can see her."

"How did you know? How could you tell?" The words topple out of me. "Can you tell from just looking at me that I can do that?"

"I'm psychic, not fucking Merlin," he says grumpily. "Of course you can see her. You were properly staring at the poor old bat."

"Fucking hell," I say again.

He huffs and turns to Levi. "Shame he didn't spend more time looking at a thesaurus up there rather than reading the rude bits in Jackie Collins books and sleeping."

CHAPTER 9

*L*evi
 I stare in amazement at the old man behind the counter and then turn to look at Blue.

He's sheet white apart from two spots of bright red on his cheeks, his expression both freaked out and excited.

"Have you ever met anyone who can do what you can?" I ask him.

He shakes his head. "No. Fuck no, apart from my mum. I've met loads of pretenders though."

The old man sniffs. "Some of those idiots who used to wait for you outside the shop, I expect." Blue nods dazedly, and the old man rubs his forehead. "They couldn't read the bloody tea leaves if you stapled their head to the cup." He leans forward, looking at Blue intently. "There are plenty of people who can see the dead, lad."

"But how can I tell who they are?" Blue says crossly. "I mean, I've been coming in here for years, and I never guessed about you."

He shrugs. "I'm not the easiest person to read." I can't help the snort, and he looks at me wryly before turning back to Blue. "Did your mam or dad never tell you any of this?"

Blue shakes his head, sitting down on the stool across the counter from the old man. "My mum died when I was young. There wasn't anyone else."

"Nobody in foster care?"

Blue gives him a look.

The old man shrugs. "I figured you were in care or not happy at home and came here for a bit of a getaway."

"Why?" I ask.

"Because he was clean enough but he never looked cared for properly."

"He wasn't in care," I say crossly. "He was homeless."

The old man looks startled for the first time, paling and sitting down on his chair with a thump. "Homeless?" he echoes, looking at Blue who shakes his head crossly at me before shrugging and nodding. "Ah, lad, I'm sorry."

"What for?" Blue now just looks freaked out.

"I figured you just wanted an escape. I never asked because you didn't seem to want to talk about it."

"I didn't, and it wasn't your problem anyway."

The old man sighs. "And not my business. That's what I've always told myself. I work best when I'm on my own. I can't be looking after people."

I'm sensing that there's a story here, but I don't think it's one I'll ever hear.

Blue shrugs. "I'm the same." He looks intently at the old man. "But I would love to know more about what I can do." He leans forward. "I mean, I can see them and they look like they want to talk to me and sometimes their voices get through, but other times I can't. And then there are the colours and sometimes if I touch objects…" He stops and inhales. "I just really need to know," he says passionately. "I can't protect Levi if I don't know."

"Protect me," I say, revolted. "I don't need *protecting*."

The old man ignores me and looks at Blue for a long second before he sighs resignedly. "Blue, go and put the closed sign on the door, and Levi can make a cup of tea for us." He points to the back of the shop. "The kitchen's through there, lad."

Blue winks at me before running off happily to do the old man's bidding. I stare after him, already feeling the lightening in his mood that someone shares his gift. That he isn't alone. I smile, and when I look back at the old man, he's watching me.

"Is he homeless now?" he asks abruptly.

"No, he's staying with me." His gaze holds mine. "He can stay as long as he likes," I say firmly.

He nods slowly, his expression enigmatic. "Okay then, go and make the tea."

I blink and jump to action, finding the small kitchen at the back of the house where he indicated. It looks down onto a cobbled yard surrounded by high brick walls, and I stare out at the view while I wait for the kettle to boil.

I hope this man has some answers for Blue and for me too, I suppose. If we can get some advice about the house, we can maybe do something to stop the activity. I pour the water into the old red ceramic teapot. *But if the ghost stuff stops, then Blue will go.*

I put the kettle down with a thud. I don't want him to go, I realise with a start. He's only been in the house for a night but already it feels full of him. Full of life and colour replacing the perfect shell it was before. Just the sight of his jacket slung over the newel post, his combat boots kicked off, and the smell of peaches on the air makes me happy. Even the blue dye smudges from his hair make me feel more alive than ever.

I've never felt so alive as I have since I came here. I've lived a fairly boring life. Mason and I never really had any highs or lows until he started shagging another man. Ghosts and a fey-looking, blue-haired man have certainly given me a new perspective on life.

I snort and grab the mugs. Blue and the old man are seated at the counter talking intently, and when I step through, Blue looks up and grins at me. It's a warm, familiar smile that makes me feel good. I smile back and, plopping the mugs down on the counter, I go to sit on a ratty old orange velvet chair.

"*No!*" Blue and the old man shout in unison. I jump and pause with my bum hovering over the chair.

"What?" I gasp.

"You'll sit on her," Blue says.

The old man nods. "Come to the counter, lad. All the other chairs are taken."

I look around the empty room. "Okay," I say slowly.

Blue snorts, and I grimace at him as I sit on the stool he pushes towards me with his foot.

"You can call me Tom," the old man says as if conferring a great honour upon me. I stop myself from grinning and incline my head respectfully. "Blue was telling me what house you own."

I nod. "Do you know it?"

"Of course I do, lad. I've lived here all my life and my mam and dad and my grandparents were the same. There isn't much that the Pattisons don't know about York."

I lean forward. "So, what can you tell me?"

He looks regretful. "About as much as you know already." I sag and he sips his tea. "My great-grandmother was in service to Rosalind and Alfred though."

I jerk. "The maid who said Rosalind's brother was unkind to her? The one who discovered the bodies?" He nods. "Did she have the..."

He smiles. "The second sight. Call it that. No, she didn't. It was my great-grandfather who had that, and, although he was courting her, he was never allowed in the house. Rosalind was a stickler for appearances."

"I'm not sure murdering your own brother fits in with that concept," I say.

"It's a mystery. It was a mystery to my great-grandmother too." He stares into space. "She never really got over finding the bodies. It changed her. Apparently, she was a confident, happy woman before, but afterwards she'd have depressions and she was always nervy. Can't say I blame her."

"Did she ever say anything apart from the bit that Blue told me?"

He shakes his head. "Knowledge culled from the books upstairs, I suppose."

Blue grins and nibbles on a biscuit.

Tom looks deep in thought for a second. "I don't think so. She didn't like to talk about it and so my great-grandfather always shut it down. I know Rosalind and her brother were very well liked in the community. They were regular churchgoers and did a lot for charity. The family were wealthy, but Alfred had vastly extended that through his knowledge of banking. Rosalind spent her days visiting the sick and trying to save women from prostitution by finding them work. Now, why this lovely lady that did so much for charity took a cutthroat razor to him, is something nobody knows. I will tell you one thing though." He leans forward. In the gloomy light of the shop, his eyes gleam mysteriously.

"I went in the house one day as a lad. It was empty at the time. It never kept owners and was always changing hands. The lower window was broken and my friends dared me to go in and stay for fifteen minutes. I didn't want to lose face, but I should have known better. I was already different and could see things they couldn't, so why I thought it would lead to anything good is beyond me."

"What happened?" Blue asks.

Something crosses Tom's face. It looks very much like fear. "I got in easily enough and went upstairs to one of the bedrooms. It was a sunny day, no shadows, nothing to frighten me." He huffs. "Yet I was so scared, I wet myself."

"What was it?"

He shrugs. "I don't know and that's the truth. I didn't see or hear anything, but it just felt like something in that house was listening and waiting for me in one of the rooms, and I knew if I stayed any longer I wouldn't get out and my ghost would join everyone in that house, because make no mistake, the house was alive with the dead."

A shiver runs down my spine. "What room was it?" I ask.

His brow furrows as he straightens a book stack with gnarled fingers. "Not the front room. That was alright. It was the smaller front bedroom."

"I saw someone in there," I say suddenly. "It was a figure watching me."

"*What?*" Blue bursts out. "Why didn't you tell me?"

"I forgot," I say shamefacedly. "It was my first day here, and I planned to camp in the house. I thought I was seeing things."

"Hmm," Tom says. "And did you go back in?"

"No, I went straight round the corner and stayed in a hotel."

"I think that was a good thing," he says slowly. "Have you ever seen anything before, lad? Ever seen anything strange? Like a ghost?"

I'd like to say that I think seeing ghosts ranks as a strange occurrence all on its own, but I don't due to the present company. Instead, I shake my head. "No, nothing."

"The fact that you did shows how strong the apparition is." Tom looks at Blue with a worried expression crossing his face. "And you're staying there," he says. "That's not a good place for a psychic to be."

"I'm not leaving," Blue says firmly. I open my mouth, and he shakes his head fiercely. "No, Levi. I'm not leaving you alone in there." He shrugs. "Anyway, nowhere is safe from ghosts. Wherever I am, they're immediately there."

"Well, that's not surprising," Tom says, sitting back on his stool. "You're very powerful."

"I'm very what?" Blue says.

"Powerful. You say you can see and hear them, can feel emotions and can see auras?"

"I never said I saw auras."

"You can see colours around people?" Blue nods. "Those are what we call auras, lad." He stares at him. "What colour is mine?"

"Blue with a bit of red," Blue says immediately.

"Hmm, that sounds appropriate." I laugh and Tom grins. "What about your boyfriend, Blue?"

"He's not my boyfriend," Blue mutters, a flush dappling his sharp cheekbones. He looks at me. "Gold," he says. "With silver and bright pink running through it."

Tom stares at Blue, an almost wistful expression crossing his face. "That's a rare one," he finally says.

Blue stares at him, and the old man shakes himself. "You're a medium, lad, as well as being a psychic. All that means is that you can make contact with the dead. I was always taught that there are three main kinds of mediums. Clairvoyants who can see the dead, clairsentients who can feel energies from spirits, and clairaudients who can hear the dead. Some mediums have one or two of these gifts. Others, like you and I, have all three. There are other gifts that come with the territory, but I won't know yours until I've seen more of you."

"But I can't use any of them properly," Blue bursts out. "I can't control anything. How can I help people? How can I help Levi if I can't do fucking anything right?"

"Do you *want* to help people?" Tom asks, an arrested look on his face.

"Of course," Blue says. "I'm not saying that I've always done good things, but I like not doing bad things quite a lot." His expression firms. "And helping Levi is not negotiable." He stares at Tom imploringly. "Can you help me? Tell me what to do?"

"I can't help you." Blue slumps, and Tom stirs. "I can't help you, but I *can* tell you what I know. It's what my mam and dad did for me. I can tell you how to control it, but it's up to you to find your own way. The ghosts are flocking to you because you're extraordinarily bright. You're almost glowing with unchecked power. It's raw, and they sense it and need it. Most of them don't want to hurt you. They just want you to hear them. When you do that, they'll go away happy."

"Not so different from people, then," I muse and Tom smiles crookedly at me.

"They are people. Just dead ones."

"But how can I stop them?" Blue says.

"There are many ways. You need to do a few simple things and take some precautions, but it's easily learnt." He stares at him, his eyes piercing over his long, crooked nose. "There's only one way really to be in control of yourself."

"How?"

"To be happy and content. It gives us confidence and surety."

Blue looks discomposed, as if being happy has never even occurred to him. I swallow hard, my heart hurting.

The old man yawns. "It's late," he says abruptly. "I'm old, and I need my dinner."

"Oh." Blue looks nervous. "Could I come back at some point and see you?"

"You can come back tomorrow," he says tersely, easing into his coat. "Nine o'clock sharp. Don't be late."

"Late for what?"

"Your first day of work."

"*Work?*" Blue echoes.

"I hope you haven't got a hearing problem. Most of the customers are old and deaf. We don't need a staff member being the same."

"*Staff member?*"

Tom nods. "You can start work tomorrow. I'll teach you what I know while you work around here."

"Doing what?"

"You can shelve these books, for a start," he says, gesturing at the teetering stacks. "It's a fact that you know what's on the shelves." He looks at Blue. "You can work the till, put book orders in, make tea. I'll pay you fifteen quid an hour."

That's way over the minimum wage. I shoot a look at Tom. He winks but Blue misses it.

"You'd really let me do that?" Blue asks.

"Of course," Tom says, his eyes gleaming under bushy eyebrows. "Did you think I was talking to the tall lad here? He can't make bloody tea to save his life."

Blue's face lights up, but then it falls. "But I haven't got an NI number. I haven't—"

"I can help you with all that," I say quickly. "We can get on the phone when we get back. Once we have your birth certificate, you'll have everything else in a few weeks, if Tom doesn't mind waiting."

I look anxiously at the old man and he shrugs. "I'm old. Waiting for the government is preferable to waiting for death." He pauses. "Or at the least, it's remarkably similar."

"Oh lovely," I say, faintly unsure what else to say. Blue and Tom look at each other and immediately break into laughter, and for some reason they look suddenly alike. I shake my head. Two of them to deal with. That's trouble.

. . .

*B*lue
       The next morning, I stand outside the shop, biting my lip and worrying my lip ring.

I can't quite work out why I'm so nervous. I was ecstatic to wake up and think that I'd got an honest job to go to, and the thought of working with books put an even shinier shine on my morning. But between the house and the shop, I seem to have discovered my nerves.

What if I'm no good at the job and Tom fires me? What if I can't find out enough to keep Levi safe?

The thought of Levi brings an instant smile to my face. Yuck. I'm ridiculous. But he was just so pretty this morning curled up in a nest of covers, his skin warm and smelling of early morning, his hair a mess of brown waves, and his full pink mouth pouted in dreams.

Normally, I roll out of bed. Okay, normally I roll off the mattress ready for the day, but it had been hard to crawl out of Levi's bed. It was just so warm and comfortable. The duvet thick and crinkly around me, the pillows full.

I'd woken to sunshine playing on my face, not the cold drip of water and that horrible musty smell that got everywhere at my old place. I'd lain there for a while, reluctant to leave, especially as the bed had Levi on the other side. Well, not really the other side. After two nights sharing a bed, I can positively say that Levi Black is a bit of a cuddler. Not just a bit—he's like a wonderful octopus who wraps his limbs around me when he's asleep.

The first time he'd done it, I'd frozen, convinced he was putting the moves on me despite his promise. When I'd heard a soft snore, I relaxed a little. And last night as he'd cuddled up again, I'd nestled into his arms and listened to the Minster bells sound the hour, and I'd realised he was a man who kept his word.

Inhaling the scent of lavender from his sheets, watching the moonlight lay stripes across the floor and the play of shadows on his sharp-boned face, I'd felt something stir inside me. I'd wanted to keep him looking happy and innocent something fucking awful.

And it's also awful, because I know that I can't stay at Levi's house for long. I have to move on. It's the way I've always done it. No ties and ready to move at the drop of a hat.

Levi has stability and a settled air about him that's as much a part of him as his wavy hair and slightly crooked nose. I'll move on once he's safe, and in a few years I'll look back and think of him as some sort of distant dream of warmth and contentment.

Maybe I'll see him around in a pub in York. He'll be with the man he's supposed to be with, and we'll smile, and I'll buy him a pint to say thank you for helping me that one lovely autumn. He'll be kind as normal but still wrapped up in his man, and eventually I'll have to leave because the sight of him with his perfect bloke will hurt me somewhere I didn't think was vulnerable anymore. A place with a door I closed off years ago that's obviously somehow come ajar.

I'd tortured myself in Levi's bed with all of those thoughts, but the pathetic thing is that I still snuggled close. As usual, I heard my mum's voice of warning about not trusting people because that way lies disaster, and I still cuddled close and pretended for a few sweet hours that Levi was my bloke and his house was ours. That we'd get up in the morning and argue over toast and household jobs the way people did on the TV shows I'd watched at one of my mum's boyfriends' houses.

I'd been as fascinated by those shows as if they were about aliens and watched them raptly, taking note of the messy houses full of possessions that just sat there on tables and in cupboards. Photo frames with happy pictures, toys and books and games and objects that obviously meant something.

To me, holding on to possessions was strange. Why keep hold of stuff when I knew it would just get left behind when my mother got the urge to run again?

My mum always told me that the only things we needed were each other, and for a long time I'd believed her. Until I lost her. Not through the suicide—in reality I'd lost her long before to drugs and alcohol and anything else she could find to blot out the things she could see.

A crotchety voice interrupts my thoughts. "You coming in or doing some strange sort of dance on the pavement?"

I smile at the sight of Tom in the door, his grumpy face welcome because he'll distract me from my thoughts.

He shakes his head. "Get in here, lad. The books aren't going to shelve themselves."

I grin at him and run up the steps, following him into the first room where the cash till is. I stop at the foot of a mountain of books strewn over the counter and in piles all over the floor.

"What the hell is that?" I breathe, forgetting the lecture I'd given myself on being polite to my new boss.

"That, lad, is your work for the morning. I figured that you've got young legs, and they're probably less tired than mine considering the amount of time you spent resting them while sitting in my shop."

I think most other people would be horrified by Tom, but strangely enough I like him. He's funny and he's brusque and I like that attitude.

"You know," I say, taking off my combat jacket and unwinding the scarf that Levi had forced on me yesterday, "in *The Empire Strikes Back,* Yoda didn't make Luke shelve books." I chuck the scarf and jacket on a chair.

"Had Yoda got a bad back?"

"He had a stick," I muse. "But he still managed to walk around."

"He didn't have a bloody book shop and ridiculous customers who persist in taking books off the shelves and then changing their minds. Bloody nuisances."

"I think Yoda probably had a better customer service ethos than you," I tease.

He grunts. "If he'd run a bookshop, he wouldn't have had that. He'd have had dreams of hitting people with his walking stick and using the force to throw them out on the pavement."

I roll up the sleeves on my jumper and pick up a stack of books. "I think it might be a good idea to train me on the till, old man, before you murder someone." I suddenly remember who I am and flush. "Only joking," I say quickly. "I'll just shelve the books."

He stares at me from under his bushy eyebrows that seem to be taking over his face. "What are you fluttering about now?"

"I don't *flutter*," I say, revolted.

He raises the eyebrows so they merge into the grizzled mass of his hair. "Oh, I think you do." He pauses and looks at me wickedly. "Like a little butterfly."

"Take that back," I say.

He shrugs. "No, I don't think I will. Butterfly Blue. You'll be waving your hands in front of your face soon like you're trying not to cry and blinking your eyes and scowling."

"That was oddly specific," I say slowly. "I think that's something you've encountered in the past." I narrow my eyes. "Probably with a customer."

He shrugs, looking innocent. "Can't imagine what you mean."

I shake my head. "So, when I've shelved the books, are you going to train me in the ways of a psychic?"

"That's a book title in your head, isn't it?"

I grin. "I can't help it. I'm imagining myself on the cover already. The plucky hero with the wonderful hair, his gaze trained on some noble quest in the distance."

"Why would a noble quest be in the distance? It's not a bus."

"Ssh," I say sternly. "You're blunting my buzz."

"Perish the thought," he says faintly.

"Staring into the distance," I continue loudly. "With one hand placed on his hip and his eyes raised to scan the skyline while he contemplates the meaning of the universe."

"And what is the meaning of the universe, Butterfly Blue?"

"I'm sure that sounds like a serial killer's nickname." I shake myself as my stomach rumbles. "The meaning of the universe is a bacon buttie."

He blinks. "I think I might be just the trainer you need, Blue." He digs in his pocket. "First things first, pop down to the bakery and get a couple of bacon cobs—I like mine well done with brown sauce—and maybe get some of those ring doughnuts and a hot chocolate each too."

I stare at him. "Are you actually hungry or are you just trying to feed me?" I'm amused to see a blush on his wrinkled cheeks. "Oh my God, you are," I say wonderingly. "I'm pretty sure you'll be wanting to adopt me next and we'll live together for the rest of our days." I pause and look around. "Until a stack of books collapses on us and we're smothered to death."

He waves a ten-pound note in my face. "Less talking and more going for food. In fact, just less talking altogether."

"It's how I express myself," I say sadly.

"Well, learn to do it silently," he offers, ignoring my plaintive sigh.

For a second we stare at each other, and then, as if synchronised, we both smile and I know I'm going to enjoy working with this grumpy old man. It's a little bit like getting to meet my future self.

Over our breakfast of bacon cobs, which is broken up occasionally by Tom being appallingly rude to customers who have dared to stray into his shop, we talk about the house. I tell him more fully about what's happening, and he seems interested in the woman I saw.

"I never saw her," he muses. "I smelt the perfume, but it was something else that scared me."

"I know," I say, biting into my cob and enjoying the salty bacon and melted butter. "I'm just not sure whether that something else is her too."

"Another manifestation of the bad side of one spirit?"

"Why not? She managed to keep her murderous side very well hidden. You ever seen that?" I ask through a mouthful of food.

"I'd say close your mouth," he says disgustedly. "But I don't think its genetically possible." I swallow and grin at him, and he shakes his head and returns to the conversation. "I've seen many things, lad. Too many to discount anything."

I put my cob down. "And you'll really train me?"

"I can't train you," he says. "I can only tell you what I was told and what worked for me. Everyone is different."

"Could you always see ghosts?"

He nods. "Right from a child I'd see people who shouldn't be there."

"Were you bullied?"

He looks shocked. "No." He considers the question. "I didn't tell people though. My parents and grandparents had the sight and they told me to keep my gift a secret right from the start, the way they taught me how to tie my shoelaces and clean my teeth."

I wonder what that must have been like. Everything I've learnt, I've had to teach myself. And that includes tying my shoes and cleaning my teeth. Something must show in my face because Tom's expression becomes complicated. I interpret a large part of it to be anger. Then it clears and he nods at the chair behind me.

"What do you see?"

I turn. "An old lady with a lacy cap snoozing in the chair."

"And what do you hear?"

I turn back to him. "Nothing." I stare at him. "Can you hear something, then?"

He nods. "She's snoring."

"How do you do that?" I lean forward over the counter. "Sometimes they try and talk to me. I can see their mouths moving and nothing. It's like they're miming."

"You're too agitated," he says, tapping his fingers on the counter. "You draw them because you're a bright light and full of energy, but it's the wrong kind."

"Wrong?"

He nods. "It's a passionate and jumbled mess. Like a storm."

"Oh lovely."

He gazes at me. "You need to learn to be calm and focus. They'll still come to you, but you'll hear them and control the situation." I stare at him and he shrugs. "It's like you have your fingers in your ears and you're shouting. Be still in your mind and mouth and you'll do it." He nods at the woman. "Try it."

"Try what?"

"Breathe in through your mouth and out through your nose. Ignore everything else and just listen. You'll tune into her when you do."

I look at him doubtfully and then turn to the woman. She's

sleeping peacefully, her mouth slightly open and a book balanced on her lap. I do as he says and try to ignore everything. It's easier here in the quiet of a bookshop. I breathe in and out through my nose, concentrating on the breaths. For a second there's nothing and then there's an audible pop and the smell of burning, and I hear her. Faint rumbling snores and the catch of her breath at the end of it.

"Oh my *God*," I shout out loud. "Oh fuck, I did it." The ghost jerks and flickers, and with an angry glare at me, she pops out of sight.

Tom sighs loudly. "Well, that's just brilliant. The old bird's cross now. When you come in tomorrow, all the books will be on the floor waiting for you."

I stare at him. "Why the emphasis on me?"

"Well, you'll be shelving them," he says grumpily. He can't quite hide the smile though. "How do you feel, lad?"

"It's bloody amazing." I stand up and start to pace. "So if I do that every time, I'll hear them?"

"Not always. Sometimes you can't no matter how hard you try. I think that's down to them and not us. You should try yoga. The breathing and the focus might help you."

"Is that what you did?" I'm trying not to imagine him in yoga clothes.

He grimaces. "Bloody hell, no. Can't be doing with that hippie nonsense. I just concentrate and don't talk. It's a dying talent in your generation."

I ignore him. "So, I could hear Rosalind if I tried?"

"Not yet," he says quickly. "You're not ready to try that, lad." He leans forward urgently. "I don't want you trying anything in that house yet."

"Okay," I say faintly. "But I need to help Levi."

"I know, Blue," he says gently. "But not at the expense of yourself."

He leans under the counter and pulls out a bundle of what looks like herbs tied together.

"What's that?" I ask curiously, sitting down to pick up my food again.

"Sage. You light the end of it and walk through the house burning it."

"Why? Is that some sort of dark art ritual? Oh, will Levi and I have to be naked?" I ask enthusiastically.

"God help me," he breathes. "No, it's not a satanic ritual. It cleanses the house. You need to do that until you're a bit more confident about your abilities." He looks hard at me. "You being in that house has been worrying me."

"I knew you cared," I say smugly, finishing my cob and thinking longingly of eating another one. His mouth quirks and he pushes his own towards me.

"I've had my breakfast," he says nonchalantly. I narrow my eyes, and he grins. "Silly old me. I must be getting senile. I completely forgot about it when I asked you to go to the bakery."

"Hmm," I say, but it doesn't stop me tearing into the food.

"You staying with Levi for a bit, then?" he asks innocently, sneaking a look at me.

I grin and watch his moue of distaste as my mouth is full. I swallow and nod.

"Just for a bit until we've sorted him out. Then I'll be off. I don't want to outstay my welcome."

"I didn't get the impression the lad was like that." He shrugs. "Seemed like a kind boy."

"He is," I say darkly. "Too kind."

"For you?"

The question makes me jerk, and I look at his sharp eyes. I consider it for a second and then shrug. "Yes."

"Why?"

I stare at him in astonishment. "You know the sort of people I hung around with, Tom. I know you remember Spud's shop and the readings because I saw you shouting at him one day, and you kicked Fay out of here many times." I pause. "Why not me?" I say slowly. "You never kicked me out."

He takes a sip of his drink. "You weren't like them," he says simply.

"How did you come to that conclusion? I'm *exactly* like them."

"No, you're a kind boy who got caught up in stuff you shouldn't have because you knew no better. You've got a conscience, lad. Albeit one whose voice must be hoarse with shouting and screaming to be heard. It's permanently exhausted, but it's still there."

I nudge him. "Who knew you were so funny?" He looks at me, and I wink. "I mean it. Who did know?"

He shakes his head, but he can't hide his smile. Then he stares at me. "I'm sorry I didn't do anything before. I didn't realise that you were homeless."

I stare at him in astonishment. "Why would you?"

"Blue, you break my heart," he says softly. "The question should always be *why* didn't I know that, not why would I." He breathes in, as if preparing for battle. "I'm not one for mushiness."

"Thank God," I breathe.

He nods. "I'll just say this. That when you decide to leave Levi ..."

"I'm not with him."

"Oh really," he says innocently, and I glare. "Anyway, where was I before I was so abruptly interrupted by a member of the rude generation?"

"I'm not sure how you can even say that without breaking into hysterical laughter."

"Anyway," he says loudly and quickly. "When you leave him, I don't want you back on the streets. I've a flat at the top of the book shop. You can have that. It has a thick door so I won't be subjected to any of your aimless prattling and at least you won't be dead on a shop doorstep." We exchange glances, and I swallow hard which makes him look panicked. "And we will never speak of this again," he warns me.

"Okay," I breathe fervently and we nod at each other in perfect accord.

CHAPTER 10

*B*lue
    I hurry down the cobbled lane, the cold wind pinching at me with icy fingers. I pull my coat around me and smile as I see home all lit up warm and welcoming. I come to a stop, ignoring the cold. *This is not my bloody home,* I remind myself, and my inner voice sounds positively shocked. *Get that thought out of your fucking head now.*

Home, the voice scoffs and I nod. It is ridiculous. It's a home, alright, but I am never going to forget that it's Levi's and not mine.

Nevertheless, I pick up my speed. My stomach gets light and squirmy as I use my key for the first time to get in. I smile down at it. It's shiny and all mine. A key to a house. I shake my head and put it carefully away in my mum's wallet before shrugging off my coat and hanging it on the hook.

The house is toasty warm and smells gorgeously of something cooking. "Levi?" I shout.

"In the kitchen," he calls.

I wander into the room which is warmly lit. The blind is closed against the night and one of the wild fig candles that he loves so much is burning on the breakfast bar. Pans are bubbling on the hob, and I sniff appreciatively.

"Oh my God, what are you cooking?" I groan.

He grins at me. He looks appetizing himself, barefoot in a black T-shirt and a pair of ancient jeans that appear to be held together by willpower. "It's gnocchi with a tomato sauce," he says. "Nothing very complicated."

"I didn't know you could cook."

Levi shrugs. "My mum taught me. She was very insistent that I know how to cook. Said no son of hers would be useless in the kitchen."

He smiles, but it has that soft edge to it. A downturn to the full lips that happens a lot. I look at the dark shadows under his eyes anxiously. He doesn't sleep well. Even accounting for this fucked-up house, he still tosses and turns in his sleep. It's so obvious that he's mourning but Levi doesn't realise. He thinks he's moved on. I watch him tenderly as he stirs something in the pot. He's going to reach a breaking point soon and I'm going to be here for him.

He chuckles, distracting me from my shockingly fervent thoughts. "What is it?" I ask.

"I was just thinking of Mason. He couldn't cook to save his life. He once started a fire in the kitchen because he let a saucepan burn dry."

"How silly," I say, gritting my teeth at the mention of Mason. He's another fly in the fucking ointment. Levi doesn't mention him much, but he must be thinking of him. Five years is a long time to be with someone, and from some of the things Levi's dropped about him, Mason appears to be both funny and successful. He was at college with Levi and features in a lot of his stories.

I also saw a photo of him last night when Levi was looking through a box to find something he needed to frame. The stupid bastard is good-looking too, with dark hair and a slim build and a big smile. Just the thought of him makes me feel less because I am none of those things, being scrawny, and a walking fucking disaster.

I stare at Levi. But I'd still treat him well if he'd let me. What sort of idiot had Levi in their life and fucked it up? If he'd been mine, I'd—

I break off the thought very quickly and rub my hands together. "Shall I lay the table?"

We eat at the little table in front of the window. I fall further into some sort of quicksand. It's just so good to sit here together and make him laugh with my ghost-tour stories. To see his tired face light up and know that later we'll climb the stairs and get into bed with one another.

I know I should be in the other room, but Levi was very stubborn last night, insisting forcefully that I couldn't stay in there, and I'd agreed, not just because of what happened in the room, but mainly because I love lying in bed with him feeling warm and safe and lit up from the inside.

I want him so badly. It's a constant fluttery feeling in my stomach and it spreads so that sometimes when I'm near him I think I must be glowing. However, it's not going to happen yet. If at all. He's seems set on keeping boundaries between us and I'm torn between thinking that it's either to give me a safe place or to keep me at a distance.

~

I come awake in the middle of the night as fingers slip through my hair and down my face. They're fucking freezing and my first thought is that Levi needs to warm his hands. My second thought is pure joy because he's finally making a move. My third thought is *Oh shit*. Because as my brain sharpens, I realise that Levi's hands are actually around my waist. He's snuggled up behind me, snoring gently.

I open my eyes warily. *What the fuck just touched me?*

The room is filled with moonlight and the shadow of the tree outside moves on the wall opposite the bed. There's nothing here that's out of the ordinary.

Then I hear the crying. At first, it's very soft. Gentle hiccups of grief that barely disturb the air. Then it gets louder, and, even as I sit up, the cries fill the air in a raging torrent of grief. Sobbing and wailing until I want to put my hands over my ears.

"Please stop," I whisper.

I glance at Levi. *How is he still sleeping so peacefully?*

I look around the moonlit room again and can't stop my instinctive jerk when my gaze lands on the woman sitting on the end of the bed. She's darkly shadowed, and her long hair hangs over her face as she leans forward, her shoulders shaking.

"Hello," I whisper.

She carries on crying, only now it's completely silent, like I'm looking at her through a wall of glass. I get out of bed slowly and wince at the coldness in the room. My nipples tighten into raised nubs under my T-shirt and I wrap my hands around myself, seeing my breaths crystallise on the air. *This is not normal.*

I shake my head at the irony. The fact that a ghost woke me with a creepy touch and is now crying at the end of our bed is not the weird bit of all this. The weird bit is that Levi Black's house is cold right now. The man is obsessed with making sure that I'm warm, to the extent that he pays more attention to the temperature than a hibernating hamster.

I edge closer to the woman. She continues to cry silently, her hair a dark curtain over her face and her shoulders shaking in a paroxysm of grief.

"Rosalind," I say warily. "Rosalind, is that you?"

I backpedal with a loud scream as her head shoots up. Where there should be a face is nothing. Just black, moving shadows.

She raises her hands to me imploringly and blood drips from them, falling and landing on the carpet in splots that shine sticky and dark in the moonlight. She rises, her movements so quick and jerky that I shout out again.

The light clicks on, and I turn to find Levi sitting up and staring at me sleepily. There's a pillow mark on his cheek and his eyes are bleary.

"What's going on?" he says, his eyes sharpening. "Blue?"

I point a trembling finger. "Can't you see her?"

My hand drops, dead weight. Where the spirit had been is nothing.

"She was just here," I say wildly. "She had no face." I cross quickly to where she was sitting. "There was blood," I mumble, looking down at the carpet. It's pristine now. "B-But," I stutter. "She was here."

"I believe you." He throws the covers back and comes to my side. He pulls me into a hug and I nestle into him, burying my head in his neck for a second and inhaling the warm, sleepy smell of his skin.

After a few minutes he pulls back and brushes my hair from my face. There's a tenderness in the gesture which is so alien to me and so typical of him. He always treats me with care. It makes my teeth hurt with the wish for it to carry on.

"Alright now?" he asks softly.

I nod and scrub my hands down my face. Exhaling slowly, I feel calm settle on me now that he's awake and with me. It's bloody nice not to be on my own with this shit.

Always before, I've curled into a ball and pulled my sleeping bag over my head, enduring the nights when spirits have silently raged at me. To have someone stand with me is weird. But nice.

"There was a woman weeping at the end of the bed," I say finally.

His mouth twitches. "Not something that's ever happened to me before."

I give a soft snort of laughter, to my surprise. "Well, she was there."

"Was it Rosalind?"

I shake my head. "I thought it was, but I was wrong."

"How do you know? Didn't you say she had no face?"

I tap my fingers gently against my teeth, thinking hard. "I just know it wasn't her. This one was thinner, and I got the impression she was young." I shrug. "Who the fuck knows?"

"You do," he says firmly. "Don't doubt yourself. Tom said you were powerful. I think you'd better start believing it."

"But if she wasn't Rosalind, then who was she? What other spirits are here?"

"Maybe we've got a house full," he says thoughtfully. "Maybe that's the problem."

I shake my head. "I don't know, but I think we need to do something."

"Would that something be to drink ourselves silly?"

I snort. "That sounds very attractive, but no. We're going to do some smudging."

"We're going to do some whatting? Is that some sort of sexual kink I've never heard of?"

"No." I laugh. "Very far from it. We're going to light a smudging stick and purify the house."

"Okay, my life has just taken a very strange turn. Can I think about this?"

"No," I say firmly. "We need to do it now, Levi."

"Why?"

"Because that frightened me," I whisper, feeling a sudden certainty that whatever is in this house is listening and shouldn't hear this. "I think it was meant to scare me too," I continue. "That woman was sent to me, and that's sufficiently worrying that I don't want to go to sleep until we've sorted out protection."

"And this smudging is protection?"

I nod.

He sighs. "Okay, we'll smudge, but I'm going to get dressed. I'm not comfortable smudging in my underpants."

I laugh. "So says every smudger."

"Is that an actual thing?"

I watch him pull on some soft-looking grey sweatpants and a white T-shirt, secretly mourning the loss of the view of him in his boxers.

"Blue?" he says.

I jump. "What?"

"Get dressed," he says, looking me up and down where I stand in my briefs and his T-shirt that I refused to relinquish, and this time I know I'm not imagining the heat in his gaze. My cock stirs and I leap into action, pulling on my own sweatpants and leaving his shirt on. It still smells a little bit of him and that gives me strength.

When we get down to the kitchen, Levi moves automatically to switch on the kettle. I repress a smile. It's almost his default setting to make tea in any emergency. I sit down at the breakfast bar and open his iPad.

"What are you doing?" he asks, bustling around and setting mugs out.

"I'm looking at YouTube."

"Why?"

"To watch videos on smudging."

He stops what he's doing. "You're watching a YouTube video on how to purify my house from vengeful spirits?" I nod and he shrugs. "My life is very weird."

"Tell me about it."

I choose a video and press Play. Levi sets a mug at my hand and peers over my shoulder. We watch the video of a woman going through the smudging process as the wind howls outside the kitchen window. When it's finished, I close the video.

"So, we need an abalone bowl to burn the stick in and a feather to waft the smoke," I say slowly. "Do you happen to have either of these things lying around your house?"

He snorts. "Alas, that my days of using feathers in kinky sex and eating from abalone bowls are gone. No, I've got a baking tray and a handkerchief. Will that do?"

I sniff. "It's not very dramatic, is it?"

He collects the tray and hanky while I undo the bag containing the smudge stick.

"Pooh," Levi says immediately. "That's pungent. What is it?"

"White sage."

"Ugh! Won't that make the house smell like a casserole?"

"No," I say patiently. "This is a different sage and even if it did, would you rather have casserole air or dead women crying everywhere?"

"My choices in life seem to have got a lot wider this year," he muses.

I put the bundle of sage on the baking tray and take the lighter that he hands me before pausing and looking up at him. "Do you think we should have some music playing?"

"Why? Are you making your own soundtrack?"

"No, it just might be nice."

He fiddles with his phone and a song blares out.

I turn my head slowly. "What the fuck is this?"

Levi bites his lip, fighting a grin. "It's the battle scene music from *Gladiator*. I used to play it before I got into a row with Mason to get me in the mood."

I shake my head. "The more I hear about your relationship, the more I think it's better all round that you're single." I listen to the music for a few seconds. "Is this supposed to fill the ghosts with dread?"

He shrugs. "Well, it is Russell Crowe."

"Point taken." I wrinkle my nose. "Don't you have something with the sound of rain? I like that."

"No way. That stuff just makes me want the loo."

"I think for the sake of our sanity we'll turn off the warmongering music and do this in silence."

"You're the boss," he says peacefully.

I wink at him. "That is true. How much better the world will be when it catches up with that notion."

"I can't believe I'm going to say this, but shall we get on with smudging my house?"

I tap his hand gently. "I really think that a large part of you isn't taking this seriously."

He pulls himself up to sit on the worksurface, swinging his long legs idly. "I know it's happening. I've seen and heard it all. I've seen the effect it has on you. But…" He pauses.

"But?"

"Well, a large part of me is still hoping that there's been a chemical spill and we've been inhaling hallucinogenic drugs for a while."

"That would be *so* much more fun than smudging at three in the morning."

He nods, holding out his fist, and I oblige with a fist bump. I draw back and set the lighter to the edge of the sage. We watch it burn for a few seconds and then I stub it out. Very slowly, white and grey smoke rises up and drifts about.

"Shit," I say as I accidentally inhale some and start to cough.

"You alright?" he asks.

I nod, still coughing. "Maybe open the window a couple of inches."

He obliges and the smell goes back to a decent level. I pick the tray up. "Okay, are we ready?"

He nods solemnly and tracks me as I walk upstairs, following me like a shaggy-haired shadow.

We start in his studio, him standing watching curiously as I move around wafting the fragrant smoke into the corners of the room. When I've finished, we both stand back and wait but nothing happens. It's a bit of an anticlimax.

Levi sighs. "I thought the spirits would be throwing themselves out of the windows by now."

I nudge him, trying not to laugh. "Come on. Bedroom next."

When we leave the studio, I stop dead on the landing. "What is it?" he asks immediately, and it doesn't escape my notice that he puts himself in front of me.

"It's too quiet."

"Is that a bad thing?"

I look around warily. "Yes." A shiver runs down my back. "We should get on with this," I say urgently.

He nods and we walk down the stairs in a solemn procession, not counting the fact that I'm holding a baking tray full of smoking sage and a hanky. When we reach the landing, we pause.

"Which room first?" Levi asks as the smoke curls above us, oozing along the walls. I open my mouth to reply but stop as I hear a faint noise.

"What's that?" I ask.

He looks around wildly. "I don't know." The noise becomes a low rustling sound. He looks back at me. "It sounds like people talking."

I cock my head to one side. He's right. The rustling turns into the low hum and mutter of people talking to one another—they're close by, but we can't quite hear their conversations. If we strained hard enough, we could hear them and—

"I need to hear what they're saying," Levi says, an urgent tone in his voice. He steps closer to the wall and my hand snaps out instinctively and stops him.

"Where are you going?"

"To listen," he says, his eyes dreamy and unfocused. "I need to know."

"No, you don't," I snap. I tug on his arm and when he doesn't respond, still staring intently at the wall, I pinch his arm.

"*Ouch!*" he says, holding his arm. "What did you do that for?"

"I need you here, Levi. Not edging off to listen to walls. With our luck you'll go into a trance and Rip van Winkle yourself for the next few years."

The whispering gets slightly louder, as if someone is turning the volume up on the speakers.

"We need to do this quickly," I say urgently. "Follow me and stay close." I end up shouting the last bit because the noise has become very loud.

He nods determinedly and takes hold of my waist, his fingers cold against the skin above my sweatpants. And that's how we do it. Joined together, we pace through the house as I use the hanky to waft the smoke into the corners of the rooms. The noise gets louder and louder.

"I can't hear myself think," he shouts as we leave the lounge. Then he spins around, looking wildly about. "What the hell is happening now?" he gasps.

The sound of footsteps echoes through the house, loud and disjointed like a whole party of people is on the move. The steps come down the stairs. Distantly, I note that my hand is shaking.

We both jump as the front door slams open with a bang. It hangs there swaying as the footsteps move past us and the voices and laughter get louder. I feel a draft on my face and the door slams shut decisively, leaving us in a silence that's still ringing with noise.

I realise that Levi is clutching me so tightly that my ribs hurt. "Levi," I gasp. "Can't breathe."

"What the fuck was that?" he asks, wild-eyed.

I shake my head. "I have no idea. The good news is that the invisible party appears to have vacated the building."

"What's the bad news?" he says warily.

"Last room to cleanse is the cellar."

We both shudder as if choreographed. He takes a deep breath. "Okay, let's do it."

I nod and there are no smiles now. I don't know what it is about the cellar, but it feels wrong to me down there. Wrong and bad.

He opens the door, and we hover at the entrance, looking down the staircase. It's too dark to see anything.

I stir. "Get the light," I whisper. "Let's do this." I look hard at Levi. "We have to be really quick down here," I warn him.

He doesn't bother to respond. Just reaches out and flicks the switch.

The cellar is immediately bathed in a dirty yellowish light that falls on the boxes on the floor and the bags of stuff left by the builder. It doesn't manage to penetrate the back of the room, though, and I swallow hard at the sight of the inky shadows.

"I'll go first," he says decisively.

I nod, but I stick tightly to his heels as we descend. *It's so cold down here.* I shudder and bunch my hand in the back of his T-shirt. When we get to the bottom, he stays close to me as we walk around the perimeter of the room. The smell of the sage starts to overpower the cellar's cold dank scent.

Within seconds the smell changes, becoming warm and light. Levi feels it too—he sniffs a couple of times.

I'm about to tell him that we're nearly done, when there's a sudden loud skittering behind the far wall. We swing round.

"What the fuck was that?" I gasp.

Levi shakes his head, staring intently at the wall. The odd disjointed skitter happens again. The hair on the back of my neck rises.

Levi's eyes are very wide in the dim light. "That doesn't sound good," he whispers. "It also doesn't sound like rats."

The noise comes again, filling my head with the image of giant rats pattering around inside the walls looking for a way out so they can eat us. I shake my head. Not a good idea to give voice to that thought.

The skittering travels along the wall, moving away from us and towards the—

"Levi," I say urgently. "Go up and stand at the door."

"Why?"

"Because I don't want to be locked down here. At the moment I can't think of anything worse."

He glances at the wall and I can see the moment he realises the noise is heading for the staircase. He sprints across the room, taking the stairs in twos. He's only just in time because even as he nears the top, the door starts to close. I gasp as he throws himself into the opening and the door rebounds off his body.

"Do it quickly," he shouts, the strain evident in his voice. "You're too far away for me to help if you need me."

I move quickly around the cellar, wafting the smoke. Everywhere that it touches, the dark retreats a little.

At first the draft around my feet doesn't register but then it gets stronger, rising to my knees.

"Blue," Levi yells. "*Come on.*"

"Trying," I gasp.

The dust on the floor rises as if summoned by a cyclone. I race around the room, wafting the sage smoke at the walls. I'm not doing this properly—I'm not sure if there even is a proper way to do it—but Levi and I need to leave this place as soon as possible.

"Blue," Levi says in a frantic voice. "Leave it."

"But I—"

"Leave it," he thunders. "Get up the stairs and don't look back."

My instinct is to look back, but the urgency in his voice has me racing towards him, darting up the stairs and almost dropping the baking tray as I go. He grabs my hand and pulls me up and past him.

I whirl to see what's happening behind me. The dust has transformed into a huge shape. It ripples and eddies, like it's being blown by a stiff wind. I get a glimpse of something dark inside it. Then Levi slams the door and locks it before sliding down the wall and sitting on the floor.

I set the baking tray on the floor and slide down beside him, and he grabs me tightly, his clasp almost painful. Silence falls for a while disturbed only by our panting breaths. As they start to ease, I look up at him.

He shrugs with a shockingly wry look on that clever face. "Okay, I think I believe now."

"I'm so thrilled that no more fairies need to die, Wendy," I say grumpily.

He snorts and pulls me even closer. "Is the house clean now?" he whispers.

I shudder at the feel of his breath in my ear before casting my senses around the house.

"For now," I say slowly. I bite my lip. "I don't think it'll last long though."

He hugs me, lowering his face onto the top of my hair, and we sit in the silence.

CHAPTER 11

One Week Later

Levi

When I wake up, the morning is dull and dreary with an overcast sky and a wind that batters against the house as if it's trying to get in. I shuffle downstairs in my boxers, yawning so widely my jaw creaks. The house is quiet. No music playing, no clattering pans or tuneless humming, so Blue is definitely at work. He has a way of filling the house with little noises, and I love knowing that he's somewhere close by, and I'll see him any second.

There haven't been any strange noises or occurrences since the night of the smudging, but he's still been sleeping with me. After the old man's revelations about the possible danger of Blue staying in this house, I didn't think he should be anywhere near that strange room.

As if by silent agreement, nothing has happened between us since that kiss on the street. I don't want him to feel obligated to please me like I'm some version of one of his old customers. That decision has been made immeasurably more difficult due to the fact that each night he's slept in his briefs and my T-shirt that he's taken a liking to. The same briefs that hug his narrow hips and show off that long, lean body. And the same T-shirt that makes some caveman part of me love how it's my clothes that are keeping him warm.

Instead of shagging, we've lain peacefully in the silent bedroom. It's been a haven lit by warm lamplight as we've read our books and discussed anything that seemed relevant. He's related incidents from his day at work, and we've laughed.

And when I've switched the light out, he's snuggled into my side. Rather than rolling away or telling him no, I've wrapped my arms around him and felt him fall asleep. They're the tamest nights I've ever spent, yet they've felt far more intimate than if we'd spent our time in the bed fucking. I like that intimacy far more than I should.

However, while he's slept peacefully when we've switched the light out, I haven't. Whichever position I've lain in, Blue has ended up snuggling into me, almost pinning me to the bed.

I'd lain awake for hours last night, my cock throbbing in my underwear and the scent of peaches in my nostrils and my arms full of him. I'd finally fallen asleep at dawn this morning and hadn't noticed when he'd got up. I'd woken very late to a note telling me he'd gone to work with lots of exclamation marks that made me smile.

In the kitchen, I set about making tea and putting on some toast while the radio plays. When "Red Light Spells Danger" by Billy Ocean comes on, I make an automatic move to switch it off. This was my mum's favourite song. She used to dance around the kitchen with me to it when I was little, both of us doing silly dance moves and laughing so hard we'd end up bent double.

I haven't been able to bear to hear it since her death, but for some reason today my finger hovers over the Off button before moving away. I forgot how catchy it is. I try to concentrate on making the tea but the song starts to pick up speed, and as Billy begins to sing, I start to sway. I add a twist and my socks slide over the wooden floor. *Wow, this floor is perfect for dancing.*

The song builds to the first chorus and before I can even think about what I'm doing, I slide across the floor and wave my hands in the air. I whoop loudly, and suddenly the music catches me again, and I'm dancing—doing stupid dips and weaves, boogieing in a way I'd never in a million years do in a club or actually in front of any living person. Only my mum.

The music fills my head, and I start to sing the words, shouting them out as we used to do, and suddenly the kitchen fills with light as the sun comes from behind the clouds and bathes the room and me in slippery sunbeams. The warmth fills me and I sing louder, holding my arms up and twisting and turning.

When the song finishes, I stop in place, panting and sweating. But as the DJ starts to talk, I hear a throat clearing behind me.

I spin around with complete dread. "*You!*"

Blue is standing there leaning against the door, his arms crossed and one hand holding a paper bag that's giving off wonderful aromas.

"Me." His tone is serious, but it's slightly spoilt by the mirth brimming in his eyes. "Tom closed up to go to some meeting, and I don't need to be back until lunchtime, so I brought you some breakfast. I never realised it was cabaret time in this house. I'd have dressed up if I'd known."

I rub my hand down my hair, very aware that I'm wearing my oldest pair of boxers and just made a total twat of myself. "Sorry," I say sheepishly. "It was my mum's favourite song and…" My voice cracks in the middle of the sentence, compounding my embarrassment.

Instantly, the humour in his face dies away. He slings the bag down on the counter and comes towards me.

"Oh no," I say hoarsely, feeling my throat close up. "There's no need. *Oof!*" I stare up at him from the chair he's just pushed me into. "What are you doing?" I say faintly as he scrambles into my lap, his weight light on my legs.

"Giving you a hug," he says seriously. "It's medically advised."

"I don't…" I start to say and then give a huge sigh as he folds into me, his scent weaving around me. I've learnt that the peachy aroma comes from his shampoo. A friend of his makes the stuff from natural ingredients.

His grip is just right. Not soft, but firm and implacable.

"I just felt like she was here," I say softly, burying my face in his shoulder.

He grabs my chin to make me look at him. "Babe, she was."

"*What?*"

He nods furiously as if for some reason I won't believe him. "She was just here watching you. Wavy brown hair with blonde streaks, glasses on a string round her neck?"

"Oh my God," I say, looking around frantically. "Where is she?"

He pulls me back gently. "She's gone, lovey," he says softly. "Can't you feel the way the light has left? She knows you're going to be okay. It was what she was waiting for. She couldn't leave before she knew. She really loves you," he says in an awed tone as if he'd never realised that a mother could love a child.

"But I don't want her to go," I say hoarsely.

Blue cups my face in his hands, his expression fiercely gentle. "We never do, lovey, but it's time."

"It can't be. Can't you call her back and…" I choke on the words, feeling the tears in the back of my throat.

I haven't cried since she died, but suddenly I can't keep it in anymore. I give a great sob, and then I'm crying hard. Sobs shake my whole body while he croons nonsense and holds me, and I find that it's actually a relief.

The spot between his neck and his shoulder, although sharp with his bones, is actually the best place for me to hide my face from the world and mourn my lovely mum.

I don't know how long I cry, but he stays with me, not saying anything, just stroking my hair and holding me in his arms. When the sobs eventually peter out, I stay with my head on his shoulder for a few minutes.

"I've soaked your shirt," I say slowly, my voice thick and hoarse.

"I've got others. You know us millennials. We're all about the clothes."

"I am aware."

He chuckles and sits back, pulling my head up to face him. He looks around, undoubtedly searching for a cloth, but his action when he can't see one stuns me. He just shrugs and, lifting his fingers, he clears away the tears on my face. He's tender and thorough and works with a concentrated look on his face while I stare at him.

I have shot my load over men's faces before, had another man's come on me, but I have never had anyone perform such an intimate act for me.

Blue seems oblivious, humming under his breath until I'm tidied up to his satisfaction. "How do you feel?" he finally asks.

I shrug awkwardly. "Hollow."

He nods. "That's good. It means the grief has gone."

"For forever?"

He looks sad. "No, babe. It never goes. But it does get easier and the times in between the sadness get longer and longer. But you'll always love and miss her." He pauses. "Maybe that's good. It's certainly a fine way to honour someone."

"When did you get so wise?" I ask.

He gives that impish grin. "Always. Everyone should know this but for some reason they resist the realization."

"It's scary," I offer.

Blue laughs and eases from my lap. I instantly want to drag him back, and for a second I consider it. I think he'd let me even though he's as prickly as a porcupine. But I know I won't. Not yet.

"Come on," he says, offering me his hand and pulling me up.

"Come on, where?"

"Out. I need to show you something."

"Oh no," I immediately protest. "I look like I've gone ten rounds with Mike Tyson."

"Ten *rounds*?" he asks, lifting one eyebrow. "Well, you're certainly a confident sort of person. I'd have given you ten seconds max."

I shake my head. "Thank you so much. What are we doing?"

"You are going to get dressed, splash some cold water on your face, put on those sexy glasses I saw you in last night, and get your coat. Chop chop," he says as I hesitate.

I abruptly give up and do as he says, knowing it'll be easier.

Before I leave the kitchen, I grab his hand. "I'm sorry," I say.

"For what?" His face is a picture of surprise.

"For asking you to get her back. That was wrong."

His face softens, and he lifts up one thin hand to cup my face. "If I could get her back for you, I would," he says, not a trace of a smile on his earnest face. "I want you to know that. Don't ever be sorry for wanting one more moment with your mum."

"Would you like that?" I ask softly.

A complicated expression crosses his face. "Your mum and mine were very different," he finally says. "It would take more than one moment with my mum."

I open my mouth to question this, but he shakes his head. "Go and get ready," he says.

Fifteen minutes later, I head downstairs to find Blue waiting by the door. I feel strangely shy. "How did you get in, anyway?" I ask, curiosity stirring. "I didn't hear your key."

His mouth twitches. "You were a little busy," he murmurs and I flush. He smiles at me and pats my arm. "I didn't need the key anyway. The door was wide open. You need to start being security conscious."

"It was closed when I came downstairs."

We exchange glances. Locking the door and testing it three times, I follow him out onto the street. He walks quickly, stealing occasional glances at me that I'm probably not meant to see.

"Can I ask you something, Blue?" I say.

He shoots me a bright glance. "Anything."

"Why has my mum gone now?"

He stares at me in incomprehension.

"I mean," I say, "according to Tom, the house is dangerous. Why wouldn't my mum stay to protect me?"

He looks thoughtful. "I don't know," he finally says. He comes to a stop and pulls me to face him. "Maybe it's because you've got help now with Tom and me. Maybe she hung around until you weren't alone. Whatever it is, I think it takes a tremendous effort for spirits to resist moving on. She must have loved you very much, Levi."

"She did." It feels nice to acknowledge that without the huge weight of grief that's usually behind it. I know he's right. The grief will be back, but I don't think it'll ever be the same as that again.

We start walking again, and I wrinkle my nose as we start down Goodramgate past The White Swan pub.

"What are we supposed to be looking at?" I pause. "Is it the Tesco Express because I've actually seen that before."

He shakes his head. "I'm saving that for a special occasion."

As I laugh he stops on the street, coolly ignoring a couple's curse as they have to abruptly steer around him.

He gestures theatrically, and I'm almost positive that he's missing his hat at the moment. "Here we are. The Holy Trinity Church."

He points at a set of ornately carved iron gates in a narrow opening. He waves me past him, and I walk down a little path that opens into a space with a small church and what was obviously once a graveyard but now looks a little bit like a garden. Lichen-covered gravestones lean drunkenly over planted areas like an irritating uncle at a wedding. A few hardy people are sitting and eating on the benches dotting the area.

Despite the bustle of the streets beyond, in this tiny corner I can only hear the sound of the leaves in the trees rustling in the cold wind.

"*Another* church?" I say as Blue comes up next to me. "What is it with York and all these churches?"

He shrugs. "People will say it's because it was a rich area with wealthy merchants who wanted to secure a place in heaven despite being wealthier than Richard Branson."

"And you'd say?" I prompt.

He shoots me a look before turning towards the church. "I'd say that maybe the people of York have always known that wickedness and evil are a lot closer to the surface than everyone thinks and having sanctified ground might come in handy occasionally."

He disappears into the church, and I stir myself into following him.

The dimly lit church smells of damp and wood. It's dark and so cold that I can see my breath, and the flagstones are uneven and worn beneath my feet.

Blue smiles, and I turn to see a man in a North Face fleece walking towards us.

"Morning, Simon," Blue says.

The man smiles a greeting. "You okay, Blue?"

"Fine. Just showing my friend around."

"I'll let you get on with it, then. We're meeting in the Hole in the Wall after work if you want to come by before the ghost walk."

"Maybe," he says, smiling warmly.

I wonder who this man is to him. Blue definitely isn't the type to waste time on false pleasantries. My hackles rise. *Is this an old lover?*

I square my shoulders and move closer to Blue, but then I remember he's my quirky and slightly wonderful friend, not a prospective boyfriend. I wonder when that feeling started to feel old and redundant.

Blue moves away and I follow him, whistling under my breath at the oak pews around us. They're scratched and worn, probably by generations of children kicking their heels as the lengthy services droned on.

"These are box pews," I mutter. "Wow! I've read about them but never thought I'd see them. They're very rare."

He smiles back at me and despite the mocking edge there's a fondness there too. "You read about *box pews*? Levi, you have to get out more."

"I can't believe these are still here," I say, ignoring him. "A congregation could damage them."

"This isn't a workable church anymore," he says knowledgeably. "It closed its doors in the seventies when it was declared redundant. Like you said, too many churches. It stood empty for a bit and then the Churches Conservation Trust took it over. They keep churches open like this all over the country so they don't get sold off so some rich person can put their Aga in the altar."

I dodge a group of people clustering around a guide. "You seem to know a lot about it?"

"I should do. I volunteered here for a while."

"You did?" I don't know why it surprises me. I'm coming to learn that Blue is much more than sharp words and an eye to making money.

He winks. "I did. They give you free biscuits with your tea."

"Oh, okay, that makes sense."

He grins and punches me lightly on the arm. "I like old places," he says, looking around the dank church as if it's Buckingham Palace. "They've got character." He comes to a stop at the side of the church. "Here it is."

I look around. "Here what is?"

He shakes his head. "The window. Look at it."

I stare at it. "It's a stained-glass window," I say cautiously, not wanting to offend him.

"Wait a minute," he instructs me, and suddenly the sun pours through the window, bathing us and the flagstones with colour.

"So pretty," I breathe.

Blue shakes his head. "Look at the figures."

I look closer and then closer still. "There's a woman's face on a man's body," I say slowly. "And what looks like a griffin with chicken legs."

He beams at me like I'm a prize student. "It's actually Mary's head on a bishop's body."

"Why is that? Was it a political commentary?"

He laughs. "Much more mundane. This window was originally in front of the altar and they took it down to move it. But once it was down they realized that they didn't know how to put it back together, so they just did a bodge job."

I laugh, staring at the window. "That's brilliant." When I turn, Blue is smiling at me. "Thank you for showing me."

He grins. "You're *so* polite. You can't quite bring yourself to ask why I'm showing you this, can you?"

I exhale in relief. "Thank you."

He laughs and then sobers. "I wanted you to see it because I think this is what grief is really like. After we lose someone, we're like this window. We're broken in pieces. Eventually we put ourselves back together, but it's never the same as the original us. Instead, we're a jumbled-up version with funny angles and new faces to show the world." He turns to face the window. "Still beautiful and still whole. But just in a new way. Even if we're a griffin with chicken legs."

I study him, watching the rich reds and blues and greens gild his face and turn those sharp features wild and almost magical. "Thank you," I say softly. "I needed this."

"I know," he says, and we stand together comfortably, neither of us quite ready to confront the subject of how close we're now standing to each other and how he knows me better than anyone I've ever met after such a short time of friendship.

~

*T*he next day I sit in my studio staring out of the window. It's late afternoon and a miserable overcast day. I'm supposed to be drawing up the latest strip in my series for the magazine, but instead I'm doodling idly. I look down at the tiny figure of a blue-haired man fighting ghosts with a lively expression and a snark bubble. Not exactly idly doodling, then.

I grab a black pencil and quickly sketch a figure rising up behind the tiny Blue figure, his arms extended to grab him. A shiver runs down my spine. That is entirely too close to home, so I rub the monster out, and instead draw a ghost rattling his chains at Blue who has a sceptical expression on his tiny face. I brush my fingertip gently over the sharp features.

It's too tender a gesture, and I shake my head and stand up to stretch, my bones creaking after sitting too long. It hasn't been a productive day. It hasn't been a productive week what with rushing around with Blue visiting psychic bookshop owners, having a mini breakdown, and kissing him.

I swallow hard at the thought of that kiss and fling myself onto the sofa. I can't stop thinking about him and about how soft his lips were.

I toss my rubber-band ball up into the air and catch it. I could have him. I know without being conceited that he's just as attracted to me as I am to him, but I can't get his past out of my head. Nor can I forget the fact that he's staying with me, and if I made a move, he might think that he had to reciprocate because of the roof over his head. The thought makes my balls shrivel up. And it's this that's given me the courage to keep everything on an even keel.

He's like a cat, I think, throwing the ball again. At first he was scrawny, but already that's changing with regular, healthy meals. He's starting to look sleek, but there's still a slight trace of feral—that hidden wildness in cats that waits for the right moment to show its face.

However, it's his happiness and enthusiasm that gives me the strength to keep him at arm's length. He goes off to work excitedly and comes back bubbling over with stories about what happened at the shop that day, how many customers Tom was rude to, and what he's learnt.

Tom is good for him. They're very alike, both of them self-sufficient and cynical, and the only thing that seems to separate their characters is their fifty-year age difference.

I like the things Tom's told Blue to do. There's an almost holistic approach to being psychic, it seems to me. Tom has encouraged Blue to eat properly and to start yoga and meditation for the breathing and spiritual awareness.

Blue went to a yoga class last night and came back laughing about it, but I saw the look of fascination on his face, so I know he'll go back. I'm coming to know Blue very well.

The house has remained fairly quiet, although yesterday when we came back from the church it was to find every kitchen cupboard open and the contents strewn all over the floor. Blue looked worried, but there hasn't been any reoccurrence of the big stuff.

I'm relieved, I tell myself as I toss the ball. Relieved and scared shitless that Blue will go if it turns out that there's no need for him to stay anymore.

Perfume suddenly floods the air and a floorboard creaks in the corner. It happens every day, and the regularity of these "visits" keeps me from nearly shitting myself. Nothing else ever happens. Just the perfume and that strange creaking as if someone or something is standing on a loose board.

I throw the ball again. The front door slams loudly, and I miss catching the ball. It hits me in the face, and I hold my cheek. "Fuck. That bloody hurt."

"Levi?" Blue shouts.

"In the studio," I call out, getting up as his thundering footsteps come up the stairs. He bursts through the door, and my thoughts scatter as if I've tossed them over my shoulder.

"Oh my *God*," I say. "When did you do that?"

He grins at me and runs a self-conscious hand over his hair. "This afternoon. Tom paid me, so I nipped to the hairdressers after work."

I move closer almost unconsciously. "Is that your real colour?"

He nods. His hair gleams under the ceiling light. Where it was blue, it's now a dirty-blond colour. It's still long and shaggy, but now it's shiny and a huge contrast with those big wolf eyes and dark eyebrows. Combine that with the healthy glow on his skin and the full lips and high cheekbones, and he looks edgy and cool.

My heart sinks. What on earth would this interesting and cool man want with me? I'm hardly party central.

The only thing I'll ever be to him is a friend. My stomach twists. I should remember that.

His smile fades. "Don't you like it?"

"Oh no," I say quickly. "It's lovely." I realise my hand has drifted towards him only when I feel the silky coolness of his hair between my fingers. "Sorry," I mutter, moving back. "I shouldn't grab your hair like that. It's a bit creepy."

"No, don't." His hand jerks out and stops mine. "I like it," he says huskily, coming closer.

We stay in some sort of stasis for a long moment, the room

cloaking us in shadows. Me with my fingers in his hair, him looking up at me, his eyes dark. Then he moves. Grabbing the back of my skull gently, he pulls my head towards him and presses his lips against mine.

His mouth opens immediately, and he groans under his breath as I open my lips and our tongues tangle. I pull him close, feeling his lithe strength against me and inhaling the scent of shampoo that clings to him. Then I realise what I'm doing and pull back, ignoring his mutter of protest.

"No," I gasp out, holding his wide shoulders in a loose grip and feeling the bones still too close to the skin. "We shouldn't do this."

He has flags of colour over those high cheekbones and his lips are full and red. At first his eyes are bleary but then they clear. "Why?" he asks baldly.

"Well, because you're staying under my roof and I don't want you to feel obligated to sleep with me because you've nowhere else to go and…" I falter at the *what the fuck* look on his face. "It wouldn't be right," I finish, and there's more of a question than I'd like in my last statement.

He holds his hand up somewhat imperiously. "Levi, have we somehow slipped into the pages of a book written by Charlotte Bronte?"

I bite my lip. "No," I say somewhat hesitantly.

"Then why are you acting like you should have a ruffled shirt and be holding me to your manly chest?"

My lips twitch, but I rally, thinking of how awful it would be if he did something he didn't want to. "I just don't want you to feel obligated. I mean, I know what you used to—"

"Levi," he barks out. "For fuck's sake, stop talking."

I nod obediently and then gasp as he jumps into my arms. The movement knocks me back into the wall, and he promptly winds his long legs around my hips and rests his elbows on my shoulders.

"Oh," I say, tightening my grip on his hips so he doesn't fall. He's still light, so there's no danger of me dropping him. "I'm not sure this is what you need."

"Levi, did I just tell you to stop talking?"

I stare into his face, fascinated by those huge light eyes. This close I can see the dark striations around the pupil that make them so unusual. "Yes, but ..."

He sighs in a long-suffering manner. "I can see I've got my work cut out for me. How can I persuade you that I'm not some poor unfortunate forced to sleep with the master before being slung out to make his living on the street?" He clicks his fingers. "Oh, I know."

Then he lowers his head and kisses me, sending his tongue rubbing lazily against mine.

I inhale sharply. Grabbing him close, I finally and gladly go under and kiss him back. He wraps himself around me tightly, and I groan at the feel of his cock hard and wanting against my belly. Cupping his buttocks, I press him closer to me and he breaks away to moan lustily before coming back to kiss me again.

I kiss him back feverishly as I stagger over to the sofa. I try to unwind his legs and arms, but he mutters a negative and rains kisses on my face before going back to my lips and I give up, falling backwards onto the sofa, the springs squeaking under our combined weight.

He pulls back, his pupils blown and his face flushed and happy. Happy to be with *me*, I think wonderingly.

"You have the best ideas," he says huskily.

I chuckle before sending my hands on a search-and-find mission up the back of his jumper. I rub my fingertips over the sleek skin of his back before grabbing his shoulder blades and pulling him into me while lifting up so he'll kiss me again. He stares at me for a long second before bending to obey my urging.

He seems to be all over me now, his small arse sitting snugly in my lap, his cock against my own and his arms around me. I ruck up his jumper impatiently, and he pulls it over his head, leaving all that pretty hair in staticky shock waves around his face. Then he bends back to me, moaning and kissing me.

I don't even recognise my needy cry of disapproval when he sits up again, stopping our kiss. He laughs, his face alight with passion.

"Just need to get this off you," he says, pulling at my long-sleeved navy T-shirt until I put my arms up. He takes it off and throws it somewhere behind him. There's a crash and the sound of something breaking.

"Oops," he says huskily. "Naughty me."

I shake my head and rub my thumbs roughly over his pale pink nipples. They're the colour of the iced sugar mice in sweet shops, and when I run my tongue over them I'm sure I'm not imagining how sweet they taste.

"Fuck," he mumbles, holding my face against him. "Do that again."

I obey, and he gives a high. reedy cry, undulating against me. "More," he urges, and I open my mouth and bite down gently on the nubbin. "Fuck," he whispers.

His eyes are closed, his face wild and transported. For a second I wonder whether he's magic and I'll lose him, but then he looks down and smiles lasciviously before moving his hands and letting his long, thin fingers unbutton my jeans.

The denim falls open, and he moans under his breath and leans in, grabbing my cock from my briefs and pulling it gently out of my jeans.

"Fuck," I gasp as he strokes it, his hand a hot, tight grasp. "Oh fuck, yes."

His panting breaths are loud, and I lift my face up so he can kiss me while I fumble with his jeans. I'm a lot less graceful than him, and for a fraught couple of seconds, I get my fingers tangled up in fabric, but then I draw him out and he gives a high cry, riding my lap as I pull our cocks together and start to rub them.

He leans back, resting his hands on my thighs and offering me his lean body to look at. "Yes," he pants, his hips swivelling on my lap and his cock rising from its nest of dark curls, a sleek, ruddy-tipped, slender rod.

It takes me a second to realise that the ringing noise I hear isn't my brain exploding through my ears but is instead the doorbell.

"What the fuck?" I mutter.

He gives a wordless cry of protest as I stop stroking our cocks. "What?" he mutters. "What's going on?"

"There's someone at the door."

"*Now?*" He sounds enraged and disbelieving, and, unbidden, I start to laugh.

"Whoever it is has terrible timing," he says crossly.

My smile fades as my worries roar back along with the blood to my brain.

He shakes his head. "Oh, Levi, don't bother," he says sharply.

"Don't bother what?" I ask.

He buttons his jeans with furious movements of his fingers. "Don't bother trying to put the barriers up again."

"I wasn't going to," I say. "I'm just not sure this is a good idea."

He glares at me, the mood moving quickly from passion to irritation. "Why? Because of my status as an ex-prostitute or because I see dead people? I'm sure that's discrimination."

"I'm not sure that's how that works." I sigh as the bell goes again. "Fucking hell." I stand and button myself up quickly and pull my T-shirt on. "We'll talk after I've got rid of whoever that is," I say, pointing at him.

He shrugs sulkily, and I'm alarmed to see the old *I don't give a shit* look come over his face. It's extraordinarily horrible to have that dismissiveness directed at me again. "Whatever," he mutters.

"What does that mean?" I say, following him as he leaves the room and clatters down the stairs.

"It means that I don't see the point," he says coolly. "All you see is someone who hooked for a living. It's not something *nice* people can get over."

"Don't call me nice in that shitty tone of voice," I hiss as we near the front door. I can see a man's silhouette through the glass. "I'm just looking out for you."

"Or for yourself." He grabs his coat and the suit bag that contains his ghost-tour uniform from the hook. "Because who knows what you'll catch from people like me." He pulls open the door, forestalling my answer.

It fades away anyway as I see who is on the step. *"Mason,"* I gasp. "What are you doing here?"

My ex smiles widely, and Blue looks back and forth between the two of us. A surly look replaces the brief glimpse of something that looked very much like hurt.

"Well, I'll be off," Blue says coldly. "Now you've got someone nice and normal to play with."

And with a swirl of his coat and an angry expression he's gone.

CHAPTER 12

*L*evi

He leaves behind a stunned silence as both Mason and I stare down the lane at his vanishing figure. Then my shocked immobility breaks and I step out of the house.

"Hey," Mason says, putting a hand on my chest. "Where are you going?"

"After him," I say, bemused, and grit my teeth as he stops my forward motion again. "I'm not sure why you're holding me back."

He puts his hands up in a gesture of surrender. "Hey, sorry. I've travelled all this way up here and you're just going to take off after some random bloke."

"He's not random. And why *are* you here?"

He gestures at a box at his feet. "I brought your stuff."

"The stuff I told you to bin?" I stare at him until he shifts awkwardly on his feet. "What's going on, Mason?"

He shrugs and sticks his hands in his pockets. "I just need to talk to you."

"And you couldn't do that on the phone?"

"No, because every time I ring you seem to have a drama going on," he says sharply and then visibly tries to relax. "I wanted to see you," he says softly, giving me his patented Mason smile.

It used to always work on me. Well, until I came home early one day and found it directed at another man. In our bed. Nevertheless, we have a lot of history between us and as much as I hated him at one point, I'd also loved him deeply too.

I look down the empty lane. Blue is long gone now and there's zero chance of finding him if he doesn't want me to.

"Ten minutes." I sigh, and he grins almost triumphantly at me. I shake my head. "That's it. Take it or leave it."

"I'll take it." He follows me in and walks past me, staring open-mouthed. "Jesus, Levi, this is gorgeous." He pokes his head into the lounge and dining room and then the kitchen. "Did you do all this?"

I shrug, walking into the kitchen to put the kettle on. "Not me personally."

He laughs. "Yes, I still have memories of the time you decided to bleed the radiator."

"I didn't know it would actually take my blood to get the thing to work. I thought bleeding was a technical term."

"I thought flood was too."

For a second we smile at each other, and I remember all the good times we had together. It's strange how far away they seem now. He was my first love, and it's a relief to suddenly know that he won't be my last. He was a rung on my ladder, and I feel a weight release as I realise that he hasn't broken me.

He looks at me quizzically. "Not giving me the decent stuff?" he says, nodding at the instant coffee.

I shake my head. "You won't be here long enough for me to brew a pot."

"Ouch." He holds his hand to his chest. "You wound me, Levi."

"I don't think so." I pour hot water into the mug and pass it to him. "What do you want?"

He fiddles with his mug, his long fingers almost delicate looking. "I've finished with Sean."

I jerk. "Really, why?"

He shrugs. "It wasn't right for either of us. I couldn't stop feeling guilty, and he expected more."

"Ah," I say, spooning sugar into my mug. "Those pesky expectations. How they do trip us up." I laugh humourlessly. "Like expecting monogamy. That surely caught me out."

"I'm sorry," he says passionately. "I'm *so* sorry. It was a really shitty thing to do."

"It was," I say quietly. "But maybe in the end it did us both a favour."

"What?" he jerks out, sitting back.

I tilt my head curiously. "Well, it's for the best. We'd have probably ended anyway. At least this way it was sooner rather than later."

He pushes his chair back and paces over to the window. "Why would we have ended?"

"Well, I'd say the fact that you couldn't keep your dick in your trousers might be an indication that we had problems."

"And your absence from our lives didn't?" he says sharply.

I sit forward. "My *absence*? Makes me sound like I went off on my holidays. Not that I was nursing my dying mother."

He scrubs his hand through his hair. "I've said I'm sorry."

"Mason, you remind me of a small child sometimes. It's like you think that saying sorry really does make everything okay. News flash, it doesn't. When you cheated, it broke us and we're Humpty Dumpty now." I spread my hands out and stand up. "We can't be put back together. And you know what? I'm glad of that. I'm happier now than I've ever been."

"What, with the bleached blond greb that just left?"

Incredibly, I laugh. "Blue would actually like that."

"*Blue*? That's his name. Fucking hell. Does he wear hemp undies and smoke a bong?"

I raise my eyebrows. "That's a hell of a lot of stereotyping in one small sentence."

"Oh, fuck off," he sneers. "Are you having a midlife crisis?"

"I'm twenty-seven. That would be quite early for one of those."

"Babe, you lost your mum, and I broke us." He comes to me so quickly that I stumble back. I hit the cupboard, and he boxes me in before I can move. He frames my face with his hands. "I want you back," he says passionately. "I made the biggest mistake of my life, and I miss you so fucking much. I want what we had."

"Mason, I *umpf*," I get out as he kisses me fiercely, our teeth clashing together.

I raise my hands to his shoulders to push him away, but at that second there's a tremendous crash, and we jerk apart. Mason's mug is smashed to pieces on the floor, his coffee steaming and dripping off the table.

"What the hell?" he says. "How did that happen?"

The kitchen fills with the scent of lily of the valley.

Mason makes a face. "Have you got one of those plug-ins? You know they're terrible with my asthma."

"Hmm, and obviously that means I'll never be able to use one again even though we split up a year ago."

He starts to respond, but at that second a door slams upstairs and then another one. "What's happening?" he says. "Have you left the windows open?"

"Yes," I say quickly. "And I should go round and close them before it starts raining. Let me show you out."

He allows me to lead him out and stops on the doorstep. "It's really over, isn't it?" he says, and something in his voice catches me with sadness because once this man meant everything.

"It is," I say quietly. "There's no going back from it, Mason. I'm sorry."

"Why are you sorry?" he chokes out. "It's my fault."

I shrug. "What's done is done. Let's not go over it again."

He reaches out, and I hug him, knowing it's for the last time. "Take care," I say softly. He gives me a lopsided smile, lifting his hand and running his fingers over my lips.

"You too."

The lounge door slams behind me and I flinch.

He looks at me curiously. "I'd go and shut those windows before the glass smashes."

I smile. "I think once you've gone it'll be fine."

He raises his hand, and with a wave, he's gone.

I shut the front door and lean against it. "I know it's you, Rosalind," I whisper. "I'm not sure what that was about but thank you. You got me out of a tight spot." I inhale the scent of perfume and shake my head. "Now I'm talking to dead people," I whisper. "I really am Haley Joel Osment, minus the bad haircut." The kitchen door slams crossly. "Okay, okay," I say. "Sorry, that was rude."

I grab my phone from my back pocket and try Blue's number. It goes straight to a generic answer message. I click End and try again. And again. Finally, I leave a message. "Blue, it's Levi. I'm sorry for whatever happened earlier." I hesitate. "To be honest, I'm not exactly sure *what* happened." I sigh. "I think you're convinced that I don't want you because of your past. You couldn't be more wrong. I do want you. It's got nothing to do with what you did or who you were, but who you are now. You're funny and sharp and complicated and I... I like you. I like all of you, and I don't want to spoil stuff. And I definitely don't want you to feel that you have to do something because you're staying in my home." I laugh mirthlessly. "I'm not convinced you do anything you don't want to, but *I* need to be sure." I pause. "Anyway, I hope I see you soon," I finish lamely and end the call.

"Shit," I mutter, scrubbing my hands through my hair. "That is the single lamest thing I've ever done."

I clear up the kitchen and then wander around downstairs for a few minutes, picking things up and putting them down and feeling restless. The house is quiet. It's been like that since Blue burned the sage, but now it's weirdly quiet like it's waiting for something. I shake my head, feeling uneasy for the first time in a week.

"Fuck it," I finally say. "You can't find him, so you should do something productive." I nod. "And well done on talking to yourself. It's just great."

I wander upstairs but avoid my studio. If I tried to do anything creative in this mood, I'd fuck something up. Instead, I wander into my bedroom, inhaling the scent of peaches that clings in here already.

It's dark as the promised storm approaches, and I switch the bedside lamps on and walk over to the window to look out, hoping stupidly to see Blue walking down the street towards home. But it's empty and suddenly I'm sure I'm the only person who's alive at the moment. I sigh.

As I raise my gaze from the street, a reflection flickers in the window. A shout erupts from my chest. I can quite clearly see the figure of a man standing behind me.

"Shit!" I spin around but the room is empty.

I look round wildly. Completely empty. I turn back to the window and then rub my eyes. Nothing. Just my wild-eyed face and messy hair. I consider actually checking the wardrobe and under the bed, but then shake my head disgustedly.

"What the fuck? Get it together, for fuck's sake. You are not looking for monsters under the bloody bed." I pause. "And I really ought to get a dog and then it won't feel like I'm going loopy when I talk out loud."

The words die away into silence. The house listens.

I need to get out of here, go for a walk. It's got to be safer.

That word runs around my brain. *Safer.* Since when do I not feel safe in my own home? A shiver works down my spine. Now, is the answer. I was curious about my house before – cautious about approaching the unknown. But the cold lump growing in my stomach right now is genuine fear.

As I reach for my shoes, there's a loud crash of thunder and the sky opens. I walk to the window again, watching rain bucket down. The tree on the lane sways, the wind blowing the branches around like it's dancing. Rain falls harder, cascading down the window and blocking out the outside world. It's as if the house is under water. The normal sight of rain in England seems to dissipate the eeriness and my fear and I abruptly feel very stupid.

"I'm not walking in this." I say out loud and throw myself onto the bed. "Get yourself together, you nutbag," I chide myself. "You live here."

I stroke one finger down the blue stain on the pillowcase and smile softly before reaching for the pile of books I bought from Tom's shop. I might as well do some research if I'm not good for anything else. Then I'll make some dinner and maybe Blue will be home by then. His mood might have improved after doing his tour. I look at the rain. Or maybe not.

I reach for the book about the house's history and try to sink into it, but the dry details make my eyes cross, and instead, I grab the murder book that Blue was reading in the shop. It's much more lively with lots of gratuitous detail, and I read happily for a while, but eventually my yawns get bigger and my eyes get heavier and I close them. *Just for a second,* I think sleepily.

The unmistakeable slam of the front door wakes me up with a jerk. "Fuck." I wipe at the drool on my chin and inadvertently clock myself in the face with the book as I do it. "Shit." I rub my face and then memory returns. Blue's back.

I jump up as I hear him call, "Levi," up the stairs.

"Coming," I shout, racing to the door. I've still got the book in my hand. I step onto the landing and immediately go still.

It's very dark and cold and I can hardly see in front of my face. "Blue?" I say hesitantly.

"Levi," comes the fainter call from downstairs.

"I'm coming." My shout is swallowed by darkness.

I move towards the stairs. A chuckle sounds from behind me, and I jump like a startled horse. I turn around slowly, certain there's someone here with me in the dark hallway.

Even knowing that, the sight that faces me makes my heart pound like it's trying to explode out of my chest.

A man stands by the back bedroom door, his stance calm and steady, as if, like the console table beside him, he has every right to be there.

I'd sensed his presence, had been prepared to see *something.* But as his tall, broad-shouldered form looms, stark lines limned with an eerie light, my veins fill with ice. My breath, my heartbeat, my skin— they've all gone numb.

Lightning flares from the bedroom window. His eyes glow blue-white, and his outline flickers. And, fuck, even as the lightning passes, he still flickers.

He's a spirit. A ghost. The parts of my brain that are trying to convince me that he's a burglar or a neighbour who's got very lost— they can shut right the fuck up. I am looking at a ghost for the first time in my life.

And those eyes. They can see me too. I take a slow step back, blinking.

He's suddenly in front of me. So close I could touch him. The chunk of ice in my throat melts and bubbles up in a garbled shout.

I stumble backwards, and a smile plays on his thin lips. My left foot hits air, and I flail. The banister's gone. The stairs are gone too.

I don't reach for him, don't even cry out for help. He wants this, wants me to tumble to the floor below.

My senses twist into a jumble of red-hot pain. There's a bang. The darkness that descends after is welcome.

*B*lue

Will enters the pub, stooping a little under the low ceiling. Sitting up slightly from my slumped position, I wave to him and catch his quick grin as he weaves around the people towards me.

"Nice hair," he says eyeing my head with a funny sort of smile. I shrug, unable to think of any light conversation, and he reaches down and hugs me tight. "You okay? This is a bit of a surprise."

"Why?"

"Well, I thought you'd be tucked up tight with your sugar daddy on a night like this."

"He's not my sugar daddy," I say automatically. "Seeing as he was a toddler when I was born. And what do you mean on a night like this?"

"It's raining cats and dogs out there. Has been for an hour." He stares at me. "Didn't you notice?"

I shrug, avoiding his clever eyes. "I've been here for the last hour and a half."

There's a long pause before he sits down on the stool opposite me. "Okay, what's going on?"

"Nothing," I say immediately. "Just killing some time before the ghost walk."

"In here?" He looks at the table of empties. "Jesus, how many have you had?"

"They're not all mine," I say sharply. "Even I can't put that amount away. The owners are shorthanded at the moment." I shoot him a look. "They could do with some good bar staff."

Will shakes his head. "Bloody hell, you're like fucking Jiminy Cricket."

"In what way?" I frown. "That had better not have been a crack about my size compared to you, the man mountain. Although you could definitely have been Pinocchio with the length of your nose that's always poking into my business."

"Oh, chill out," he says lazily. "I meant that you've gone straight and want everyone else to do the same."

I shudder. "I can assure you that the last thing I'll ever do is go straight."

He laughs. "I meant now that you're respectable with a man, a job, a house and everything, I've just been waiting for you to start nagging me to do the same."

"It's not my house," I say sharply. "It never will be. It's Levi's." I draw in a slightly too shaky breath. "And Levi isn't my man. I'm not too sure how long I'll be there for anyway. Is there any space in the squat?"

There's a very loud silence, before he sighs noisily and heavily. "Okay, what the fuck is going on?"

I open my mouth to deny everything, but I catch his intractable expression and close my mouth carefully.

"Good idea," he says coldly. "What happened, Blue? Why are you sitting in a pub on your own when you have a very pretty man at home?"

"I made a pass at him." Unable to hold his gaze, I trace my finger through a puddle of beer on the wooden table.

"Well, I can't say that's surprising. I saw that coming from a mile off."

"Oh, did you also spot the bit where he said he couldn't sleep with a retired prostitute, and his ex-boyfriend turned up?"

"He said that?" His voice is deadly.

I think back and frown. "Not *exactly*."

He shakes his head.

I burst into speech. "But he mentioned my past, and I know that's what he was thinking, and then his ex turned up, and he was so gorgeous and expensively dressed and they went so well together."

"How did he mention your past? Did he say 'Blue, you're a filthy little whore'?"

I blink. "Have you been listening at my bedroom door again?" He glares, and I relent. "Okay, he didn't say that exactly. He said he knew what I'd been through and he didn't want me to feel like I was doing anything out of obligation."

There's a stunned silence, and then he reaches over and flicks my forehead.

"Ouch! Why did you do that?"

"Because you are a complete and utter twat. What the fuck is wrong with him saying that?"

"Well, he just sees me as shop-soiled. I fucking hate that. I don't want pitying."

"It doesn't sound like he pities you. It sounds like he really likes you."

"*What?*" I jerk and spill my pint onto the table.

We both leap back and after a few futile glances around for a member of staff, he uses his sleeve to mop the spillage.

"How did you work that out?" I hiss.

"Using my eyes," Will hisses back. He sits back, tapping his fingers lightly on the table.

I sigh. I'm probably not going to like what he says next as this is his brutal honesty pose.

"Blue, sex is an obligation for you."

"What?"

165

He shrugs helplessly. "It is. It used to be about money and survival. Now, it's just because it's expected of you, and you're too fair-minded to disappoint people."

"Oh my God," I say faintly. "Please make it stop."

"I wish I could," he says miserably. "I hate heart-to-hearts. They make me itchy." He braces himself and carries on talking quickly. "I see that about you, so why shouldn't he? Difference with this one is that he isn't willing to say yes just to get his balls emptied. This one wants to make you feel happy too."

I stare at him, feeling the revelation wash over me. I remember Levi's earnest expression and the fumbling way he tried to explain himself, and I remember how he held me so hard against him when I was in his arms and the way he looked at me. I'd heard his words but not taken the whole picture into consideration.

"Shit," I say, sighing and scrubbing my fingers down my face.

"Well, that about sums it up," he says gloomily.

I rally slightly. "Well, okay then, but did you happen to hear the bit about the ex-boyfriend turning up?"

"The ex who has been an ex for a whole year? *That's* the one he looked like he went so well with?"

"Hmm," I say somewhat sulkily.

He sighs. "Blue, this bloke is a good one. I think he's maybe like a unicorn to us which is why we can't quite believe that he's real. We're waiting for the other shoe to drop all the time. What if it never does? What if this is the real deal?" He grabs my hand and squeezes it. "What if this is the one for you?"

"You don't believe in shit like that," I scoff.

He shakes his head. "Not for me, but I've always believed in it for you."

"*Why?*"

"Because there's something different about you, Blue. There always has been. Stands to reason that someone like you would have someone special waiting for him."

I stroke his hand. "And what if I've just fucked that up?" I say softly.

Then I catch the time on his watch. "Shit, I'm going to be late to meet the group if I'm not careful."

"I'll come with you. We can walk and talk."

"Oh joy," I say acerbically, hearing his laughter follow me out.

It's raining heavily by the time we get to the meeting point.

He pulls his hood up and looks around curiously. "Don't you normally finish with the Devil?"

"Not this week," I mutter. I try to fasten my long overcoat and ignore the woman with no eyes who is drifting closer to me. "Hugh and I did a swap."

"Where is everyone, then?"

"It's raining. I'll be lucky if anyone turns up." I watch the ghost of the devil victim.

"What are you seeing?" he asks.

"Emily, the last victim. She's a bit agitated tonight."

"Maybe she didn't win on the lottery."

I shake my head. "Your sense of humour is actually a fault in your character."

I keep my gaze on Emily. Normally, she just stands there looking sad and displaying the tears in her flesh. Sometimes they're bleeding. Other times they're just rents in her skin showing a darkness within. Tonight, though, she looks almost agitated, pacing up and down the dimly lit road.

Making sure there's nobody around apart from Will—he doesn't count as he's seen me do this more times than normal—I approach her and smile.

"You okay, Emily?" I finally settle for saying inanely.

Will snorts. "What the hell? You're not chatting her up in the pub."

I shake my head, my concern growing. "You can't see her. She looks really worried."

"What would a ghost have to be worried about? Ghost bills, ghost laundry, not winning on the ghost horses?"

"Ssh, don't be rude." I leave him thinking about that one while I edge closer. "Emily?" I say softly.

She looks at me, and I blanch as blood seeps redly from her empty eye sockets. She makes an imploring gesture and inky shadows spill from the hole in her chest where her heart once was. Remembering Tom's words from the other day, I close my eyes, focusing on drawing in my breath slowly through my nostrils and then sending my worries out with an exhale.

When I open my eyes, she's all I can see. The rest of the world has faded away. For a wild moment I want to ring Tom and tell him it worked, but I focus on her. She's stopped pacing and is standing quite still. There's an almost inaudible pop, and I suddenly know she can see and hear me.

"What is it?" I say in my head. *"Tell me, Emily."*

As clear as a bell I hear a light voice with a Yorkshire accent speak. *"Help him."*

"Help who?"

"Powerful again. Help him. Too late."

The last is said on a wail. I jerk, breaking the bubble surrounding us.

"What?" I say out loud.

She gestures at me, but I can't hear her anymore. It's like watching the TV with the sound off as she opens and shuts her mouth.

"What is it?" Will asks, coming to my side and grabbing my arm.

"She says I have to help him."

"Help who?"

I stare at Emily, and the answer comes immediately. "Levi. I have to help Levi."

A raging panic floods my senses. *"What?"* I shout at the spectre. "What's happened to Levi?"

But it's no use. She fades slowly and within a second she's gone.

"No," I say, darting forward.

Will grabs me. "Your ghost-tour people are coming," he says.

I shoot a panicked look down the road at the two men approaching. I grab my hat and stuff it into Will's hands. "You do it."

"What?" he says, and it's so loud it echoes around the small close.

"I have to go. Something's happened to Levi."

"And you know that because a ghostly woman round the back of Tesco's told you so?"

"Don't take the piss."

"Oh, I'm sorry." He sounds slightly panicked now, his voice gone high. "I thought that's what we were doing. *Joking*."

"I need you to do the tour. Please, Will, you've been round with me loads of times. I have to go." The last is frantic.

He nods immediately. "Okay, but if he's just sitting on the sofa with indigestion you have to promise to come back and rescue me."

"I will." I grab him and hug him.

"Be careful," he whispers. "Please be careful in that house."

I nod and without wasting another second dash off, peeling around the two men approaching me and splashing through a puddle. "Sorry," I shout and leave them behind.

It's very busy for a Friday night in October, and I race up High Petergate, dodging around groups of people standing looking at the menus in the restaurant windows. I take the Snickelway to the left of the Hole in the Wall pub and race up the close, slipping and sliding on the slick cobbles. The Minster bells chime the hour, the sweet notes a sharp contrast to the dread in my heart.

I shouldn't have left him. I knew the sage was too good to be true and the trouble was going to start again. I should have been there, rather than wallowing in a fit of the sulks because he wouldn't fuck me and his perfect ex-boyfriend turned up. I think of the house's previous owner and the way he died, and I pick up speed, pounding down the lane until I hit the front door with a crash, panting and sweating.

The house is dark. Dark and foreboding-looking with no signs of life. Normally, when I come back from a ghost walk there are lights on and music playing. Now, it's as still as the grave. I shake my head. *Don't use those words.*

Fumbling for my key I twist it in the lock. I push but nothing happens, and my nose bangs painfully on the wood.

"What the hell?" I whisper. I turn the key again. It's unlocked, but it won't open.

For a wild second I wonder whether Levi's locked the deadbolt so that he and Mason can have an uninterrupted shag. Pain coils in my stomach.

I shake my head. "No," I say out loud. "He wouldn't do that. Levi is not like everyone else. He isn't."

I push the door again, and to my amazement, it opens as smoothly and easily as a knife sinking through butter.

I hesitate briefly, but then step into the hallway and stand stock-still, paralysed with a sudden overriding and desperate fear. The hallway is as black as night, and I can't see anything at all. It's like I've suddenly gone blind.

Apparently, I've gone deaf too, because I can't hear a single sound. The door is open behind me so there should be noises from the street, but there's nothing. It's like I've stepped into a black hole.

One of my mum's boyfriends hit me on the head with a saucepan when I was a kid. I stood there for a second feeling nothing, but then suddenly became aware of something cold running down my skull and face. It was blood, but it was icy cold.

That's what my fear feels like now—cold streams of terror flowing down my body seizing me with the certain knowledge that something waits for me in the dark. If I go any further, I won't ever be able to get out again.

Tom spoke of the fear he felt in this house as a child. The same entity waits for me.

A cold chuckle sounds from the blackness. I shudder at the evil in that noise. The evil of something that died bad to the bones. It's waited out the years here, growing steadily worse in the cold and dark. Waiting for life and blood to reanimate this house and give it strength.

I can't go in. I can't make my feet move. I'll be grabbed as soon as I move a muscle.

There's a shuffling noise in the shadows. That low chuckle sounds again, and I'm suddenly so angry I could spit.

"How dare you?" I say in a low voice. "How fucking *dare* you. Where is Levi? You can't frighten me away."

The darkness seems stunned into silence. A shaft of moonlight pierces the gloom. Shadows swirl and boil. Then I see him.

"Levi," I cry out. "*Levi.*"

He's lying at the foot of the stairs crumpled and still. Any fear I had is long gone as I dash though the dark, feeling it lighten and fall away.

"Oh fuck, sweetheart," I choke out, falling to my knees and sending a shaking hand out to feel his skin. He's cold and pain hits me. *He's dead.* But then my fingers trace his neck and feel his pulse beating thinly.

"Levi?" I call out.

I'm afraid to move him in case he hurt his back or neck. I fumble for my phone and I'm amazed to see bars, a part of me so sure that we've been trapped away from the outside world, no reception, the doors slamming shut to close us off forever.

I don't care though. Levi and I will be together. I'm not leaving him here.

I dial the emergency services. The woman listens calmly as I spill out a story of my roommate falling down a flight of stairs. She promises to send someone.

I put down the phone and take a deep breath. The atmosphere has an underlying sense of thwarted rage there now, rather than the menace I'd sensed earlier.

I stroke Levi's thick, shiny brown hair. His face is white and still. Before I can second-guess myself, I bend and kiss his face. "I won't leave you," I say vehemently, hearing the tears in my voice. "I won't leave while you need me, Levi. Not *ever.*"

A tinkling comes from directly above me. I look up to find the chandelier is rotating. Slowly at first and then faster and faster, it spins around, the crystals jingling.

A creaking noise begins as the pictures in the hallway sway. They move from side to side, picking up speed until one falls, the shattering glass as noisy as a bomb. Another one falls, the glass exploding outwards.

"No," I shout, hovering over Levi, protecting his face. "I'm not going. I will not leave him."

The scent of lily of the valley floods the hallway, so pungent that it brings tears to my eyes. The chandelier comes to a gentle stop, and, on the wall, the remaining pictures are as upright and unmoving as a chaperone at a ball.

I take a breath and go still. The perfume smells different tonight. There's a coppery taint to it that's very much like blood. I look around warily, assessing the changed atmosphere. Rosalind has scared the other entity away.

"For the time being," a woman's soft voice says in my head. *"Not for long though."*

I nod grimly and sit down. My foot scrapes something that Levi is half lying on, and tugging it out, I find the murder book he bought me at the shop. It seems like a lifetime ago now, but warmth fills me at the thought of him solemnly adding it to his pile. The cover is now creased but it's intact, and so I put it into my pocket as delicately as if I was handling the crown jewels. Then I settle down to wait for the ambulance to arrive, Levi's hand held firmly in mine and my body hovering protectively over his.

CHAPTER 13

*L*evi

The first time I come awake it's to a blur of pain and cold and somewhere the sound of Blue's voice. I cling to it like it's a rope in the dark, but it vanishes, and I sink back down.

The second time is slightly easier. I open my eyes a slit and gingerly test for pain. It's centred in my arm and my head, but it isn't as bad as it was, and I cautiously open my eyes.

I'm in a bed with a curtain drawn around it. The smell of disinfectant tells me it's a hospital. Blue is curled up in a chair next to the bed, sleeping with his mouth slightly open. He looks thin and drawn and worried even while asleep.

I stir and the bed creaks. Blue's eyes shoot open. When he sees me looking at him, he moves so quickly that he nearly falls out of the chair.

"Levi," he gasps. "You're awake."

I nod and immediately regret it. Pain clangs sharp and bright like a bell tolling the hour. "Oh shit," I mumble, hearing the slur in my words. "Hurts."

"Stay there," he instructs me sternly. "I'll run and get someone."

My mouth twitches. "Not going anywhere," I whisper.

He hesitates before leaning forward and dropping a kiss on my lips so quickly that I think I've imagined it.

"I'm so glad you're awake," he whispers and then vanishes, the only sign he's been there the gentle swaying of the curtain.

I close my eyes and when I open them again, a tired-looking doctor is bending over me.

"Let's have a look at you, Mr Black," he says kindly.

The next five minutes are excruciating, and I can't keep back my gasps of pain. Blue hovers, looking fraught and grabbing my hand and squeezing it when he's not in the way, and sometimes when he is.

Finally, the doctor stands back. "Well, you're a *very* lucky young man, Mr Black. You have a light concussion, a broken arm, and lots of bumps and bruises."

"Lucky?" I mouth.

He smiles. "Lucky because people have been seriously hurt in the type of accident you had. Can you remember what happened?" he asks carefully.

I draw a complete blank, and I'm fully frightened for the first time since I woke up. *What did happen?*

Then the man's face from the hallway comes back to me. The dark, the cold, and the whispers that surrounded me when I resurfaced for a second at the bottom of the stairs.

If I tell the doctor that, I'll probably end up being sectioned.

"I must have missed the step," I say hoarsely, my throat pained. "It was dark and I didn't put the light on, and the next thing I knew I was falling."

The doctor smiles at me, looking somewhat relieved. God knows what he thought had happened.

He directs a less cautious smile at Blue. "Well, you were lucky that Mr Billings found you."

"Who's that?" I ask blankly.

Blue snorts. "That's me, you idiot. That's my surname."

"Oh, I remember now. The Mysterious and Amazing Blue Billings. It's a cool name," I say, my voice slurring again.

The doctor laughs. "It was a good job that Mr Billings came home when he did. If you'd been lying there much longer, it might have been a very different story."

"Good timing," I whisper.

The sound of Blue's laughter and the feel of his hand on mine remain with me until I fall asleep again.

When I next wake up it's dark outside the window. The ward is lit low, and it's very quiet, telling me it's probably the early hours of the morning.

Blue is sitting beside the bed, one hand clasped around mine and his nose buried in a book. Squinting, I can make out the title of the murder book I bought him—the one I was reading last night. *The night before last? Whenever.*

"How are you still here?" I say sleepily. "Don't they kick visitors out?"

He jumps and drops the book into his lap. "Shit, you startled me," he whispers, getting up and standing by the bed. He strokes my hair back, his face darkening as he looks at me. I wonder what I look like but dismiss the concern. It's a million to one I've looked better.

"I know one of the nurses," he whispers, answering my earlier question. "He says if I'm quiet and stay out of the way, he'll pretend that he can't see me."

"If you know the nurse, he must surely have an inkling that it's impossible for you to be quiet and stay out of the way," I mutter.

He laughs and then astonishes me by bending forward and kissing me gently. It's a soft almost butterfly kiss that still manages to pack a wallop. I blink as he draws back.

"What was that for?" I ask sleepily.

"Because you're *here*," he says fiercely. "And you might not have been." He shudders.

I reach out to squeeze his hand but stop as pain knifes through me. "Shit," I jerk out. "That hurts." A plaster cast encases my left arm up to the elbow. It's pink.

"It's bound to hurt," he mutters. "You've broken your arm."

"Why is the cast pink?"

"To remind you to look after yourself. I chose a bright colour because sometimes you don't seem so bright."

"I think I remember." I try to smile but close my eyes as pain floods around me. When it's receded, I open them to find him watching me carefully.

"What happened, Levi?" he whispers. "I know something did."

"How?"

"Because…" He falters slightly but rallies. "The ghost of the Devil's victim told me you were in trouble."

I blink. "Am I on morphine?"

He chuckles. "No such luck, or I'd have asked to join you. No, I was about to start the ghost walk and she appeared. Told me you were in trouble. So, even the ghosts of York are warning me now."

"She *told* you."

Pride crosses his face. "Yep. I did what Tom said, and I heard her." He leans forward, his thin, mobile face alight with enthusiasm. "It bloody worked." He pauses before honesty obviously compels him to add, "For a few seconds, anyway."

"Well, I'm grateful for the few seconds," I mutter, trying to sit up and subsiding back down as he puts a gentle hand on my chest. A thin hand that nevertheless manages to push me back firmly.

"Nope," he says. "No moving around yet. Lying still."

I smile up at him. He grimaces as if suffering a strong emotion. Then his expression clears, and he perches his arse on the side of my bed. I feel the warmth of his body and edge a little closer. He smiles at me as if he knows what's going through my head and cups his hand on my hip over the blankets.

"I got to the house." He pauses and breathes in. "You were at the foot of the stairs." He bites his lip, nervously toying with his lip ring, his face pale. "It was horrible. So dark and fucking terrifying. There was something in the dark."

"And you *stayed* there? Why? You could have been hurt, Blue."

He looks indignant. "I wasn't leaving you. *Never*."

My stomach warms, and I smile at him. It falls away as I remember. "There was a man," I say slowly.

"A man?"

The pain in my head flares. He strokes my hair tenderly and the touch of his cold fingers is lovely against the hot skin of my face. "He was standing outside the bedroom." I grab his hand suddenly. "He laughed. It was that horrible laugh I heard the first day in the house. What is going on? I thought the only murderer in the house was Rosalind." I pause, gathering my thoughts. "Maybe she didn't do it after all. Maybe someone else was in the house that night."

"Oh no, she did it," Blue says with a grim certainty. "Her hands were covered in his blood and her prints were all over the razor."

"How did you know? Ah, the ghost tour."

He shakes his head. "No, that book. It was by your side when I found you."

"I was reading it," I say slowly. Then realisation flares. "Oh my God," I gasp. "I heard the door open and you called my name."

"I couldn't have done, babe. When I got back you were at the foot of the stairs."

"Where did you go?" The question is out before I can pull it back.

He grimaces, looking shamefaced. "The pub to meet Will."

I relax slightly because I'd imagined him going to find someone else, but his eyes sharpen.

"And you definitely heard me calling your name?" I nod and he frowns. "Jesus, that means it impersonated me to lure you out."

"Lure me out? I'm not a bloody trout," I say, trying to smile, but his expression stops it dead in its tracks.

"Levi, it pretended to be me because it wanted you at the top of the stairs. Maybe that's what happened to the previous owner."

I stare at him. "This isn't about the Victorian murderess, is it?" He shakes his head. "And do you have any idea *what* it's about?" He shakes his head again. "Okay, good chat," I say slowly.

"Go to sleep," Blue says softly. "All this can wait until morning."

"Will you stay?" I ask, fumbling for his hand.

"I will."

The promise in his voice follows me into sleep.

~

J realise that hospitals start their day obscenely early when a nurse pops her head around the curtain to take my breakfast order at six o'clock in the morning.

I stare at her. "I'm not sure I can eat anything at this time of the night."

She laughs and straightens the bed covers over me. "It's the middle of the morning." She looks slightly stern. "And you must eat something, Levi. We won't be able to release you until you do."

I look over at Blue who is fast asleep and crunched up in the uncomfortable-looking hospital chair.

"Could I just have some toast and marmite?" I ask.

She nods approvingly. She looks at Blue, and her eyes soften. "I'll bring him a cup of tea too," she whispers.

"Thank you for letting him stay."

She smiles. "It wasn't so much *letting* him stay, as just giving in. That's one determined young man you've got there."

I smile at him. "He is that," I say softly.

She tweaks a corner of the sheet and is gone, the curtain swaying in her wake like she's a nurse made of a tornado.

"I thought you didn't like marmite. You said you threw up in your mouth when you smelt it," Blue says, blinking at me blearily.

"It's not for me," I whisper. "It's for you."

He looks confused. "Why?"

"Because you need to eat. You didn't have tea yesterday, and I bet you didn't eat while you were out. No wonder you're so thin."

Astonishment is written all over his face, and I flush.

"You ordered me breakfast," he says wonderingly. Then his mouth quirks. "And I didn't even have to give a blowjob."

I shake my head and immediately regret it, closing my eyes as my headache pulses red-hot in my temples. When I open my eyes, Blue is leaning over me.

"Sorry," he says in a shamefaced manner. "I shouldn't have said that."

"No, you shouldn't," I say sharply. "You never have to perform for me. I like you just the way you are."

His eyes open a bit wider, the colour startlingly light. "Really?"

"Of course." I sigh. "You're funny and quick-witted and brave. Why wouldn't I like you?" I hold my hand up. "Oh, I forgot, because you traded sex for money once upon a time."

"That would stop most people."

"I'm not most people. I'm me. And I don't mind. I understand why you did it, and I understand why you stopped, but my liking you has zero to do with any of it."

"Does it have anything to do with why we're not sleeping together?" He holds up a hand to stop me answering. "It's absolutely fine if you don't want to. I should have said that yesterday instead of storming off like a twat. We can just be friends, but I need to know so I don't push some boundary."

I stare at him long enough for him to look apprehensive. "I want you so much, Blue," I finally say, my voice hoarse. "All the time. But I couldn't sleep with you because it would have put you in an impossible position. You're staying with me because the alternative is a squat. I don't want you thinking that you have to have sex with me in return for a bed. I want you to want me, but if you don't, I still want to be your friend. I'll always want that."

Something flares bright in his face but then he shutters it. "So, you're not thinking for me, then?" he says mildly.

I blink. "What?"

"So, you're not making decisions for this clever and brave person that you seem to think I am? That's good to know."

I stare at him and his mouth quirks.

"Oh, I see what you're doing," I say darkly.

He laughs. "I'm just saying I make my own decisions. I always have." He swallows. "I'm sorry I was so shitty yesterday and left like that. I'm so sorry I left you on your own. I know you're trying to think of me, but you must realise that it's hard to get used to because I've done all my own decision-making since I was ten. Probably earlier. Some of them have been shit, admittedly, but I own them all."

"I'm sorry about yesterday too," I say softly, grabbing his hand and squeezing the cold fingers.

His expression clouds.

"What?" I ask. "What's the matter?"

"I didn't think," he says, trying to pull his hand away. "Do you want me to call Mason?" He pauses. "Actually, where was Mason when the homicidal ghost was on the rampage?"

"Gone," I say, lifting his fingers and dropping a kiss on them. "He left about ten minutes after you stormed off." Incredibly, I manage a smile. "Rosalind smashed his cup and the doors started their usual chorus."

He gapes at me. "*Rosalind* smashed his cup?"

"I know." I stare at him. "I know I can't see ghosts and have zero input, but I really don't feel threatened by her. I got the impression she did it because Mason tried to kiss me and she was warning him off."

"He tried to *kiss you?*"

I shouldn't be so thrilled with the jealousy written on his face, but I must be a bad person because I totally am.

"Didn't get far," I whisper. "What with all the cup smashing going on."

"Well, considering her last warning led to her slitting some poor bloke's throat, he should count himself lucky with caffeine withdrawal," he says tartly.

I chuckle and wince at my head. "I'm okay," I say as his hands fly over me. "Just my head."

He sits down on the bed, gifting me with a waft of peaches. "I know what you mean about Rosalind. It's a bloody mystery to me."

"It's a mystery we need to solve," I say slowly, feeling tiredness sweep over me again. "I'm going to contact Mr Fenton," I say sleepily. "The lawyer in charge of the will. He said to phone him. Looking back, he seemed like he might know something." I sigh. "They're likely to discharge me today, and I'm not sure I even want to go home."

He immediately shakes his head, making me feel slightly better about how cowardly I just sounded. "I don't think you should go back yet. I think we need to find out what's really haunting that house. Up until now we've just gone along with what's happening. I think it's time we did some research and maybe hopefully then we'll be able to come up with a plan of action." He shifts, seeming suddenly awkward. "So Mason's out of the picture," he says casually. "Why? You two looked good together."

"Because I don't want him anymore," I say simply. "He's my history, and I have to say a lot of it was good history."

"Would you still be with him if he hadn't cheated?"

I consider that. "I don't think so, because whatever made him cheat would still be there. A bit like a crack in brickwork. It spreads after a bit." His shoulders relax slightly, and I smile almost shyly. "Besides, I'm very interested in another man."

"Oh yes?" He smiles, and it's glorious. Big and vibrant like his spirit. "Who's that, then?"

"Some bloke I met. Too thin and extremely challenging."

He laughs and leans down to kiss me.

"Enough of that," the nurse says behind us, making us jump apart. "No shenanigans before breakfast."

"And after breakfast?" Blue says, winking at her.

She grins. "That'll be your own business once the doctor has seen him this morning."

"I can go home?" I ask eagerly.

"You're hurting my feelings," she says wryly. "Yes, if he's happy with you, then you can go." She looks around. "You'll need something to wear though. Your clothes had blood all over them from the cut on your head."

She puts the tray down on the table in front of me and leaves us with a smile.

Blue stands up. "I'll go back to the house and grab us both a few changes of clothing."

"No," I immediately protest. "I don't want you going back there."

My voice has risen and he motions for me to quieten down. "I've got to," he says. "I need our wallets and some clothes." He smiles at me. "I'll be absolutely fine."

"I'm sure that's what the other bloke said," I say sourly.

"Well, I've got a little bit of an advantage over the two of you because I can actually see them coming." He shakes his head at me. "Will you feel better if I ask someone to meet me there?"

I relax back into the pillows. "Yes."

"Okay, then I will." He pushes the plate towards me. "I'll share the toast with you and to show you how much I like you, I'll only put marmite on half of it." I open my mouth to say that I'm not hungry but shut it quickly at the sight of his stern face. "I know you don't want to eat, but you need food in you so they'll let you go and so you're alert for our planning meeting."

"Sounds like the council," I say gloomily and he laughs.

"Well, that's a cheerful sound for a hospital," a gruff voice says from the curtain.

Blue's face brightens. "Tom," he exclaims and races over to hug the old man. I repress a smile at the way the old man huffs yet is so obviously thrilled.

Tom looks over at me and his face clouds with concern. "You okay, lad?"

I try to hitch myself up on my pillow, but the sharp twang of pain stops me in my tracks. Blue rushes over to help me, and I manage a smile for the old man. "I'm fine," I say, leaning back against the pillow with a sigh of relief and giving Blue's hand a squeeze of thanks.

Tom sinks into the chair that Blue indicates.

"How did you know I was here?" I ask.

He jerks his head at Blue. "Boy Wonder over there rang me late last night and told me what had happened." His bushy eyebrows meet in a frown. "You can't go back there, Levi."

"I said that," Blue says, leaning against the bed. "We're going to stay in a hotel. I'm going back to the house in a bit to get a change of clothes and some money."

"I'll go with you," Tom says. Blue looks like he's going to protest, but Tom shakes his grey head firmly. "Don't argue, Blue. You shouldn't be in there on your own either. You're even more vulnerable than Levi, and that's saying something because he's like a kitten on the bloody railway tracks."

I blink. "I think I'm offended," I muse, but Tom and Blue ignore me.

"I don't want you to get hurt, Tom," Blue argues predictably.

"I won't," Tom says irritably.

"Last time you were in the house you said you were scared you'd be stuck there."

"I was bloody twelve," Tom retorts. "I've learnt a few tricks since then."

"Let Tom take you," I say, closing my eyes briefly when the headache flares. When I open them, Blue is leaning over me looking at me with concern. "I'm okay," I say slowly. "Head hurts."

"You need to sleep."

"I will, but only if you take Tom with you." Blue stares at me, and I try a smile. "Safety in numbers," I slur, feeling sleep dance and blur my mind.

"Okay," Blue finally says with a sigh. "I'll do that."

"Promise?"

"I promise." He leans down and kisses me softly. "I've never made promises to *anyone* before," he whispers. "So you know I'll keep that one. Now sleep."

*B*lue

Tom, Will, and I stand outside the house staring up at it dubiously.

"It looks so normal," I marvel. "Just like an average house."

"Well, so did Amityville," Will says comfortingly. "And look what happened there."

Tom shakes his head. "Never take a job with the Samaritans."

Will snorts. "Hardly likely. I'm at the pub when most people want to ring."

I snort and pull out the key that Levi gave me the other day. I'd been so thrilled with it at the time. It was a symbol of trust and a sign that I was standing on the rung of a ladder ready to climb out of my old life. I sigh. Seems like my old life just hitched a ride along with me.

I look at the two of them. "Ready?"

Their smiles fall away and they nod seriously.

"It's a bit of a mess," I say, pushing the front door open and stepping gingerly in. "There was blood everywhere and glass from the pictures and—"

"Good imagination, lad," Tom says, stepping in behind me. His back is straight and his gaze goes everywhere.

My eyes are trained on the hallway. "What the fuck?" I whisper. "Who did this?"

The hallway is immaculate. The carpet is straight, and there's no trace of blood anywhere. The pictures are hanging on the walls again and the glass that had littered the floor is completely gone. I rub my chin and stare disbelievingly.

Will steps next to me. "Smells of perfume," he observes.

Suddenly I can smell it. Lily of the valley.

"*She* did this," I whisper, afraid to even say her name in this house now.

Tom looks over at me, and I don't need to read his mind to know he's troubled. He starts to say something and then reconsiders. "Get the stuff," he orders me. I take a step, and he grabs my arm. "Make it very quick," he says forcefully.

I share a troubled look with Will, and we leap into action. Leaving Tom, we dash upstairs. I show Will into the front bedroom. This room is immaculate too, the bed made neatly and no clothes anywhere. I bite my lip.

"Grab me and Levi a few changes of clothes," I whisper. "I'll go up to the studio and get his art stuff."

"You sure you're okay up there on your own?"

"It's the safest place in the house," I say without thinking and pause. "Why is that?" I whisper.

"I wouldn't stop to consider it, Blue. I might not be fucking psychic, but even I can tell there's something wrong in this house." He shivers. "We need to get out of here."

I nod and book it up the stairs. The studio is an oasis. It's star-tlingly warm and sunny in here with none of the lowering feelings of the rest of the house. For a second I rest against the door, my eyes closed, and when I open them, I gasp. Rosalind is here as clear as day, standing against the back wall.

"Rosalind," I gasp before I can think better of it.

She doesn't seem to hear me. She stares down at the floor, seem-ingly absorbed in whatever she's looking at. Usually ghosts are slightly see-through, but she's as clear and real as if she were another human being.

A few strands of her hair have escaped her bun to curl softly against her rounded chin. The faint lines on the sides of her eyes are clearly visible and the violets on her dress are a light purple.

"Rosalind?" I try again, but she ignores me.

I get the impression that she actually can't see or hear me, so instead of running back downstairs, I grab Levi's rucksack and start to stuff his books and pencils into it and anything else I think he might need.

When I'm done, I edge to the door. She's still standing there like a sentinel for something I can't see, but just before I leave I whisper, "Thank you, Rosalind." I hesitate. "I know you tried to help him last night. I smelt your perfume in the hallway." I remember that it had seemed to be mingled with the smell of blood and swallow hard. "I hope that it didn't hurt you to help, but I'm so grateful to you for protecting Levi. He's very special."

She's still examining that piece of floor as if it has the key to world peace. Maybe it's something she did a lot in real life. Ghosts do seem to cling to routines.

When she lifts her head and looks at me, it's such a shock that I nearly hit the ceiling. I gasp and put a hand to my chest as she exam-ines my face intently. I open my mouth to try to speak but thundering footsteps sound behind me.

Will shouts, "Blue!" I look towards the door and when I turn back Rosalind has gone, leaving only the scent of her perfume.

"Shit," I whisper.

"You alright?" Will asks, coming into the room. He brandishes a bag at me. "I've packed everything I think you'll need." He winks. "I've even included the condoms and lube, seeing as the two of you seem to be sharing a bed very cosily."

"Will," I say warningly.

He chuckles, but his smile dies when Tom shouts, "Blue!" from downstairs. There's an urgency in the call.

"Coming," I shout, and we race down the stairs. Tom is standing at the bottom. His face is pale and set. "You okay?" I ask breathlessly. "What's happened?"

"We need to go," he says abruptly.

I suddenly become aware of a knocking noise coming from the cellar. "What's that?" I whisper.

Will shifts awkwardly.

"I don't know," Tom says. He shrugs. "I opened the door and I think I disturbed something because that started a few minutes later."

We listen as the banging gets louder. It sounds like someone is hammering something. I tilt my head to the side, trying to read the air and gauge the feeling on it. I blink when I do. Absolute rage and hatred.

"Fuck," I breathe.

For the first time since I've met Tom, he looks worried. "I know."

"What?" Will asks. "What are you getting?"

"It's not nice." Tom turns towards the door. "I shouldn't have opened it," he mutters. "But I couldn't help it. There's something down there and it's powerful and…" He shudders.

"What?" Will whispers, his face pale.

"Wicked," he says abruptly. "There's wickedness down there. I opened the door and couldn't go down even a step—"

The banging stops. It's ridiculous, but the sudden cessation of sound is the most startling and frightening thing that's happened since we arrived.

"Okay," Will finally says, making me jump. "It's stopped. Can we *please* go now?"

The second he finishes the plea, a footstep sounds on the cellar stairs.

Then another. And another. The slow steps, deliberate and purposeful.

Then Tom says hoarsely, "We need to get out now," and we're a flurry of movement.

Will and I get stuck in the narrow doorway trying to leave the house, and it's almost comical, like a cartoon. But there's nothing funny about the grit of fear that lingers in the back of my throat, making my mouth dry. And still the footsteps sound from behind us.

The cellar door bursts open, and looking back automatically, I see the chandelier starting its mad dance again, spinning, the sound of tinkling glass silvery on the air.

Tom grabs me and pulls, and Will and I shoot out of the door like a cork from a bottle and fall on the ground in the silent street. The door slams behind us, shaking the house with the force of its movements.

For a second we don't move, Will and I sitting on the cobbles and Tom staring up at the house. Then Will sighs and turns to me.

"You know when you said there must be something wrong with Levi and I pooh-poohed it?"

I nod.

"Well, this house is what's fucking wrong with Levi." He pokes me. "Why can't you just take up with a cheating arsehole with an alcohol problem like normal people?"

CHAPTER 14

*L*evi
        Blue lets us into our hotel room and guides me to the bed.
I groan as I lower myself onto the mattress. "God, that feels good."

He dumps the bags containing our supplies on the desk and marches back towards me, determination in every line of his body. He pulls my jeans off, leaving me in my boxers and T-shirt, and then lifts my feet gently onto the mattress. Grabbing a pillow, he puts it under my arm and fusses with it until he deems it perfect. Finally satisfied, he steps back. "Nice view," he says.

"Why thank you, Blue. Although, I have to say you're not seeing me at my best."

"Idiot," he says almost affectionately and nods at the window. "I meant out there."

I look past him at the perfect view we have of Clifford's Tower. "Lovely," I say disinterestedly. "I think I'm more happy about the fact that you've booked us into a modern hotel. At least we'll have a night off from ghosts tonight."

He turns on the TV and starts running through the channels. "I wouldn't be so quick to relax," he murmurs. "A ghost coach and horses has been spotted here at midnight."

"Oh great." I sigh. "With my luck, one of the horses will kick me in the fucking head."

He chuckles and, giving up on the TV, he places the remote carefully by my hand. "You're in a whole box of half-empty glasses sort of mood today, aren't you?" he says, toeing off his shoes and climbing onto the bed beside me.

I raise my good arm and try not to get too giddy about the fact that he instantly curls into my side and lays his head on my chest with a happy-sounding sigh. Something has changed between us since our talk this morning, and it feels real and right. I tighten my hold and kiss the top of his head, inhaling the familiar scent of his shampoo.

"You seem happy?" I say softly.

His wide mouth tilts at the corner. "I am. I finally listened to my answerphone messages."

I stare at him uncomprehendingly and then realisation floods in at the memory of my rambling message before the accident.

I rush into speech. "Can't you find anything?" I ask, nodding at the TV. My voice is slightly too high in my agitation.

He stares at me for a long second and then obviously decides to let it go. "Nah, I'll read for a bit."

When he was staying at the house, I'd noticed he had little interest in the TV, probably due to all his years living without one. He'd watched one episode of *EastEnders* in horrified silence before pronouncing that he'd rather live in the squat than watch another. When he's still, which doesn't happen a lot, he prefers to read.

The life he's led has given him strange holes in his cultural references. He knows virtually nothing about children's television, but more than most twenty-four-year-olds ever will about the *Carry On* films. Like a magpie, he's picked up bits and pieces of things from wherever he's landed or lived.

He does, however, love music. He and Will seem to have been to hundreds of concerts. Apparently, one of their friends is a roadie. Consequently, Blue has an encyclopaedic knowledge of music and his tastes are wide-ranging, picked up from a life of moving from place to place, meeting new people all the time and absorbing their likes and dislikes.

I switch the TV off and we both lie there for a second. It's lovely. The mattress is firm, the air smells of furniture polish, and Blue's body is warm against mine.

"This is lovely," I say slowly. "God, I don't know why I'm so bloody tired."

"You fell downstairs, had a head injury, and broke your arm. Not to mention the last few weeks of interrupted sleep. The miracle is that you've not fallen asleep while crossing the road. Go to sleep."

I sigh and fidget. "I don't think I can. I'm *too* tired, if you know what I mean, and I hurt all over."

Blue comes up on one elbow and gives me a slow smile that instantly wakes me up.

"What? Why are you smiling as if my pain pleases you?" I say warily. "What sort of monster are you?"

He reaches out, and I watch in a stunned silence as he lowers his hand and lays it just above my cock which immediately stiffens.

"Is this okay?" he asks.

I groan. "If it's what I think it is, then oh my God, yes."

I don't have the slightest inclination to stop this now. He's an adult, and I think I've finally accepted that he's attracted to me and wants this. Maybe that bang on the head shook some sense into me, or both of us.

He chuckles and slides his hand inside my boxers, bringing out my dick and scrambling all my thoughts.

"Shit," I whisper fervently as his warm hand surrounds my cock.

He winks at me. "I read once that giving someone an orgasm takes their mind off their pain."

"Oh fuck."

He wriggles down the bed and his hot breath washes over my dick.

"I'm so glad you pursued an alternative education," I babble. "The English curriculum would *never* have covered that."

"Shame on the British education system." He's still laughing when he takes my cock into his mouth, and the vibrations wash over the sensitive flesh.

My groan is loud in the quiet room. He looks up at me, and it's so fucking hot to see those wolf eyes studying me with his full lips stretched around my cock.

He pulls off and, with capable hands, strips off my boxers and manoeuvres them down my legs before throwing them off the side of the bed. While he's busy doing this, I gingerly take off my T-shirt, accompanied by a lot of wincing.

"Careful," he chides. "If I do this, you have to stay absolutely still. I'll do my thing and you just watch your head."

"I'll watch the top one. You focus on the little head in front of you," I advise.

He laughs, and then leans forward and licks up and down the length of my dick, making it sloppy before pulling back and blowing cool air across the sensitive skin. I can't help the arch of my spine as I push my cock towards him, but I groan at the sharp pain that follows.

He shakes his head before holding tight to the base of my dick, studying me intensely. "Can you be still? Because I'm not doing this and hurting you."

"I can," I say.

The words echo in the room like a vow. His lip twitches before he lies on his front, pressing into the mattress and shoving gently at my legs. He helps me spread them, and then I close my eyes and pant out a gasping breath as he nuzzles my balls before taking each one in his mouth and sucking gently.

Meanwhile, his hand continues to jack me, his fist a tight grasp. He lets my balls go and nuzzles into the space behind them. His tongue roots into that space, pressing firmly before licking up my taint and kissing my hole. He plays there for a second, and I cry out as he licks over the wrinkled opening, giving it soft suckling kisses.

I force open my eyes. He's lying full length on the bed as he licks me. His arse cheeks clench and release, and I realise that he's rubbing his cock against the mattress. The thought rushes through me like lightning that he's turned on. From what he's said before, he's always viewed sex as a transaction. To see him taking his pleasure honestly is so hot.

"Oh God," I breathe out. "Blue."

He pulls away, moving up onto his elbows. "Cock's getting dry," he mutters, and I watch, fascinated, as he spits on my cock and uses it as lube to fist the length. We stare at each other for a long second.

"Why am I the only one naked?" I finally say hoarsely.

He studies me, those wolf eyes very intent, before a smile dawns. It's like the sun coming out. I grin as he levers off the bed and strips off his T-shirt. I don't even try to hide my ogling. He's lean and I can still see his ribs, but his shoulders are wide and his arms taut with muscle.

He smiles at me, and I clutch the base of my cock.

"*Really?*" he says.

"I'll go off if you even look at me funny, so get undressed quickly."

He cocks his head, and then his long fingers unbuckle his belt. I swallow hard at the musical jangling and watch in a riveted silence as he undoes the buttons on his jeans. He slides them off his narrow hips, and then he's standing there in just a pair of blue briefs. They cling to his body, barely containing his cock which is pushing up, the head peeping over the waistband. His pelvic muscles are clearly defined, and he watches me intently before slowly slipping his underwear off. It falls to the floor in a small fabric puddle.

For a long few seconds he stands there lit by the golden glow of the lamps. His skin is the colour of cream and shines in the light, and his cock is hard. It's slender but long and throbbing visibly, the blunt head an angry red colour and slick with pre-come.

Then he stalks towards me, and I gulp as he lowers himself over me. He hovers there, his arms supporting his weight so that only our cocks touch. It hits me like an electric shock, and I arch up towards him. And then I subside with a pained groan as every bone in my body seems to protest.

"Exactly," he says smugly. "That's not going to happen, Levi. This is not a team sport tonight. You're going to stay very still."

I run my hand over his chest, feeling the smooth silk of his skin underneath my fingertips. I trace his tight stomach muscles, trailing down to his pelvis and the skin there which is as taut as a drum. Then I stroke over his cock, tracing the veins with a soft touch. He shudders under my fingers and pulls back.

"No," he chides. "It's not about me tonight," he warns, helping me move and then settling back between my legs. "I'm not drawing this out. Just be aware that you will not be seeing my best work."

I shake my head gently and then screw my eyes shut as Blue takes my dick into his mouth. He's not messing around anymore and starts a tight suction around my cock, pausing only to pull back and suckle the flanged head, his lip ring rubbing against my sensitive shaft. He sticks the tip of his tongue into the slit and then pulls back as I groan for him to take me in his mouth again.

He's sucking hard now, and saliva pools at the base of my cock in the pubic hair. He gives a stuttered moan around my dick which feels incredible, and when I open my eyes, I find him on all fours. His head is bent over my groin, his arse in the air, and his other hand busy between his legs. He's fisting his cock and masturbating furiously.

"Oh shit," I breathe.

He pulls off my dick. "What do you want?" he says hoarsely.

"I want to come," I slur. "And I want to watch you come too, Blue."

He nods, flags of colour high on his sharp cheekbones, and bends back to my dick. He lifts his fingers to my mouth and, obeying his unspoken command, I suck on them messily until they're dripping with saliva. Never stopping the movements of his mouth, he lowers his hand and tickles the edge of my hole.

"Ungh," I say intelligently and brace myself as he slides the tip of his finger into my hole. He takes it slowly without any lube, settling for playing with the edges of the opening, sending pleasure tickling around the base of my spine. Then he starts to suck hard, fluttering his tongue around the head, and within seconds I feel my balls draw up.

"Blue," I say hoarsely to warn him, but he sucks harder. I give a garbled shout and start to come, filling his mouth. I clench my arse, spurting again, and he looks up as spunk slips from his mouth.

When I've finished, I settle back onto the bed. "You too," I say thickly.

I groan as, with those wolf eyes intent on me, he opens his mouth and spits my semen into the palm of his right hand. I swallow hard as he uses it to masturbate his cock.

"Come here," I say softly, pulling his hips, and he moves obediently to straddle my waist. His hand moves frantically and he looks over my body with an avid gaze.

"All over me," I direct. "Come all over me, babe."

He groans and clenches his eyes shut. His cock spills ribbons of creamy come over my chest, the liquid burning hot on my skin. Then he collapses to the side of me, nestling into me with a happy sigh, and silence falls.

After a bit, he stirs. "I want you to know that I've always been careful," he whispers. I open my mouth to protest, but he shakes his head fiercely. "We should have spoken about this earlier. You know my past, Levi. You need to be more careful." He looks at me almost nervously. "I'm clear of everything," he finally says.

"Me too. I got tested after Mason, because we weren't using condoms when he was with the other bloke."

Thoughts run over his mobile face—too fast for me to decipher. "I've never come while doing that before," he suddenly says in a very observational tone of voice. "I don't think I've ever really come that hard. I'm usually too worried or scared during sex to relax."

My stomach clenches at the thought of him being scared, and I tap his face. When he turns it to me, I kiss him softly, sucking lazily on the full lower lip and savouring the feel of his lip ring. "I'm glad."

"Thank you," he mutters.

I shake my head. "There's no need to thank me," I say, feeling the pulse of my headache return.

It must show in my face, because he kisses me gently. "Go to sleep," he whispers, pulling the covers up around me and tucking me in. "I'll be here."

"Will you save me from the coach and horses, Blue?" I ask sleepily.

"Always."

When I come awake, the sky outside the window is dark, only a distant glow coming from the spotlights illuminating Clifford's Tower. The skin on my chest itches where his spunk covered it.

"How long was I asleep?" I say hoarsely.

He checks my watch which is on his wrist after I gave it to him for safekeeping in the hospital. "A couple of hours. How do you feel?"

I test myself gingerly. "Quite a bit better," I say in surprise. "My head's stopped hurting, at least."

He winks at me. "Told you I knew a solution to pain."

"Thank you, Doctor Billings. Goodness, I hope I don't lose you to the NHS."

"They couldn't afford me," he says loftily. He looks at me with bright eyes. "Now you're awake, I'll nip out and get us something to eat. I didn't want to leave you alone when you were sleeping."

"I'm a big boy. I'm sure I'd have been fine," I say mildly. I eye him. "What are you doing?"

He's curled up against me on the bed with my iPad perched on his knees and my earbuds in his ears. He's dressed in his briefs and my T-shirt again. He smiles distractedly at me. "Watching *Supernatural*."

"Really?"

He nods. "I like it."

"Is it true to life? Are you picking up tips?"

Blue laughs. "In all my years living in the squats I've never seen *anyone* who looked like Dean. They'd have been a lot more crowded if that had been the case." He winks. "I see what you mean about his arse though."

"I know," I say happily. "It's a peach. Let's have a look."

He eases into my side, his head resting on my chest, and balances the iPad on my stomach. I kiss his head, seeing the curve of his full lips. "Don't go out," I whisper. "Let's order room service and watch this. Then I need a shower."

He grins at me. "Cool."

I smile at him. He's happier staying in than most men would be if I'd bought them an all-expenses trip to the Bahamas.

There's the beep of a phone. "Is that you or me?" I ask.

"Yours, I think," he says, yawning. He puts a hand on my chest as I go to get up. "Stay where you are," he scolds. "I'll bring it over and order the food while I'm at it."

I watch him, rather than Sam and Dean. He paces over to where my phone is charging on the dressing table. He brings it over, and I check the display.

"What do you want?" he asks as he chucks me the room service menu.

I give it a careless look. "I'll have a burger and a chocolate milkshake if they can make one."

He shakes his head smilingly.

"What?" I ask.

"You're such a child."

"No, I'm all man," I tell him seriously. "I know this because I pay a gas bill."

"I must be Peter Pan then in this equation," he says wryly. "Because I've never paid one of those in my life."

"You're more like Nana," I tell him. "Looking after people so well."

He shakes his head. "You just compared me to a dog, Levi. Don't ever rely on your charm to pick up men. Work on your tactics instead."

I laugh and look at my messages as he picks up the room phone and dials for room service.

"It was Mr Fenton," I say after he finishes the order and puts the phone down.

"The solicitor?"

I nod, dimly noticing that my head doesn't hurt when I do it. "He says he'll meet us here tomorrow afternoon in the bar." I purse my lips. "He's bringing someone with him, apparently."

"Who?"

I shrug and pass him the phone to put back on charge. "Who knows. We'll find out tomorrow."

～

*I*t's a young woman. She's very pretty with long dark hair but she's also very thin and pale. She and Mr Fenton are sitting at a table with their heads close together, talking quietly.

"Is that his daughter?" Blue whispers.

I don't know why I didn't see it. They both have the same nose.

"I wonder why he's brought her," he says.

I shrug. "Let's find out."

When we get to the table, Mr Fenton gets up immediately and shakes my hand.

"This is Blue," I say, drawing him forward. He comes slightly reluctantly but gives me a small smile.

The girl with Mr Fenton looks intently at Blue. "You're the ghost-walk bloke," she says.

His smile widens. "I am. Have you been on one?"

She smiles, and it looks a little sad. "At one point in my life it felt like I'd been on every ghost walk in York."

Mr Fenton makes a fussy gesture. "I'm so sorry. Levi and Blue, this is my daughter Amelia."

We nod and smile, and as we sit down at the table, the waiter bustles over.

"I took the liberty of ordering afternoon tea," Mr Fenton says. "Is that okay?"

I shrug. "I'm not terribly hungry, but I'm sure Blue will enjoy it."

"You need to eat," Blue says firmly. "No arguing."

"Wouldn't dream of it," I say meekly.

He grins at me and winks.

Mr Fenton and his daughter are looking at us with interest. Mr Fenton doesn't seem to know what to say about the obvious intimacy between us, but Amelia smiles kindly.

After we've ordered our drinks, we all sit back while the waiter sorts out the food. There are tiny sandwiches and an assortment of prettily iced cakes.

Ignoring the sandwiches that Blue places on my plate and gestures imperiously for me to eat, I look at Mr Fenton. "I'm sorry for calling you. I couldn't think of anyone else to ask."

He glances at his daughter and smiles somewhat sadly. "It's not a problem, Levi. I've been expecting your call." He hesitates. "In fact, if you hadn't rung me, Amelia was insisting that we meet with you anyway."

"She was? Why?" The incredulity is rich in my voice.

He starts to answer, but Amelia puts her hand on his arm. "I think maybe I should do this, Daddy."

"Are you sure?"

She nods and turns to me. "The truth is that I've been worried about you." She eyes my arm and my slightly battered face. "Seems like I was right to be concerned."

"I fell down the stairs," I say.

Mr Fenton gasps loudly and Amelia goes so white that she looks like she might pass out. I'm shocked by their reactions. Falling down the stairs is something that happens to people every day. I'd chosen my words carefully too. There had been absolutely no mention of murderous ghosts. "Are you okay?" I say to her.

She nods, biting her lip, and I watch in horror as her eyes fill with tears.

"Oh shit, I'm sorry." I'm not quite sure what I'm apologising for but feel the same panic I used to get when my mum cried. When I'd do anything to make it stop. "I'm quite okay," I say lamely.

Blue lays his hand on my arm. "It's not about you," he says quietly.

He's staring intently behind Amelia, and oh shit, I know that look. I follow his gaze surreptitiously, but I can't see anything. Everything's so clear to him that it still amazes me that I can't see it. It's almost infuriating.

"How do you know?" Amelia says.

Blue shakes his head. "I'll tell you, but you have to promise not to freak out." He and Amelia are staring at each other intently. When she eventually nods, he leans forward. "He's standing near to you. Brown hair, tall with very blue eyes."

"What the fuck?" I mutter.

Mr Fenton stares at Blue with doubt and anger in his eyes. Amelia starts to cry quietly. There's a flurry of movement, and Blue kneels down beside her chair.

"He wants you to know that he loves you very much and he's sorry. He should have taken your advice and left the house, but he couldn't. He wants you to know that he's safe, and he wants you to be happy. He likes that you're still wearing the blue beads."

I sit back in shock, and Amelia grabs Blue's hand. I see him wince at the pressure.

"Did it?" She hesitates. "Did it—?"

"No." Blue shakes his head. "It was a second of falling and then nothing."

She sags slightly.

Mr Fenton leans forward. "Would you care to tell me what you're talking about," he says coldly.

There's a challenge in his voice but also incomprehension. I think he wants Blue to be a charlatan, but even a second spent with Blue would tell him otherwise. Honesty is written all over Blue.

Blue looks at me, and I shrug. "I'd quite like to know too," I say mildly.

He squeezes Amelia's hand and stands up, edging back round to his seat. "Connor," he says simply. "The previous owner of your house, Levi, who fell down the stairs."

I'd somehow known the words were coming, but they still slam into me, knocking my teeth together and taking my breath. Like being smashed in the face by one of the slamming doors in my house.

"You were engaged?" he says, talking again to Amelia.

She nods and blows her nose. "Yes." She smiles mistily. "We met when he bought the house and my father dealt with the sale." Her gaze turns inward. "He was lovely. Very kind and funny. He was a property developer." She looks at Blue. "Can you really see him?"

He nods. He's become weary—his shoulders sloped and his eyes shadowed. How draining it must be to his spirit to see the dead and spend time with the people who are grieving them. They look to him for answers, yet it's impossible for him to give everyone what they need. I'm sure it doesn't go well when people don't hear what they want.

Regardless of the company, I grab his hand and hold it tight. He shoots me a startled look, but I feel his muscles ease.

"Would you like to meet me for coffee at some point?" he offers hesitantly to Amelia. "We can talk and I can tell you what I'm getting." He hesitates. "I have to add that it's a bit hit and miss with me, so you might not get what you want."

I stare at him. "I don't think any of that was hit and miss, Blue. Has something changed? Because you couldn't have done that a few weeks ago."

He shrugs. "It feels like it. I'm not sure if it's what Tom's teaching me, or if something shook free the other night, but I can sense Connor's thoughts *really* clearly."

"Can you hear him like with the woman the other night?"

He shakes his head. "No, but I'm not trying. It's not the right place for it."

I look around to find a few people sneaking looks at us. "You're probably right," I mutter.

"I *would* like to meet you," Amelia interrupts.

Her father stirs. "Amelia, we discussed this. You saw so many of the lying buggers. I thought you'd stopped."

I straighten up, prepared to say something, but Blue kicks my ankle and shakes his head at me. "It's fine," he mouths.

"I agree with you about the false ones. But Blue's the real thing," Amelia says to her father.

"How do you know?"

"Because he knew about the blue beads. No one knows about that but Connor and me. He always called my sapphire necklace the blue beads. Taking the mickey as normal." She smiles at Blue and there's a grace and beauty in the gesture. "Can I take your number?"

He nods. "Are you okay to go on with this?"

She nods and squares her shoulders before turning to me. "As I've said, Connor was my fiancé. We were planning to get married. It would have been this year."

"I'm so sorry," I say awkwardly.

"That bloody house," she spits out, her face contorting suddenly. "It's all that house's fault."

"Can you tell us what happened?" I grimace. "I hate to put you through it, but my falling down those stairs wasn't an accident."

She breathes in deeply. "I'm glad you're okay. I don't know what I can tell you that will help, but maybe it's easier if I tell you about the last month of Connor's life and then you can ask questions?" We nod and she leans forward. "He became obsessed with the idea that the house was haunted. It started small, according to him. Doors would slam, windows would open by themselves. Things would fly off shelves for no reason." I jerk and she shakes her head. "I see it hasn't changed."

Mr Fenton stirs again, and she shoots him a sharp look. "I know you don't believe, Daddy, but this is the truth. It's Connor's truth and it should be heard."

He taps his fingers on the table. "I do believe," he says finally and very reluctantly. His daughter shoots him an incredulous look and he flushes. "I admit I didn't at first. I'm not sure I did even when Connor died and you told me. But having to spend time in that house when I was letting tradesmen in changed my mind." He shudders and looks at me. "I'm sorry, Levi. I wanted to say something to you, but it was very difficult. I'm a solicitor. We deal in dry facts and not supposition. You might have laughed in my face for all I knew." He pauses. "But it didn't sit well leaving you that day, and I've worried about you ever since."

I want to point out that it's taken a long time for him to get round to saying something, but I don't. I'd have probably done the same with no proof. "It's fine," I say. "We're talking now." I turn back to Amelia. "Can you tell us more?"

She nods. "According to Connor, it started to escalate. He was kept awake at night by the sound of something being dragged through the house. He heard weeping and screaming. At first I didn't believe him. I thought he was sleep deprived and his mind was playing tricks on him. Then I got locked in the cellar one night."

"What?" I exclaim.

She nods, her face pale. "It was awful. Connor had gone out for a takeaway. He didn't want to leave me on my own, but I laughed at him and insisted. When he'd gone I heard sounds in the cellar and like an idiot, I went to have a look. I was halfway down the stairs when the lights went out and the door slammed." Her fingers grip tightly together, her face set. "I couldn't get out," she says simply. "And there was something there in the dark with me." She shakes her head. "Nothing happened, but I could hear breathing and I knew. When Connor got back, my throat was hoarse from screaming and I'd broken my nails on the door, but he heard nothing. He'd been in the house for ten minutes before he realised I wasn't upstairs. In all that time he never heard me scream. When he opened the door, he said it wasn't locked." Her eyes are dark and haunted. "Suffice it to say, I believed him after that."

"So what happened then?"

"I asked him to leave. I begged him to sell up, but he'd invested money in the house and he couldn't or wouldn't leave. So he turned to research. He said there must be a clue to what happened in the house, that things like that don't just happen without a reason. Hence the ghost tours. We went on all of them but all we learned was that a murder had happened there. But we also learned the murderer was a woman. Connor kept insisting that he'd seen her ghost and he didn't fear her. He actually felt she was trying to protect him at times."

"He was right," Blue says.

She sighs. "Then he started going to psychics. He had no luck finding a good one until one night when he went to a shop on the Shambles." Blue jerks and I tighten my grip on his hand. "He told me the man there had been the real deal. The man advised him to leave the house as soon as possible and told him he would die if he didn't."

Blue breathes in sharply.

Amelia jerks. "Oh my God, was that you?"

He nods. "I'm so sorry I couldn't help him further. He had a dark cloud over him, making it so difficult to see. And like I told you earlier, my abilities aren't very reliable." He shakes his head. "I can't remember much about him. In those days when I talked to people, I didn't remember many details afterwards. I definitely shouldn't have told him he'd die. That's slightly against the psychic code."

"But you were right," she says firmly. "Because he did."

"Why didn't he leave?" he asks.

"He was going to, but then he discovered something. It made him really excited. He called me one night and told me he'd found an answer."

I jump. "Really?" Excitement pours through me. *This could be it.* "What was it?"

"He didn't tell me." I sag in disappointment. "I was at a conference in Harrogate and we didn't talk for long. He told me that he'd found something in a book which might be the key to the activity in the house, and he was going to London that day to do some research. I never spoke to him again after that, and he was dead within two days."

"A book." I think hard. "There were no books in the house when I moved in."

"I know. I have them," she says. "His mother gave me most of his effects. I think all of his books are in a box in the storage area."

"Could you look?" I ask urgently.

She nods. "Of course I will. He thought that if he could prove whatever he'd found then the house might be safe again." She sighs. "To be honest, it sounded like mad ramblings to me, and I got angry with him. That day he was supposed to be moving out of the place and there he was haring it off to London. I thought it was never going to end. I regret that so much now," she says finally, a wealth of sadness in her voice.

Blue leans forward and takes her hand. "He knows that. People argue. Rows go with love like toast and marmalade and scones and jam. Words said in the heat of the moment aren't what we take with us when we die. Only the love remains out of everything."

"How do you know?"

"I feel it," he says simply. "It's what comes across in nearly every spirit I've ever seen and every bereaved person who's ever come to me."

They stare at each other for a long moment and then something eases slightly in her face. "Thank you," she says softly.

I fiddle with the handle of my cup, going over her words. "Did you say he went to London on the day he died?" I ask.

"Yes."

"Do you know what he was doing there?"

She frowns. "I don't. He was in the middle of telling me when we started arguing." She bites her lip. "But I'll tell you something that was a bit strange. After the accident when I went back into the house, there was a flyer next to the phone for a Jack the Ripper walk. It struck me as strange at the time because he'd never expressed an interest in that, and it seemed so out of left field for someone who was so obsessed with what was happening in his own home."

I sit back. "A Jack the Ripper walk," I say disbelievingly. "What's that got to do with anything?"

Blue taps his fingers lightly on the table, his face creased in thought. "The only connection I can think of is that at one point the London police thought the Devil of York was connected to the Ripper case, or that he was actually the Ripper who'd moved localities." He looks at me. "You remember? I say it on my ghost tour every night that the head policeman actually visited York and studied the case." He shakes his head. "But he was convinced there was no connection. Completely ruled it out."

Silence falls over the table until Mr Fenton stirs. "Do you still have the flyer, Amelia?"

She thinks hard. "Probably. I couldn't bear to throw anything away, and for a while it comforted me because for some silly reason I thought that maybe he'd been planning for us to spend a few days in London. I liked that idea in the darkest hours." She shrugs. "Doesn't seem likely now."

Blue taps her wrist. "Maybe not, but the fact that he thought he had the answer and was going for it says a lot about his commitment to keeping both of you safe. I think that's probably a better proof of love than a city break."

She smiles at him.

Mr Fenton shoots Blue a look of gratitude. "Surely your way forward is set, then."

We look at him enquiringly.

"Why don't you trace Connor's footsteps?" he says. "Follow him to London, go on the tour he wanted to. See if you can glean anything from that." He shrugs. "It seems a logical step to me. After all, you've found nothing here."

Blue and I exchange glances. He says, "Sounds like a good plan to me."

I sit back. "This is madness, but okay. London, here we come."

CHAPTER 15

*B*lue
It's funny to be back in London after all this time. At one point in my head the city had become something awful. The scene of my mother's suicide and our worst moments.

But now it's just another slightly grimy city. I love the history of it, but I have to say I prefer York. I like how it's so easy to get around. I like the smallness of it and the way the Minster looks over everything. I like knowing the names of the local people I pass on the street. I like that Levi lives there.

Levi has booked us into a nice hotel in Kensington, and I can't help the roundness of my eyes as I look at the huge lobby with its marble floors and wood panelling. However, most of my attention is on Levi. He's done very well so far, but he's flagging after the long train journey. It's in the tightness around his pretty eyes and the way he's cradling his arm.

As soon as we get into the room, I make a beeline for the bed and draw the covers back. "Strip and get in," I instruct.

Humour flares instantly in his eyes. "Blue, I'm sorry, but I'm just not that sort of boy."

"You totally are, but only with the right pain level incentive," I say tartly.

He grins, but pain is thinning his mouth, and I help him take his coat off, noting every wince anxiously.

He stands quietly, letting me help where other blokes would protest at being coddled. I love the steadiness of him, the way he's so quietly confident. Most of the men I've been with have been full of bluster. Not Levi. He's happy in himself and looks to the good in people.

It's a testament to his mum, but I do halfway wish he weren't so prepared to accept people on face value. It's going to get him hurt. He's a gorgeous man inside and out and I'm amazed he doesn't know it. I think of the time I looked up on that ghost tour and saw him watching me, all that lovely hair messy and his coat half on. All I could see was the humour and warmth in his eyes.

I push away my thoughts while I help him with his jumper and jeans, trying not to notice his wide, smooth chest and that trail of nut-brown hair leading down from his belly button. I remember the way it tickled my nose and the rich, warm scent of his pubes at the base of his cock.

I swallow hard and force my attention back to where it's needed. We haven't even discussed the blowjob from the other night, as we'd slept all day in the quiet calmness of the hotel and then woken up late and in a rush to meet Mr Fenton and Amelia.

The added dimension to our relationship is something I haven't quite worked out. I'd thought about it all the way here on the train while pretending to read, but the best I can come up with is how close he feels now. Like we're connected in some secret and invisible way.

I'm not sure why. I've given hundreds of blowjobs and that hadn't even been my best effort. I'd forgotten all my moves and got totally lost in everything. I didn't check myself or look for potential trouble. Instead, I was absorbed by him, listening to him groan and cry out. My coming had taken me completely by surprise, but I'd been desperate for it by then.

I'm jerked from my thoughts when he taps my shoulder. "You okay, Mr Thoughtful?"

I flush as I realise I've stopped undressing him and have been staring into space. "Just thinking of the Ripper walk," I say quickly, bending down to take off his shoes and socks and then easing his jeans off.

Finally, when Levi's down to his boxers, I help him into bed. The way he settles down with a tired groan means I'm right about his pain level.

"You need some more painkillers," I say decisively and head into the bathroom to get him a glass of water. I stand over him as he swallows the tablets and then take the glass from him.

"I'm sorry," he says, grabbing my fingers as I start to move away.

"What for?"

"I'm hardly good company. We should be doing something fun while we're in London."

I reach down and stroke the warm silky hair back from his face. His eyes are as sweet and brown as a bag of Chocolate Buttons. I remember one of my mum's boyfriends buying me some once when I was little. I ate them as slowly as I could, feeling the chocolate dissolve in a sweet burst on my tongue. I made a small bag last a few hours. I shake my head to clear away all the extremely stupid thoughts. There's no point to fond memories. They don't help with the shit that life throws at you.

"Listen," I say, "the Ripper tour is tonight. There's going to be a lot of walking and then we need our A-game to question the bloke. Therefore, you need to sleep and get your strength back, Levi."

"What will you do?" he asks sleepily.

I hold up his iPad. "I've got a date with Dean Winchester."

He smiles, but within seconds he's asleep, his chest rising and falling gently.

I strip myself down to my briefs too and then ease carefully into the bed next to him, cradling his iPad and pulling the sheets and blankets over us. But rather than watch anything, I snuggle carefully into him. I've grown addicted to doing this, and I try not to think about how hard it will be to not sleep next to him when this is all over.

I've never slept well before. It was always so cold in the squats I lived in, and I had to sleep lightly in case anyone pinched anything of mine or tried to hurt me. But it's so different with Levi. He's warm and smells so good and I sleep deeply next to him because despite me telling my brain no, it clearly still believes that I'm safe with him.

I rest my head gently on the pillow and look at the elegant lines of his face. I wish I could draw like he does. I'd love to sketch the sharp lines of his cheekbones, the slightly too big nose and the plush softness of his mouth. I lay my hand very gently on his chest, holding my breath in case he wakes up, but he sleeps on and, abandoning all ideas of watching my programme, I snuggle in a bit further and let sleep take me under.

When I wake next, dusk is gathering outside the window and a glance at the clock tells me we still have a few hours left before we have to be at the Ripper walk. I look sideways and go still. Levi isn't asleep. He's nestled into his pillow watching me steadily, the lines of pain on his forehead gone and a smile playing on his mouth.

"You alright?" I ask softly. "How's the head?"

"So much better," he says and stretches, giving a grunt of contentment that hits me in the base of my stomach.

He rolls onto his side, and we study each other for a long moment. I don't know who reaches for the other first, but we're suddenly lying in a tangle of arms and legs.

The room is cool, but Levi's body is hot against mine, and I stretch out against his length, all the hair-roughened surfaces providing a delicate friction. As if synchronised, we wriggle out of our underwear, and he gives a small groan as my body moves against his. His cock rises and pushes against mine, hot and silky.

"Blue," he says softly and kisses me.

His tongue plays across the seam of my lips. I open to give him access, and the kiss catches light. He plunges his tongue inside, twining and rubbing against mine, and his breath puffs softly on my cheek.

He groans and rolls over onto me, pushing me down into the mattress. Most of his weight is on me, because he only has one arm to support him. For a split second, total fear shoots through me and I can't catch my breath. I've been held down before by johns, and I quickly learnt to avoid this position because, let's face it, when you're on your back with your legs spread and someone's weight is on you, there aren't many ways to escape.

He reads the momentary stiffness of my body immediately and levers off me, taking his weight on his elbow but still keeping body contact with his leg slung gently over mine and his big hand kneading my hip.

"You okay?" he asks. His voice is hoarse and uneven and sends a tingle down my spine, making me want to rub against him like a cat. He stays my hip as I push towards him. "Blue?"

I cup his face, feeling the sharpness of his cheekbone under the soft skin. "I'm okay," I whisper. "Really. Just old instincts are hard to forget."

As his gaze skims our bodies, realisation flashes in his eyes.

"I don't want to stop though," I say forcefully. "Ignore it."

He shakes his head and falls onto his back. I open my mouth to argue but he pats my hip. "We'll save that position for another time," he says, giving me a lazy smile. "My arm's too fucked to pound you into the mattress tonight anyway."

For a long second, I stare at him. His soft eyes and that long body stretched out on the bed, his olive skin a contrast to the white sheets. "But you will pound me at some point?" I say dubiously.

He chuckles as he gives my body a slow onceover. "I promise." The sudden heat in his gaze makes me squirm. "Roll over on your front, Blue," he murmurs. "Let me see that arse of yours."

I roll slowly over, giving him a show and revelling in the low groan he can't hide. I wriggle into position, resting my head on my folded arms so I can look at him, and then slowly spread my legs.

His eyes darken even more, and he runs one hand down my back. His fingers are soft, as befitting an artist, and they trace the muscles of my back. I shudder as his fingers glance over a ticklish spot, and the feeling seems to echo in my balls as I giggle and writhe.

"You like that?" he whispers. He smiles as his fingers return to my back, taking a different route this time and seeming to spread heat wherever they go. I wriggle and groan, and I wonder if my back is lit up under the skin, fairy lights twinkling and tracing the different paths his fingers are taking.

He doesn't go straight for my hole or my bum as other men have done. Instead, he touches me slowly and gently, tracing those invisible tracks. His fingers swoop lower every time he makes a circle, and I find myself holding my breath as they perform a lazy figure of eight over the skin just above my buttocks. I spread my legs further, trying to tempt him and not even minding the chuckle he gives as he goes back to tracing my shoulder blades.

"Teasing bastard," I mumble. I'm nearly drooling.

He smiles, and I close my eyes as his fingers glide smoothly down and this time they skim over my buttocks, making me tremble. They slide lower and brush so gently against my balls that I wonder if I've imagined it. Then up his fingers go again, but this time when they come down, he traces a long finger down the crack of my arse and strokes my balls with a firmer touch.

"Oh shit," I gasp, grabbing handfuls of the sheet under me and writhing at the teasing movement. It's almost like I'm lying in the sea letting the tide slowly run over me.

Levi carries on like this with gentle gropes and lazy caresses until I feel his lips touch my back. He kisses my shoulder blades, deviating up to press a kiss into my neck where he buries his face and inhales as if he's taking my scent in. It tickles my ears and neck, and I push my hips down into the mattress, the sheets abrading my cock.

His hand stretches down, and he traces his finger up and down my taint while pressing more kisses down my back. Each one feels like fire against my skin, and I moan and pant, lost to everything but his talented hand.

He's hard against my hip, the tip of his cock painting a wet stripe, and I sniff, trying to get the scent of him in my nose. I press against his groin with my hip and his breath stutters as he presses back, starting to slide his cock against me.

Then there's only cold air as he sits up and moves behind me.

"What are you doing?" I say blearily, swallowing the extra saliva in my mouth before I dribble.

"Tasting," he mutters and before I can say anything, he pushes his face into me and I feel the swipe of his tongue over the wrinkled skin at my opening.

"Oh my *God*," I shout way too loudly. "What the fuck, Levi?"

When I look back at him, he raises his head, his eyes going very dark, his lips full and red. "I'm going to rim you," he says hoarsely. "Any objections?"

"None that a sane person would make." He hovers, and I stick my arse out. "Come on," I plead. "Do it, Levi."

He bends down and the rough surface of his cast catches my skin. It's a stark contrast to the softness of his tongue when he slides it along my taint, and it seems to make the pleasure deeper.

"Oh fuck," I manage to get out, burying my hot face in the cool pillow. "Oh fuck, that's so good."

"Just wait," he promises. "This is just the beginning."

"I've never …" I begin before coming to a stop, not wanting to bring up my past and the fact that punters don't rim.

He kisses my right arse cheek. "I know," he says quietly. "I know, Blue."

He bends back to his task without saying another word, and I give way to the feeling of his tongue as he licks me from balls to hole before stiffening his tongue and prodding it against the opening. Then he pulls back and suckles the skin around it. Just those two movements repeated endlessly until my hole is looser and I have to push him off and grab the base of my dick to stop myself from coming.

I stay there, arse in the air, the cold air striking my hole and making the pleasure running through me even more intense.

"Oh God," I finally say. "That's the best thing *ever*."

He chuckles and kisses my hole again, bathing it in wet and getting it lovely and sloppy.

"I need the lube," he says softly. "Wait there a minute."

I turn my face on the pillow, watching him move away. His arse is paler than the rest of his body. High and tight and nicely rounded. I press my cock into the mattress and pull back with a gasp, feeling the tell-tale tingle in my balls.

He leans against the bathroom door, watching me as he opens a box of condoms. His colour is high, his eyes dark, and his hair sticks up. I lick my lips. He's so gorgeous to me.

"Come here, Levi," I whisper.

A shiver runs down his body. It gives me a sudden rush of power that I can affect him like that. With the rush, comes a feeling of tenderness and protectiveness that warns me not to abuse my power.

I swallow as he moves towards me, the muscles in his body bunching and releasing. He settles on the bed, sitting next to me, and cups one arse cheek possessively.

"Mine," he says hoarsely.

I manage a smile with far too much teeth. I try to give my shrug a careless air. "If you want it."

He squeezes the cheek. "I do," he says solemnly, and I swallow hard. He hands me the condom and lube. "You'll have to put the condom on. If I try to do it with one hand, we'll likely be here all night."

"Well, we can't have that," I say huskily, hearing the click in his throat as he swallows hard. I tear open the wrapper, and as slowly and torturously as I can manage, I slide it on, accompanied by a great deal of gratuitous fondling. The catch in his breathing and the soft groans he can't hold back are my reward. I grin up at him and he shakes his head, his eyes dancing with humour.

"Lube now, you little minx. Pour some onto my hand," he directs. "I'm likely to squeeze out the whole bloody bottle with my left hand, otherwise."

I do as I'm told, watching him rub it between his fingers, and then I bury my head in the pillow and shout out as his middle finger presses against my entrance. He circles it gently, making it slippery before sliding the tip into me.

"Oh shit," I whisper, feeling the familiar burn.

He looks up. "Relax," he directs, and there's a sudden element of control in his voice. "Let me in, sweetie." He smiles although it obviously takes effort. His chest is damp with sweat. "I'll stop now," he says steadily. "Any time you want it to stop, you tell me and I'll do it."

"That's not fair," I whisper.

He shakes his head. "There's no such thing as not fair in sex, Blue. It isn't about keeping score and it certainly isn't something you have to do to make me happy. I'm happy with you anyway."

I study his earnest face intently, and something inside me that's been buried so deep, a hard kernel that warns me people can't be trusted and will hurt me, relaxes its grip and lets warmth through.

"I trust you," I say softly. "I want you to do it."

His expression softens—he's glad. He taps his finger against my hole. "Breathe out and relax," he instructs me.

I do as he says and his finger finally slides in. I inhale sharply, because it's been a while since I did this, and it feels awkward. Then he crooks his finger gently, like he's summoning something. He brushes my insides, and fireworks go off behind my eyes.

"Oh fuck," I shout very loudly.

He kisses my back, rubbing his face against my skin as if coating himself in my sweat. It's unbelievably erotic combined with that stealthy finger movement.

I pant and writhe as he brushes the spot again and then cry out in protest as he removes the finger. But he simply holds out his hand for more lube, and when he returns to my arse, it's with two fingers this time. He plays there for a while, stroking and stretching me until I'm a panting, sodden mess. It feels like he's jerking me off from the inside, and I push my hips into the bed and grunt.

His gaze is heavy and intent on me, breaths coming hard from his slightly open mouth.

"I want you to fuck me, Levi," I say clearly. "I need it."

And even as I say that, I know I've never felt it before like this. I've *never* needed sex. It's always been the other bloke feeling desperate, but now it's like I'll explode if he doesn't get his cock inside me.

He pulls his fingers out, and I give a disappointed whine, but he lays on his back and grabs the base of his dick, holding it up.

"Climb on," he says, his smile is almost pained. "I can't use one arm, so you can ride me instead. Makes it easier."

I narrow my eyes, because I bloody well know that the only person he's trying to make this easier for is me. "And next time you'll be on top?" I clarify.

He grins, a sudden flash of white in a wide, warm smile. "Every day if you want it," he promises. He slaps my hip gently. "Come on, Blue."

I sit, sling my leg over him, and take hold of his cock. I cup both of our dicks in my hand and rub. It's intended to show him who the boss is now but it backfires slightly because even as he arches and cries out, I have to back away to stop myself from coming.

"Bloody hell, I'm so close," I say hoarsely.

Even now it's hard to believe it's me with my cock throbbing, desperate to get a man's knob in me. But it is, and I revel in it. I scoot until his cock is knocking against my backside, and then I rise up, and, steadying his dick, I sink down until the head is against my entrance. I rub against it, feeling it stir the nerves in my passage. I take a deep breath and slowly lower myself onto it.

It isn't easy despite how open I am, but he lies still, letting me edge down his cock, the only sign of his agitation the fist he clenches with his good hand in the bed linen underneath him. Finally, I sit fully on his dick, feeling his wiry pubes against my arse and the length of his cock hard and throbbing inside me.

"Alright?" he asks in a stuttered voice, sucking in a breath as I move experimentally.

I bite my lip and throw my head back, letting out a deep groan as his cock brushes my prostate. I'm drawn into a trance-like state as I lift up and sit down again. I go slowly at first, crying out as he rubs me just right, and then faster until I'm bouncing on his dick. I let out short cries as he helps me lift and lower, one hand holding my arse tight enough to leave bruises.

His dick pistons into me, the slap of flesh and the low groans of two men fucking echoing around the room. I want to spin it out and tease him, but I can't, and my balls tighten.

"Oh God, I'm so close," I mutter. "Touch me. Ungh!" I cry out as he grabs my cock in his fist, and I shuttle through it a couple of times before come bursts from my dick in three long spurts, painting his stomach and chest with spunk.

"Blue!" he shouts. He lifts his hips, battering into my arse for a couple more thrusts before he arches his back and groans. Heat blooms inside me, and for a wild moment I wish he was bare and I could feel his come in me. I've never had that before, never even considered it, but tonight the thought is enough to make me spurt another tiny amount of come.

I fall down onto him. "Christ," I whisper, trying to catch my breath. "I've never…"

"No," he mutters, drawing me close. I bury my head in his chest and he kisses my forehead and chuckles. "You now have come in your hair," he informs me.

I sniff. "I'm surprised it's not on the ceiling. I've never come like that before."

Levi stares at me, and I feel a little embarrassed. He's probably had that loads. He was in a five-year relationship. The irony is that I've more than likely had many more men than him, but in this bed with him I was almost a virgin. For a second I wish passionately that I had been. That I had come to him clean, and not dented and battered by all the years I gave this away in return for bed and money.

"Hey," Levi says softly. "Me neither," he says very clearly, holding my gaze. "It's never been like that for me before."

"Really? Wasn't Mason any good?" I say happily. I usually avoid thinking about them in bed together, but this revelation is very cheering.

"It was good, don't get me wrong. I was always very happy with the sex, but now I know it was lacking something because apparently there's another level that nobody told me about."

I try to ignore the warmth in my stomach and settle for humour.

"Were you missing the stage of getting spunk in your partner's hair? Because babe, it feels like I've got a natural hair gel in there."

He chuckles and, grabbing the base of the condom, he levers me up slightly and pulls out. I grunt at the unpleasant feeling and he reaches down with his good hand and pets my hole, massaging it gently.

When he pulls me back down to him, I protest. "I'm covered in come."

He laughs. "So am I. What does it matter?"

"It'll matter when we can wallpaper a wall with what's sticking us together."

Despite that, I don't move away from him. He pulls the covers up around us, and I snuggle in.

"Lie here with me a bit, Blue," he whispers. "We've still got time."

CHAPTER 16

*L*evi

While we wait for our guide outside the pub as we were told to, I sneak a glance at Blue. He's looking contemplatively down the road, and I can't work out whether he's seen someone alive or dead. His expression is tranquil, but those pale eyes of his are full of thoughts. And plotting, I think with some amusement. Always plotting.

He stirs, and I immediately focus on the pub sign. I shift position, feeling the slight ache in my leg muscles from the sex earlier. Heat rushes through me, and I can feel it staining my cheeks. Images of sex flick through my head. Blue's slumberous eyes, the way he lay spread across the bed, all that creamy skin on display and my fingers stuffed in his arse, and later the feel of my cock disappearing into his tiny hole.

I lick my lips, imagining I can taste him even though I know I can't. He'd tasted almost sweet. I have a sudden flashing image of his face when he'd come. Surprise and abandonment to the pleasure had been written all over him, and I swallow when I recall the feel of his come hot on my hand and coating my fingers.

I bite my lip and try to think of other things, but I can't. He's all I can think of. I've never had sex like that before. I feel almost guilty towards Mason for thinking it, but it's the truth. I was with him for five years, and, although I enjoyed sex, it had never felt as consuming as it did today.

Consuming. I roll the word in my mouth. It fits what I'd experienced with Blue in that bed. I'd felt almost burned alive, my only focus him and his scent of peaches. Having his come on my hands and his spit in my mouth felt like the single hottest thing I've ever done.

I look up to find Blue watching me. Those wolf eyes of his are peculiarly intent, and I swallow. They're filled with the same heat I know he can read in mine. We watch each other warily until he moves closer to me.

He opens his mouth to say something, but at that second we hear a loud and very posh voice say, "Hello."

I turn and see a tall man standing in front of us attired top to toe in Victorian dress. He's thin with a long hooked nose and a rather wild-looking mop of black hair, but he has a wide and happy smile on his face.

"Good evening, folks," he says in his rich voice. "Ready for some tales of foul murder tonight? Led by me, your estimable host, Julian Prince."

I want to smile when I see Blue staring at the man with a great deal of admiration in his eyes. I shake my head instead, and then I'm jerked round with the force of Blue's grasp as he propels me down the road after our guide.

The Ripper tour is fascinating, despite the fact that most of the murder sites are long gone now, lost to the encroach of time and housing and the bombing during the war. Still, Julian's voice is rich and he certainly knows his stuff. The group follow him eagerly, but none are more rapt than Blue, and the vast majority of my enjoyment is coming from watching him watch the other man. They're obviously soul mates if we count a flair for the dramatic and a love of a good story.

Eventually, the tour winds down, and he allows questions as we stand in the murky gloom of a streetlight. The usual questions are asked about injuries and who he thinks the Ripper really was, and he fields them with aplomb. Whether he's right, I have no idea because I know next to nothing about the Ripper. My attention drifts slightly to the way the breeze is lifting the silky strands of Blue's hair and how the light hits his face, turning the dips and hollows mysterious and beautiful.

When Julian's voice turns slightly anxious, I drag my attention back. He's listening to a young man who's standing at the front of the group. I noticed him earlier because he seemed to have a permanent sneer on his face, making jokey asides to his friend which set the mood of the group slightly against him. You could sense it like a slight change in the wind direction as people stood a little apart from him, disassociating themselves from him. By the last murder site, even his friend had stepped away.

"I don't know why you won't say it," the young man says insistently. Blue glares at him. "You made yourself look a right tit over that book."

"I'm thrilled that you read it," Julian says smoothly, but there's an edge to his voice, and he looks rather sad. "But let's not dwell on that. It was rather an unpleasant time for me."

I look at Blue in question, and he steps close to whisper in my ear. I shudder slightly at the feel of his hot breath and drag myself back to the conversation. "Julian wrote a book about Jack the Ripper, insisting that the five canonical murders were the least of his crimes. He claimed that he moved about the country and there were more murders that the police never connected to him. He was disproved, and he became a bit of a laughingstock." He shakes his head and represses a smile. "I *knew* you weren't listening."

I wink at him, and we both turn back to the conversation. Julian sounds increasingly desperate as the man rants on about his book, the shoddy research, and Julian's shortcomings as an author while the group shifts awkwardly.

Blue stares intently at the man, and I sigh because I can almost guess what's coming.

"Maybe you should read another book," Blue says sharply.

The man turns to him. "What?" he says crossly.

"Maybe you should read the one called 'Let's make a twat of ourselves by forcing our opinions on others despite the fact that it's fucking cold and we all need a drink.'"

The man's mouth opens and shuts, and Blue gives him an innocent-looking smile that doesn't actually manage to cover up the sharpness. "Not read that one? Shame. I think it only had a small print run. Babe, how many copies did it sell?"

"One," I say wryly. "Just the one, my love." I catch his smile warming and widening and shake my head reprovingly at him.

"You trying to say something to me?" the young man says belligerently.

Blue tenses, but I shake my head in warning.

"He's saying you're acting like a prat and to shut the hell up," I say curtly. "He just used a lot more useless words in the middle than I did."

The guide seizes the silence that follows that pronunciation. "Well, thank you for your company tonight," he says brightly. "It's been an absolute pleasure. Please leave a review on TripAdvisor."

The young man walks towards us, and I straighten to my full height which is about a foot taller than him.

"Walk away," I say levelly.

He glares at Blue, and I shake my head and smile coldly at the idiot. "Don't speak to him either."

He obviously thinks better of what he was planning to say, and giving us a disgusted look, he disappears down the street. It's a relief, to tell the truth. I'm not sure how threatening I could have been if he'd caught a glimpse of my pink cast.

An elbow in my side recalls me to Blue who is staring at me strangely, his eyes wide. "What?" I ask.

He shakes his head. "Why did you do that? You could have ended up in a fight."

"Nah." I hug him, feeling the momentary resistance before he gives in and hugs me back. "He wasn't going to fight me." I pause. "Which is probably a good job. I don't much like fighting, and I've only got one workable arm."

"Good," he says slowly. "I don't like the thought of you being in a fight." He inhales sharply and hugs me tighter. "Especially not over me and my mouth."

I smile down at him. "I can think of no better reason to fight than for you and that mouth."

For the first time since I've met him, he actually looks flustered. "Oh," he says, running his hand through his hair. "Well then. Erm."

I bite my lip to hide my smile

He shakes his head crossly. "Don't think you're getting away with the bit about *useless words* either."

I laugh out loud and hug him closer. "I know I won't."

"Thank you for the intervention." The quiet words come from our side, and we turn to find Julian standing there staring at us.

The rest of the group have gone while we were bantering, so it's a good job Julian broke it up or we'd have lost him too. The sole reason for us being in London.

"Not at all," Blue says smoothly. "He was being a prat. There's no need to be that rude."

Julian clears his throat. "Well, it was welcome anyway. People like that, I've found, tend to like the sound of their own voices."

Blue smiles at him. "I run a tour of my own, so I know what you mean."

The other man's eyes sharpen. "You run a Ripper tour?" He doesn't look particularly happy with the idea.

Blue shakes his head. "Oh no, I run a ghost tour in York."

Relief runs over Julian's face—he's likely pleased that they're not competitors—and interest replaces it. "Really? How interesting. So you cover the Devil of York, then?"

Blue looks quickly at me and I nod, unable to believe that it's running this way. It's almost too easy. He turns back to the man. "I do, and that's sort of why we wanted to talk to you. Would it be possible for us to buy you a drink somewhere?"

Julian looks at us, trepidation and caution running over his face.

Something about us must seem trustworthy though, and not as if we're black-market organ sellers, because he finally nods. "Follow me. I know the perfect place."

The perfect place turns out to be the Ten Bells pub in Spitalfields, a tall building on the corner of the busy Commercial Street.

"It's the place where Mary Kelly had her last drink," Julian breathes before insisting on taking our drink orders as a thank you for rescuing him and disappearing to the bar.

I look around. "Did she die by hipster?" I mutter.

Blue snorts and elbows me, but his busy eyes are everywhere. The pub looks like any other old place that's been done up and infiltrated by men with beards and tight jeans. Apart from a wall of pretty blue and white tiles which must date from the Victorian time, the rest of the place is standard city cosy. There are a few people drinking, but it's not too busy.

Julian comes back, sliding the drinks in front of us. "Here's to you," he says, an almost happy expression on his face now that he's not being confronted with fierce book critics. "Now, what did you need to talk about?" He stares at Blue. "Is it about the Devil of York? Because I have to say that I stand by my statement that those crimes were unrelated to the Ripper unless purely by copycatting."

"Oh no," Blue says slowly. "I wouldn't want to argue with you on that. I'm not much of a one for arguing," he says almost piously, making me snort into my beer.

The two men turn to stare at me and I sigh. "We actually need some information from you," I say, reaching into my pocket for the photo of Connor that Amelia gave us along with the Ripper tour leaflet. "It's about this man."

Julian takes it, looking dubiously down at the photo. "I'm sorry," he finally says. "I don't know him." He looks at us. "Is this a missing person thing?"

Blue shakes his head. "Please look again. We believe he came to see you. After a tour, maybe."

Julian stares down at it and then gives a jolt of recognition. "Why, I do know him." He looks up at us. "He came for a tour a few years ago, if I remember rightly. I don't think I'd have recognised him again if it wasn't for the fact that you're from York too, and we were discussing the Devil of York murders."

"We were?" I say slowly. "I don't think we've discussed them yet."

"Oh no, not us. Him," he says cheerfully. "*He* was discussing it."

I sit back, staring at Blue. Is this the connection we've been looking for? But what is it about?

Blue looks thoughtfully back at me and then turns to Julian. "Was he arguing with you over the fact that the Ripper didn't do the killings in York? I don't understand."

"Oh no. He knew the Ripper didn't do it." He looks at us. "He thought he knew the identity of the Devil."

The information feels rather like I'd imagine a small bomb detonating under me would feel. For a long second Blue and I just sit gaping at each other and then I turn to Julian who is obliviously drinking his pint.

"He knew who the Devil was?"

He nods.

Blue shakes his head disbelievingly. "And that's what he wanted to talk to you about?"

"Of course," Julian says. "I'm considered a bit of an authority on the Devil, in the sense that it was my research that proved conclusively that he wasn't Jack the Ripper. The murders were very different." He looks puzzled. "Wasn't this your friend? Didn't you know this? Can't you ask him? I must say I was very surprised that he didn't release a book about it. I watched out for one for quite a while."

Blue hesitates. "No, it's not like that," he says slowly. "Connor is dead. We don't know him apart from the fact that Levi now owns his house."

Julian puts his pint down. "Dead. That's so sad. He was so young." He stares at us. "So why are you here?"

I give Blue an imploring glance. He sighs loudly and rolls his eyes.

"Levi's house is haunted," he says.

Julian blinks but doesn't say anything, and Blue forges ahead. "Connor died there, but before the accident, he came to London to talk to you. We thought it would be something to do with the house, but it looks like he was just a true-crime fanatic after all."

I put my hand on Blue's arm to shut him up. "Wait." I turn to Julian, a sudden thought occurring to me. "Who did Connor think was the Devil of York?"

"Why, Alfred Farrington, a local businessman, of course. He lived on a side street near the Minster and Connor seemed to believe he ended up being murdered by his own sister. Imagine that," Julian says, smiling and staring at us over the top of his glass. "A vicious serial killer being murdered by his own *family*."

*B*lue
We let ourselves into the hotel room and Levi pulls off his coat, throwing it cavalierly over a chair before subsiding onto the bed with a dramatic sigh. "What the *fuck*?" he groans, scrubbing his hand over his eyes.

The journey back had been made largely in silence as we digested what Julian had told us. Obviously, that quiet period is over now.

I pull my own coat off and climb onto the bed beside Levi, something in me thrilling when he holds up his good arm for me to cuddle into him. I consider that arm for a second, wondering whether I should refuse. At some point I'm going to have to leave him and return to my old way of dealing with things on my own. But that thought makes my chest feel tight so I slide in next to him, giving a completely silent sigh of happiness when it comes down over my shoulders.

"I never thought of this," I say slowly. "To me, he's always just been this poor bloke whose sister murdered him."

His arm stiffens. "Is that why she killed him, do you think? She found out he was the Devil?"

"Nah," I scoff instinctively and then pause. "Actually, maybe." I sit up on my elbows, staring down at his face. Those pretty dark eyes of his are looking at me curiously. "I mean, no one could find any reason for her doing it, either at the time or since. It was a complete mystery why someone as well liked and kind as Rosalind could have done that to her only family."

His brow furrows in thought. "Maybe she found out, Blue."

I shake my head. "All along I've thought that whatever evil was in that house was something a lot older. I actually wondered whether it was something really evil and ancient and it made her kill her brother."

He bites his lip. "That occurred to me too."

We both look at each other in silence for a second.

"But if she knew, Levi. If she somehow found out and she put a stop to the murders…"

"If he even did the murders," he says. "There's no bloody connection at all between him and those women. Otherwise, it would have become part of the legend of the Devil. You'd have known all about it. You'd have been talking about it on your tour."

I jerk as recognition streams through me. "*Fuck,*" I hiss. I go to crawl off the bed.

His arm stays me. "Wait, where are you going? Blue?"

"To get the book. The one you were reading when you had the accident."

"Have we still got it?"

"It was under you when I found you that night. I put it in my pocket, and I'm pretty sure it'll be with my stuff in the bag."

He lets go of my arm, and I hotfoot it over to the bag, rooting through it and pulling out clothes and toiletries before exclaiming triumphantly. "Here it is."

He eyes the title. The lettering gives the impression of dripping blood. "Is that a good thing? It looks a bit over the top."

"It is," I say, riffling through the pages. "But it's also the book I used to read where I got most of the information for the tour. The Devil section is huge." I scan the words quickly until I find the relevant paragraph. I read it and then read it again more slowly. "Shit," I finally say, lifting my head to stare at him.

"What is it?" He sits in a cross-legged position, his hair ruffled.

"There is a fucking connection. Jesus," I exclaim. "I knew it all along. I just didn't know it was him."

"*Blue*," he says exasperatedly. "Tell me."

I throw myself on the bed next to him. "Do you remember I said on the tour that the last victim of the Devil was seen by her friend walking away from the pub that night?" He nods. "And an hour later the beat bobby was hailed by a man who said he'd seen what looked like a dead body on the street?"

His gaze sharpens. "*No?*"

I nod. "His name was Alfred Farrington." I shake my head. "I never connected it with the house, because it's a different surname from Rosalind's."

"Because she was a widow," he says slowly.

I nod. "Yet somehow in my head he was called Mr Cooper too. I suppose it was the brother and sister bit. Fuck, I'm stupid."

"No, you're not," Levi says immediately and predictably. He doesn't seem to like me saying anything bad about myself. He stands up and begins pacing. "Surely it can't have been him. Wouldn't the police have had him down as a suspect?"

"Who knows if they didn't, Levi?" I think hard. "A lot of the Ripper police records were lost, so any Ripper connection might have vanished. Some of it was due to bombing in the war and a lot of it because the security wasn't tight and people just walked off with stuff. Who knows if they did or didn't suspect him? As for the York police, I've never heard his name mentioned in connection with it. I think the problem was that they didn't have *any* suspects. It's why he got the name the Devil, because how else could he slip in and murder women so horrifically and never be caught?" I shrug. "Of course, he was then murdered himself, which would have taken anyone's eye off him if anyone ever did suspect."

"So if he was the Devil, and it's only an *if*, how did Rosalind know?"

I sigh. "We'll probably never know for sure."

"But you think this is it, don't you?" He looks steadily at me.

"I actually do. Don't forget it was the Devil's victim that warned me you were in trouble. I'd think she'd have to be connected to this whole mess to know anything." I shake my head at my own idiocy at not spotting that. "I also think that Connor thought it too, but how on earth he knew that, we'll never know."

"Maybe the haunting took a different theme for him, Blue. Maybe more was revealed."

I hum thoughtfully. "Maybe Rosalind couldn't or didn't protect him as well as you. For some reason she seems to have taken a fancy to you. I *knew* she didn't feel evil."

"But why me?"

"Maybe it's because you're a truly good person." Levi looks like he wants to argue but I shake my head. "Maybe it's because your mum was around you for a while. That's got to have given you some protection. When I saw her in the kitchen with you the light was blinding." I shrug. "I think that's love. I don't know for sure, but it felt very much like I imagine love would feel."

Levi winces and his soft mouth turns down as if his lips are collapsing under the weight of his grief. That sadness is becoming a little faded, but it'll never go. It's a part of him now, like his big feet with the long middle toe and the way he scratches his ear when he's thinking.

"You're tired," I say softly. "Let's get some sleep. We can think in the morning. We've got time."

～

J climb the steps to the attic and Levi's studio, but something feels different. In a distant part of my brain I know that I'm dreaming, but I can still feel the sleek wood of the handrail under my fingers. The air is scented with the smells of furniture polish and lily of the valley.

The décor has changed—that's what's different.

Levi's house is painted in shades of grey with bold artwork. Now it's papered in a flowery pattern, the details so defined that I can see the petals on the tiny roses and notice a slight tear in the paper near the top of the stairs. I try to look behind me to see any other changes, but I can't. Something is stopping me from looking back.

I know I shouldn't be here. It's dangerous. But something strong keeps me moving steadily up the stairs to the open door. Behind me, a steady thudding starts to sound. A knocking that seems to come from the depths of the house. A chill runs down my spine but still I walk on, unable to look back.

I enter the door to Levi's studio, but it's not the room I'm expecting. This is Rosalind's sewing room with the shelves full of baskets from which tumble brightly coloured embroidery silks. A dainty-looking chair is drawn up under the window where Levi's drafting table sits. A small table is pulled up next to it on which is a white cloth with coloured embroidered flowers rioting around some words I can't read.

My attention falls away from it as I spot Rosalind. She's standing against the far wall of the room just like she was a few days ago. Her dress is the same. I can even see the wisps of hair that have fallen from her bun and curled around her neck just as I did before. And, as then, her attention is on the floor in front of her.

"Rosalind," I say.

She ignores me. She kneels down and fiddles with something. There's a click and I watch her push an object into the dark aperture that's opened up at her feet.

I gasp and then try to step back. She hears me and starts to turn.

I've seen her many times now, and I know she was trying to protect Levi, but something about the way she turns and the angle of her body makes my blood run cold and every nerve tighten.

I close my eyes but when I open them, my stomach lurches in horror. I try to scream but I can't. She's standing near me, her dead eyes fixed on me. Her face is purple, and there's a livid mark around her neck from the noose. But what makes terror curdle in my stomach is the fact that she's covered in blood. It's splashed across that pretty dress, making scarlet flowers bloom hideously amongst the faded violet ones. A speckled mist of it lines her purple face, dripping from her lips, and as she moves towards me, she flicks her fingers and blood rains in fat drops onto the wooden floor, making sticky splatting noises as it lands.

She opens her mouth to speak, and her tongue lolls out just as footsteps start to sound on the stairs. Movement catches my eyes and I turn my head and stare as blood begins to run down the walls.

The sight loosens something in my throat, and I scream. And scream.

And sit bolt upright, gulping in air, another scream—this one silent—tangling in my throat and a secret knowledge hammering in my brain.

I breathe in and out noisily. *Just a dream,* I tell myself. *Oh fuck, it was just a dream.*

My hands are shaking. I'm freezing cold and a whole-body shiver passes through me. Breathing in, I reach over to shake Levi's shoulder. "Levi, wake up. I know where the diary is."

"What? Where what diary is?" Levi says sleepily, sitting up with the covers falling to his waist. He stares at me. "You okay?"

I wipe my forehead, only just realising that I'm sweating.

"Not sure, to be honest. I think Rosalind visited me in my dream." I shiver again, and he exclaims, pulling me to him.

"I smell awful," I try to protest, but he gathers me close and tangles my legs with his own, clutching me in a tight grip. After a few minutes, the shudders stop, and his warmth seeps into me.

"What happened?" he whispers.

I tell him, holding the covers up tightly over us, creating a nest. He brushes my hair back from my forehead, and my eyes sting because the gesture is so tender.

"But how do you know it was a diary?" he finally asks.

I shrug. "I just woke up knowing it."

"That's fucking creepy."

Astonishingly, I laugh, something I didn't see myself doing after that dream. "It's under the floorboards in the attic."

He scrubs his fingers through his hair. "Shit, that makes sense. I bet I even know where."

I look at him in surprise.

"There's a board that creaks in the corner of the room even when no one's standing on it." He pauses. "Only now I'm considering this new information, and I'm thinking someone dead might have been standing on it all along." He sighs. "Fuck my life."

I repress a smile and nod. "That must be the place."

He kisses my forehead. "Well, I suppose that's amazing, although we probably do need to discuss the fact that you've added a rather creepy item to your list of talents and you can now commune with ghosts in your dreams."

"Let's table that discussion for a few years in the future. Like seventy," I suggest.

He grins. "We'll go back to the house tomorrow and get the diary, take it back to the hotel, and solve the crime."

"Okay, Scooby-Doo," I hiss. "It's brilliant that you've solved the case without those pesky kids. But you're ignoring one very important piece of information."

"You're raining on my parade, Blue," he mutters. "Okay, what's the information?"

"What's the date tomorrow?"

"November the fifth."

"And what does that mean?"

"Sparklers and toffee apples," he offers hopefully.

"Yes to all of that, and yes to the fact that it's also the anniversary of the murder."

"I'd say that doesn't matter, but your expression is saying otherwise," he says slowly.

I nod solemnly. "Is it saying that it's probably the most dangerous time to be in that house?"

He nods.

"Well then, my expression is very wise, Levi."

CHAPTER 17

Blue

The Minster bells are ringing when we get back to the house, and the street is dark and quiet.

"Shit, I wish the train had been on time," I mutter, pacing behind Levi as he digs in his coat pocket for the keys. "It's dark. It's *completely* the wrong time to be doing this."

He looks at me curiously. "Is all that stuff they say about the light keeping away ghosts true, then? I always thought it had been made up by horror writers."

I shake my head. "It's based in truth like a lot of the old tales. Put it this way, it would take a strong spirit to appear during the daylight hours." I pause. "Strong or just really pissed off. Tom says that the entrance to the path between the living and the dead is covered with a very thin curtain. During daylight hours it's fairly strong, but at night it's raggedy and gaping." I stare at him. "And on the anniversary of a violent death it's almost non-existent. This is completely the wrong time to do this."

A firework goes off overhead, making us both jump. The gold and red glow from it highlights the troubled expression on Levi's face. "But I still think we have to do it, Blue. Rosalind appeared in your dream last night on the eve of the murder. Surely there must be a reason for that."

I give a long sigh. "I know." I grab his arm. "We get in and grab the diary and then we're out, got it? We can't stay here a moment too long, Levi. I won't risk you."

"You won't risk *me*. What about you?"

I bite my lip. "I'll be fine. You can't see anything. You're like a giant baby blundering around."

"What a lovely and charming image you have of me," he says dryly. "Now I see why you wanted to jump me." I shake my head as he exclaims and holds up the key. "Got it." He fits it into the door and looks at me. "Ready?"

"No," I mutter. "But let's do it anyway."

"That's the spirit."

"Literally."

The silence in the house when we go in is almost an anti-climax. Levi looks around, his gaze straying to the foot of the stairs, and a small shudder runs through him.

"Did you clean up when you were here to get the clothes?" he whispers furiously. "I told you to be quick."

"Much as I love the futility of you bossing me around, I didn't do it."

"Well, who did?"

"Who do you think?"

He opens his mouth to speak the name, and remembering, I slap my hand over it. I stare into his indignant eyes. "Do not name the dead in here tonight, Levi."

When I take my hand away his brown eyes are as serious as I've ever seen them.

"Come on," I mutter. "Stay close. We're going up to the attic." I look around. "We've got five minutes tops, and then we're out of here."

He nods and follows me up the staircase as I move swiftly, my eyes darting everywhere. The house is silent. As silent as the dead, I think morosely, and then wish I hadn't. I take the stairs to the attic even quicker, so we're panting when we barrel into the room. I flick the light switch on, slam the door behind us and lean back against it.

"I'll stay here," I whisper. "You try the board that's always creaking."

He nods. "I hope the builders didn't nail it down or we're going to need the toolbox."

"Where is it?"

"The cellar."

"Let's pray they're crap at their jobs, then."

He nods and darts over to the corner of the room where I saw Rosalind standing. I think of the crimson stains all over her and shudder. Levi pulls the thick rug back and starts to tap.

"Don't do that too much," I hiss. "It's drawing attention."

He nods and then gives a quiet exclamation. "Here it is." He looks up and grins. "Thank God for shoddy workmanship." He pushes the board and the room is so quiet that I hear the click as the board lifts up, showing a black gap underneath it. He looks up at me, his eyes bright in the light with excitement. "There's something in here wrapped in cloth."

Against my will, the same excitement stirs. This is something that has lain here a secret for well over a hundred years. "Lift it out carefully," I instruct. He pulls out a small object and lays it on the floor. Abandoning my station, I move and stand over him.

The object is wrapped in a shawl embroidered in lilac and pale mint green. I hold my breath as he unwraps the material, carefully opening the folds until a book is revealed. Made of white leather, it looks delicate and feminine, and Levi's hand looks huge as he opens the cover. Written on the fly page in small handwriting are the words, *"The Diary of Rosalind Evelyn Cooper."*

"Fuck," he whispers. "This is it."

"Okay, grab it and let's go, Levi," I whisper harshly. "We haven't got time to read it now."

My demand falls on deaf ears. He's flicking through the pages, and I recognise the fixed look he gets when he's reading.

"I just want to look," he whispers. "Shit, there are hundreds of entries."

"Well, let's read them at the nice modern hotel where the only danger we'll be in is eating too much room service or fucking each other to death," I hiss.

"How are we supposed to find anything in here?" he mutters, ignoring me and standing up. He moves towards the desk. "I'll get a pencil and we can mark the interesting passages and—"

It happens quickly. The smell of lily the valley enters the room and at the same time Levi lurches to one side as if he's been pushed and the book falls to the floor.

I dart over. "Are you okay?" I whisper urgently. "Are you hurt?"

He rubs his chest, staring past me. "Something pushed me. It fucking hurt and—"

His eyes go huge as he stares past me.

I whirl around, my own eyes bulging in shock. "What the hell?" I whisper.

The book lies open on the floor, the pages turning on their own. Slowly at first, but then faster and faster with odd pauses as if the air is looking for something.

"Blue, there is no draft in here," Levi whispers.

"I know."

"What's happening?"

"I think Rosalind is looking for the right passage and got fed up with how slow you were being." The book's pages stop moving. "Yay! I think she's found the correct passage now," I whisper.

We both move slowly towards the book, approaching it as if it's as toothy and terrifying as a fucking T-Rex. Levi kneels, and I hover at his back looking around wildly, but there's no sight of Rosalind or anything else. I wonder why I can't see her now.

"It's the last entry," he says slowly. "It takes up several pages."

"Read it out," I whisper. "I don't think we're meant to leave here before you do that."

"I'll try," he mutters. "The writing's quite small."

October 30th 1895

I know the truth. I cannot believe it. I do not want to believe it. But it is the truth.

I write these words hoping that no one will ever read them. I have not written in this diary for many years. I had no need when I was married and happy, but now I have to put down what has happened even if it is just a way of assuring myself that I am not going mad.

Last night my brother made me a drink of hot milk, announcing that I looked pale. As I've done for the last few months, I smiled and thanked him for being such a good brother to me. However, this time I didn't drink it.

My suspicions have been growing for a while because every night that he has done this I have slept like the dead and woken with great difficulty. At first I believed it to be a symptom of my illness, but gradually I have come to believe that Alfred is putting something into my drink to make me sleep.

I wondered at first whether it could be because he had found out how ill I was, and was, in his kindness, attempting to give me sweet dreams. However, a small part of me knew that this could never be true. Alfred and I were never close as children, a fact that I regarded at the time with relief because I saw what happened to the people who his attention fell on. I have always known him to be a cruel man.

I once saw him hurt an animal. It was a stray cat that used to came begging for scraps from the servants at the kitchen door. I used to wait to play with it because it was a charming little creature. I arrived late one day and saw Alfred attempting to drown it in the pond.

I ran at once to get my father, but Alfred told him a pretty story about fishing the poor scrap out of the water where it had fallen. My father believed him, and I was whipped by him that evening for telling lies. I was then forced to apologise to my brother. He accepted it with a lovely show of manners, but I saw his eyes and I knew then that I would not be forgiven.

My marriage and exit from my family home filled me with happiness and it was with great despair that circumstances forced me back into living with him. He has punished me in some small way every day since.

Curiosity, therefore, naturally filled me as to why he wanted me to sleep so heavily. That and a deep-seated knowledge that it could not be for anyone's good. So, tonight I accepted the drink and promptly poured it into a plant while he wasn't looking. I then pretended to become sleepy while watching as he became more and more agitated. It was as if he was impatient and eager, and it made a chill run down my back for some reason.

After ten minutes I excused myself. He kissed me on my forehead and wished me sweet dreams. When I got to my room, I didn't get undressed. Instead, I crawled fully clothed under the blankets in case he came to my room to check on me. I was right to do so because within half an hour I heard his heavy tread on the stairs and then came the light knock on my door. I closed my eyes and feigned sleep when I heard the door open. He gave a sigh of what sounded like satisfaction and then his tread descended.

I immediately jumped out of bed and seized my cloak. When the front door shut with a click, I ran down the stairs and stepped out into the night after him. York is different at night, as if it is given over to the dark. Tonight, however, no one was about which must be connected to the terrible murders that have been happening. I followed his heavy deliberate footsteps as he moved over the cobbles, a mist obscuring him from my gaze which was a blessing as it hid me from him too.

He moved with deliberation, as if he knew where he was going, and after a few twists and turns down side streets, I noticed that his pace had picked up. At times it was hard to keep up with him and oh, how I almost wish I hadn't. That I could have been spared my dark knowledge.

Instead, I kept pace until the area grew poorer and I almost lost him when one of my pains struck me. I leant against the brick wall for a few moments, riding out the pain and trying not to moan as the damp mist speckled my hair and cloak. Eventually the pain passed and I heard voices nearby, one of them being my brother. When I peeked around the corner, I found him talking to a young woman. Her clothing identified her as a loose woman, as did the way she was hanging from his arm and touching him indiscriminately.

At first a wave of relief hit me. He was consorting with prostitutes, not doing something worse. The idea of what he could have been doing has made me frightened this week because always I have that knowledge of how cruel Alfred really is beneath the charm. A knowledge buttressed by the fact that every time he has drugged my drink, the next morning's papers have brought news of another hideous murder.

I was about to leave and race back to the house so he wouldn't find me gone, but then everything seemed to happen at once. Alfred whirled the woman around so that her back rested against him. Something silver in his hand flashed in the weak light and in that split second her eyes found mine. At first I went to draw back, horrified that she would give me away, but then his hand came down in a swift motion and she gave a hideous gurgle that will haunt me until the end of days and sagged against him. Her eyes drained of life even as I watched and the blood on her throat fountained out in great spurts and poured down her chest. It made my breath catch and stars flash behind my eyes.

I leant there unable to look away as he lowered her to the ground. He reached for a bag that I only noticed at that point. Our father's old Gladstone bag. When he pulled out another knife and bent towards her eyes, I backed away.

I don't think I have run like that since I was a young girl, and I doubt I ever will again. I recall the burning in my chest and the coldness of the night as I flew down the lanes towards home as if the devil was after me. A laugh caught in my throat because why would he be? This devil knew where I lived. I was sharing a house with the Devil of York.

When I flew into the house I fell to the floor and spent a precious few minutes panting in a heap. Then I rallied and tried to work out what to do. My first thought was to go to the police, but much as I hated it, I had to dismiss it. I have too much knowledge of how charming and what a brilliant liar Alfred is, to trust that a group of men would see through him on the word of a woman.

For a long time I sat there until a desire to know more came over me. This was acerbated by the fact that Alfred had left the cellar door unlocked. That room has always been Alfred's sanctuary. He made it into his study when he bought the house and he has the only key. Mary and I are forbidden to enter, even to clean. He must have thought himself safe tonight with me drugged and abed.

I did not want to look, but I knew I must. At first it looked like any other room. Bookshelves lined three of the walls and his desk and huge leather chair were innocuous enough. But my attention was drawn to an opening in the far wall made possible by the removal of some bricks which lay in a neat stack next to the hole.

It took me a while to gather the courage to look in, but I knew it was my duty and steeled myself. What I saw will haunt me to my dying day which fortunately is not too far away now. Inside the cubby hole were shelves on which large jars stood. Each one was filled with murky liquid in which strange objects swam as if in a nightmare. I knew before I even examined one what I would find and what would be added tonight. That poor girl's eyes and who knows what else.

I backed away and flew up the stairs and then stood in the kitchen trying to gather my thoughts and steel my spine. It was only when I saw the glass of whisky on a tray on the kitchen table that the first glimmers of my plan came to me. Alfred always has a whisky at night and had obviously poured this in preparation for the terrible celebration he would have when he came home.

I stared at it for a long while until I remembered that Alfred would be back soon, and he must not find me awake. I raced up the stairs and once I was in bed I lay plotting. I heard the click of the front door half an hour later and his heavy steps on the staircase. They hesitated outside my door and I held my breath as I watched the handle move slightly, but he must have reconsidered, because after a few seconds his steps moved on, and I heard his bedroom door close. I lay awake for a long time turning over my thoughts, and by the time that dawn spread its light across the sky I knew my plan.

I am going to bide my time for a few days and lull him into a false sense of security. He will think himself safe and undetected and let his guard down accordingly.

Then one night I will lace Alfred's whisky with laudanum which the doctor has kindly given me for my pain. It will ensure that he is unconscious and cannot fight the difficult and dreadful thing I must do.

Once he is asleep, I will go downstairs one last time to the cellar and make sure that the tools of Alfred's terrible trade are hidden away securely behind the wall. I don't know why I am doing this, but my father's lessons about presenting a good face to the world have obviously run far deeper than I ever imagined.

I shall then retrieve the carving knife from the kitchen and climb the stairs to his room. I know it will be hard, but I must tell myself that I am ridding the world of a monster. That more poor young girls need not die because of his perverted desires.

Then I shall come back to my room. I cannot write anymore on that lest it rob me of my strength to do the right thing. I know that I am going to die soon, whether it be from this disease or from the hangman's noose when they imprison me for murdering my own brother. I cannot see that it matters either way. At least this way I will choose the method with which I leave this world and the noose will be of my own making. I shall not write in this diary again.

His voice fades away into silence as we both stare at each other.

"It's what we thought, Levi," I say slowly. "What a bloody brave woman she was."

He nods and then jerks. "Do you know what this means?"

I shake my head.

Levi gestures in excitement. "She says she went downstairs and made sure that everything was sealed away that could incriminate him."

"So?" I say and then gasp.

He nods frantically. "It means it's probably all still there." He grabs my arm. "Think about it, Blue. It's only Connor and us that have ever made this connection. No one's stayed here long, and the disruptions in the house seem to start and finish in the cellar. Remember the builder's tools being thrown around? It's like he didn't want anyone to uncover the stuff."

"He was protecting his kill mementos," I whisper. "And they're probably still there."

Levi nods. "The diary was here. They must be too, or we'd have heard about it." He bites his lip. "We have to go down there."

"*What?*" I say, and it's far too loud in the silence. "Are you fucking *mad?*"

"I think we're supposed to," he says stubbornly. "Everything has been leading towards this, and Rosalind helping us find the diary is the last step. Maybe this is the way to stop him."

"No," I say harshly. "No fucking way, Levi. This is so fucking dangerous and—"

A scream echoes through the house.

"What the hell is that?" Levi shouts, jumping to his feet, his eyes wild. "What is it?"

I put my hands over my ears, but the screams go on and on, harsh and grating and seeming to make the house shake. "Oh shit, make it stop," I yell.

The screaming stops so abruptly that it's disorientating, and my ears are ringing when I lower my hands. I open my mouth to say something, but another horrific noise erupts—a thick gurgling followed by choking.

"That sounds like…"

Levi nods grimly. "Like someone gargling mouthwash." He pauses. "Or maybe just having their throat cut."

"We have to go," I say just as the door flies open, banging against the wall like a thunderclap. "*Now*," I add harshly.

He nods, his eyes wide. He crouches to grab the diary, thrusting it into his coat pocket before we fly out of the studio and down the stairs. And into hell.

"Oh my God," I shout.

The gargling noise gets louder and louder. Glass shatters as the pictures fall from the walls and smash against the floor.

"Keep moving," I shout at Levi.

He's pointing at the red fluid seeping out of the holes where the picture nails were. It slides down the walls to the floor where it puddles and spreads, the air thickening with the scent of copper.

We race past the front bedroom, and this time it's me who stops to stare in disbelief.

Rosalind's body hangs from the ceiling light fixture, her dress drenched in red and her hands swinging gently with the movement. She raises her head and looks at me, her face black and her tongue protruding. A shrill noise echoes through the room. Levi shakes me, and I realise that I'm screaming.

"Keep moving," he shouts. "We need to get out."

Grabbing my hand, Levi pounds down the stairs and runs flat out to the front door.

"Thank God," I pant. "Open it." He fumbles with the handle, and I grip his shoulder, sending a frantic glance over my shoulder. "What are you doing?" I hiss. "Open the fucking door."

"I can't." He pulls frantically at the door, but it doesn't move. "Blue, it's locked. What shall we do? We can't get out this way."

Suddenly the noise stops, silence descending like a theatre curtain. Swift and heavy.

I turn to see the cellar door swinging slowly open.

I backpedal so fast into Levi that he sways with the impact. "What the fuck?" he breathes.

I'm sure his arm is hurting where I'm grabbing it, but I can't bring myself to let go.

"I think that's an invitation," I whisper.

Our gazes are fixed on that door. Listening for those heavy, awful footsteps to come up the stairs. Listening for that evil chuckle to erupt from the darkness. Waiting for Alfred to appear.

Nothing happens. The door stays open, taunting us, and the house is full of a heavy, waiting silence.

Levi breathes in slowly, and I copy him, feeling a modicum of calm enter me.

"There's no way out," he whispers, resignation heavy in his voice. "We're going to have to do this."

"I'm sorry."

He looks blank. "Why?"

"Because I can't do anything to help."

"You're here, aren't you?" he says softly. "With me?"

I nod.

"Then what else can you do, love?"

I want to dwell on the endearment, but there's no time. "I wish we were at the hotel eating room service, Levi," I whisper. "But I'd still rather be here with you than anywhere else on earth."

He kisses me. It's fast, but the darkness lifts a little and perfume fills the air around us, blending gruesomely with the scent of blood.

"Okay," he whispers. "Let's do this." He leans closer. "We'll get in and find the hidey-hole. From her description, it sounds like it's on the far wall. We'll empty it and see what happens."

"I've had better propositions," I say sadly and squeeze his arm. "But not from better people." An idea occurs to me. "Oh, wait here."

I dart into the kitchen and open and shut the cupboards, rummaging through them and letting the contents spill out.

"Are you *baking* something?" he hisses in an outraged whisper. "What are you *doing*?"

"Just looking for—"

I spy what I need with a hiss of jubilation, stuff it into my coat pocket, and go back to Levi.

"Okay now, Blue? Or do you have some ironing to do?"

I pinch him. "Facing possible death is not the time for sarcasm." I look at the door and any humour dies. "Let's do this," I say slowly. As he moves, I grab his arm. "Levi, I—"

He leans in to kiss my lips softly. "Me too, Blue. Me too."

Then he lets me go and moves purposefully to the cellar door, with me hanging on to his coat with a death grip.

The actual cellar is a bit of an anti-climax. Nothing sinister is there. Nothing at all.

The room is lit by the dingy glow of a single lightbulb. Boxes are stacked against one wall and the pile of tools are set neatly in the corner. Apart from that, it's just a large whitewashed room with a cement floor. I shoot Levi a glance.

He nods grimly. "Let's hope she kept it sealed in the wall and didn't have a mad half hour and bury it under the fucking floor. Otherwise we might have to ring Mr Harrison, the builder, and I'm pretty sure my bill will go up." He looks round the room. "Do you feel anything?" he whispers.

"Nothing. I don't understand it. Where is he, Levi? I thought he'd be prowling around down here." I bite my lip. "Let's find the stuff. Where did you think it would be?"

He strides to the back wall. "There's a patch over here that's slightly rougher and darker than the other bits. I noticed it ages ago." He points to it.

I bend to take a closer look. "The wall is crumbly, but the bricks seem pretty solid. How will you get in?" I ask.

"Sledgehammer."

"Oh my God, that'll make such a mess."

"At the moment I don't care," Levi says shortly. He walks over to the pile of tools and starts sorting through them.

The lightbulb flickers, and we freeze.

"Blue?" he says questioningly.

I look around wildly. There's still nothing here. It's like a vacuum with no sound. "Nothing yet," I say, making my voice very steady. "But hurry up anyway," I add in the same calm voice.

He straightens, carrying a sledgehammer.

"And how are you intending to do that with one arm?" I shake my head. "Give it to me. I'll do it."

There's a pop and the bulb explodes. We both cry out, and I raise my hands to shield my eyes from the shards.

"Blue," Levi says urgently. I open my eyes to find him standing in front of me, a dim shadow in the light coming from the stairs. "I'll do it," he says grimly. I open my mouth to protest, but he shakes his head. "I think you need to keep an eye out. That seems much more important."

The atmosphere is changing, the scent of burning filling my nostrils. "He's here," I say quietly.

He holds the sledgehammer low like a lump hammer and then heaves it at the wall. There's a crack and dust rains down, and we both jump as the cellar door slams shut.

"Shit." I stumble up the stairs to try the door. "It's locked," I call out. "Fuck, it's so dark. I can't see anything."

"Close your eyes for a few seconds," he says calmly. "You'll see a bit better when you open them. Then come down here. There's a torch app on my phone. You can hold it steady so I can see what I'm doing."

I swallow hard and shut my eyes. The dark is absolute. Like a weight bearing down on my eyelids. I clench my fists. Anything could be standing beside me right now and I'd be totally blind to the threat. But Levi told me to do it, so I stay still.

The time I spend with my eyes closed in that cold cellar might not be measured by much in the passage of actual time, but to me it's eternal. However, when I open them, I can see dimly. I look immediately to Levi to find him watching me, a faint light emanating from the phone in his hand. He gives me a half smile and strength floods through me.

"Okay," I say, and my voice at least sounds calm. "Let's do this." I descend the stairs carefully, ready any minute for a shove that doesn't come. However, the whole atmosphere of the room feels threatening now.

I pause as I get to him. "I can hear breathing. Can you?" I whisper.

He shakes his head and hands me his phone. My fingers are trembling, so I hold it with both hands to keep the light steady.

He swings at the wall again and again, grunting with the effort. He's clearly in pain.

"Your arm, Levi," I whisper.

"Never mind that," he returns.

There's a presence behind me, silent and still. "Oh my God, he's here," I breathe.

Levi stops, and I shake my head. "Keep going," I say fervently. "It's our only chance."

He swings at the wall again.

The presence I'd sensed glides closer, flickering into the figure of a man. Alfred.

He's outlined by a murky yellow light, illuminating the room enough for me to see more details. His lips are very thin and his eyes shine with a cruel light. He's stout, with muttonchop whiskers, and wearing a Victorian-looking suit and a hat. He paces around me, like a shark scenting blood in the water. I swallow hard.

Levi levels the sledgehammer at the wall again and grunts in satisfaction as bricks start to rain down onto the floor. He repeats the action again and again, bricks creating a pile of rubble on the floor.

Alfred makes a hissing noise, his face contorting into a rictus of rage. He motions with his hands and something flies through the air.

"Shit!" Levi shouts as a brick hits him on the arm.

I take a step towards him and then remember. "Keep going," I shout. "I've got something."

245

He looks over his shoulder. "What is it?"

I put the phone down on a pile of bricks so the dim light illuminates us. Then I reach in my pocket for the tube and show it to him as I fumble with the top.

"*Salt,*" he says indignantly, his voice rising. "Are you going to fucking cook him?"

I shake my head, flipping the top off. "I saw it on *Supernatural.* Dean and Sam shoot it at ghosts."

"Oh well, by all means let's pin our survival on fictional characters in a TV programme."

I throw the salt at Alfred as hard as I can. It seems to sink into him and for a second he looks almost corporeal. Then there's a horrible scream, and he disintegrates into a writhing shadow.

"It works," I shout. "That's fucking *epic.*"

"It's Himalayan pink sea salt," Levi says somewhat sniffily.

"I don't care whether it was ground on the inner thighs of virgins from the land of the faeries. It worked." Alfred's shadow starts to slowly reform in front of my eyes. "Although not for long. Keep hammering," I shout. "I've only got the one tube."

While I throw salt, he returns to his task, swinging the hammer with one hand, his casted arm steadying himself awkwardly. More bricks come loose and he exclaims in triumph. "I can see something," he mutters.

I look down at my salt tube. "Hurry up," I hiss. "There's not much left."

He swings the hammer again and a large portion of the wall collapses, bringing with it a jumble of objects. Alfred screams, loud and enraged.

Levi scrambles frantically through the rubble, sorting through objects. He tosses something in my direction. A black leather Gladstone bag. It's battered and covered in dust.

"Look in that," he shouts, dodging a hammer that flies through the air at him. He's not so lucky with the next—a tool hits him on the side of his head.

"Oh shit," I cry. "He got you. You're bleeding." Blood streams down his face.

I lurch towards him, but he waves me off.

"Ignore it, Blue. I'm fine. Look in the bag."

I fumble with the clasp and the bag falls open. Looking inside, I gag and cringe. "Fuck!"

"What is it?" he shouts as he pulls out some jars from the rubble.

"Knives and a saw. Oh my God, Levi, they've still got blood and flesh on them. What are those jars?"

I grab the phone and aim the light at the jar he holds up. We peer at its murky contents. And we both recoil as if synchronised. An eyeball swims out of the liquid and bumps against the glass.

"Oh my God," Levi moans. "There's a fucking ear in here too. What is this?"

"Rosalind guessed it," I mutter. "These are the jars with all the missing bits from the victims. Emily lost her eyes and her heart."

Alfred's shape paces nearby. The sense of rage and hate filling the air is overwhelming.

His eyes seem to glow in the light as he stares at me. My throat catches on something, and I cough. I try to swallow but the object clogging my throat gets bigger and I gag, panic swiping its claws down my back.

"You okay? What is it?"

The phone drops from my hands and sends a jagged beam of light upwards. I bend over, hacking and choking but the object won't move, my throat swelling around the obstruction.

"Can't breathe," I gasp.

I raise my hands to my neck, heaving and gagging. The room whirls around me as sparks bloom in my vision. I claw at my throat again, feeling the skin tear under my fingers as I try to get air.

"Blue," Levi screams. "Blue, breathe."

I choke, trying to obey him as he reaches for me.

Alfred appears beside us, as solid as Levi and me, his face contorted with hate. Alfred makes a gesture, and Levi rebounds off me as if he's been shoved. His arms windmill as he staggers back and, losing his footing, he falls onto the rubble.

Dust billows up in a huge cloud, and Levi cries out in pain as he rolls to the ground on his bad arm.

The jars ascend in slow motion. Then they fly and whirl before smashing onto the ground in the centre of the cellar, splashing us with things I don't want to think about.

Alfred bellows.

The obstruction in my throat shifts. I cough and gag until something flies out and lands on the ground in front of me. To my horror, it's a woman's crocheted glove, tiny and worn and bloodstained.

Did this belong to one of the victims? I taste something unspeakably vile and coppery in my mouth. I hawk and spit into the dust.

Dust from the rubble billows. I scramble through it and throw myself next to Levi. He grabs me tightly with one arm. His cast is ripped, hanging by his side at a funny angle.

"You okay? Your poor arm, Levi," I whisper hoarsely, my words falling over themselves and tangling in my throat.

"I'm alright. Where is he?" He gulps. "Oh God, I can see him. He's just staring at us, Blue."

Alfred smiles wickedly. All is still as if we've been suspended in motion. I look wildly around for a weapon, a tool, something to help us, but there's nothing. The tube of salt lies on the floor with the last granules scattered around.

I fumble for Levi's hand and clutch it tight. "Levi," I whisper. "I'm sorry."

"I don't want you to *ever* apologise to me again," he says softly.

He hugs me hard as we wait for Alfred. *This is it.*

The spirit watches us with a gloating expression on his face. He moves and I cringe, gripping Levi and pressing my head to his shoulder. He murmurs something, an instruction to hide my eyes.

The air shifts, and Alfred's expression changes to one I've never seen on him before—fear. I inhale sharply. Then slowly, like gas escaping, shadows move and seep out of the hole in the wall.

They twine around the rubble, rubbing against the broken jars before rising to hover in the air. The shadows flicker and melt into the shapes of five women. They surround Alfred. Grey and faint though they are, I can still pick out the details of their dresses and hairstyles. They stand silently watching Alfred as if waiting for something.

A low humming vibrates through the room. A wind picks up out of nowhere, blowing my hair back and sending dust clouds billowing and glittering into the air.

Alfred looks wildly around and another figure metamorphosizes. It's Rosalind, and she stands before him in full colour, as real-looking as me and Levi.

She stares at her brother and he grimaces, lifting a hand almost unconsciously to his throat. She begins to pace in a wide circle, the silent women joining her. Alfred is at the circle's centre. As Rosalind walks, a thin, sparkling line appears at her feet.

The humming gets louder, and suddenly the shadowy women start to advance, moving slowly but without hesitation. The smell of lily of the valley and blood comes to me, and I fling myself onto Levi as he rolls onto his back with a groan of pain.

"What's happening?" he shouts above the rising noise.

I shield his face with my body. Alfred screams, and the women's figures splinter and blow apart only to reform around him. The screaming intensifies as they begin to tear him apart. He vanishes underneath their writhing shapes.

"What's happening?" Levi says.

"Don't look at them, Marion!" I shout.

"What the fuck? Are you quoting *Indiana Jones* at me?" he yells, and he sounds so cross and indignant that, incredibly, I feel laughter rise in me.

It dies as I watch the women shred Alfred, bits of him flying into the air like papery cinders rising from a fire. All the while, the figure of Rosalind paces around the circle like a sentinel.

Alfred gives one last desperate scream as if he's being dragged to hell. By his balls.

Then everything falls silent. His remains sparkle in the air before twisting and falling to the ground, winking out like sparks from a firework.

I swallow hard as one of the shadows comes towards me. When she gets closer, I can see that it's Emily. She has her eyes back and the gaping hole in her chest has vanished.

"Thank you." It's so faint that it's like a whisper in the air.

I smile at her.

She raises her head as if scenting something. A sudden wind blows through the cellar, bringing with it the sweet smell of rain on dry earth. Emily and the other shadowy figures splinter and disappear, letting the breeze bear them away.

Silence descends, the only sound our panting breaths. Eventually, I roll off Levi and onto my back.

"Is it done?" he asks.

I lift my head and look around, gauging the atmosphere with my senses.

The cellar is empty again. Only the dust and bricks and various items of murderous equipment hint at what just happened. The air is still and warm.

"It's done," I say, lowering my head to his chest and feeling his arm pull me closer.

"Holy shit," he mutters.

Incredibly, I laugh. "You can say that again."

He looks over at the Gladstone bag and the smashed jars and the squishy horrible things in red water that I'm trying really hard not to look at.

"Blue, if I didn't suspect that I've broken my arm again, I'd arm wrestle you for the chance not to tell the police that we've knocked a wall down in my cellar and inadvertently managed to solve a famous historical murder."

"I have got very agile elbows, so I'd probably have won anyway," I say modestly.

He snorts.

I nudge him. "Look on the bright side. We're both gay, so ninety percent of the coppers attending the scene will think we were just having a sex party."

His laughter is loud in the silence. "We should really ring someone, though," he finally says.

I snuggle closer. "Later. Let's just lie here a bit longer and cherish the fact that it's finally over." I feel the stiffness in his body and look up. "You alright?"

He sits, wincing at the movement, and looks at me. "It's really over?"

I nod. "Alfred's gone and I think the women are at peace now."

"Maybe they couldn't rest until we uncovered the jars."

"Maybe."

My hand falls away from Levi. Realisation hits suddenly and with the force of a punch. There's no longer a reason for us to be together. As horrible as the events have been, they've also been sort of wonderful—they've brought me and Levi together—and I don't want to let him go.

He looks deeply into my eyes, and I don't know what he sees. Probably everything. He has an unnerving ability to pluck my emotions from thin air.

Finally, a smile spreads slowly over his face.

"Maybe we'd better stick close though, Blue," he says huskily. "You know, just in case."

My answering smile is a face-splitter. "Just in case," I say demurely and then spoil it by hugging him tight and kissing him lustily.

Finally, he pulls back. "Could be with me for a long time. You okay with that?"

I look into his eyes and run my finger down that gorgeous face. "I'm not doing anything special. I've got the time. Have you?"

EPILOGUE

Five Months Later

Blue

I gather my group around me, noticing with satisfaction the large number. I don't need to do the ghost tour anymore because I now have a job, but it's very satisfactory to walk past my ex, Hugh, and mentally stick two fingers up at him. Okay, sometimes I do actually stick two fingers up at him.

"So, this is the Murder House," I say in a carrying voice. "The home of the notorious Devil of York. We stopped at the scene of his last crime, but this was his home and where his dreadful career was brought to a stop when his life was ended by his sister. She had learnt of his evil ways and, knowing the police wouldn't believe her, she courageously ended his life, thus saving countless women from a dire end." I say this last bit slightly louder in case Rosalind is listening. She deserves the credit.

"Is it true that you found eyeballs in the cellar?" comes a voice from the back.

I take off my hat and flourish it. "There were indeed eyeballs. Buried in a wall along with a lot of other very unpleasant body parts and the man's murder bag."

"And *you* found them?" the voice carries on. I think it's the very earnest young man who's followed every word I've spoken tonight quite closely, as if he expects I'll test him at the tour's end.

"It was me." The group sighs and moves closer. "Well, me and my boyfriend," I add quickly. "I suppose he had a bit of a hand in discovering it too."

At that point the kitchen window shoots up and several of the women shriek. The figure of my boyfriend appears in the window wearing jeans, a blue plaid shirt, and a slightly sardonic expression.

"Oh, really?" he says silkily. "A *bit* of a hand, eh?"

I smile up at him. It's impossible not to when he looks so handsome. "Well, you had broken your arm again, babe."

He shakes his head. "You forgot your coffee." Through the open window, he passes me the travel mug he bought me a few weeks ago that says *What would Dean do?* on the side.

"Thank you, boo," I say cheerfully.

He grimaces. "For the five hundredth time, please don't call me that."

"Any questions?" I ask, evading the subject. "Me and my boo are here for you. *Exclusively and not available on any of the other ghost tours,*" I emphasise.

Levi snorts.

A few people put up their hands, and together Levi and I deal with them like a team. Eventually, the questions, which mainly seem to be about which body parts were in the wall, die out.

"Well, we should be moving on," I say.

Levi sags with relief. It makes me want to smile.

An elderly lady steps forward. "Is this the house where you see naked men?" she demands querulously. "My sister came a few months ago and she saw one."

I can actually see Levi blush. He's so adorable.

"Sometimes," I say to her, starting to usher the group along. "But he'll only appear if you're pure of heart and mind."

I turn back to wave at Levi. He's standing with his arms folded.

"Well, we must be off, folks. There's more murder and mayhem ahead of us. Say goodnight to my boo."

He waves as the group obediently mumble goodbyes, and I blow him a kiss.

I glance up and see the figure of Rosalind in the front bedroom window. No one in the group realises that they've missed a genuine real-life ghost, and I don't tell them. It's our secret. She's staring out at us with an impenetrable expression on her face.

I blink and she's gone. By now Levi has closed the kitchen window and the blind, but I know he's there still, and it makes me feel funny in a good sort of way. Like it's my home I'm looking at, even though it's not. *He's* my home.

I moved out of the house once the problems had been sorted. He argued against it at the time, wanting me to stay, but even though I was flattered, I stuck to my guns and took the flat over the bookshop that Tom had offered me.

It's small, with a kitchen that looks like it was last renovated in the fifties. It's freezing in winter and apparently it'll be boiling in the summer, but the windows look out on the narrow lane and if I crane my neck I can see the Minster.

It's a lane that's filled with both the living and the dead. Ghosts of past booksellers are always around, like the man who wanders the street in the morning with his head in a book. And not literally either, which is a relief after our last experience with body parts. The ghosts on my lane seem to be happy ghosts, which I put down to their love of reading.

In the flat I'm safe, and when I lie in bed and reach out to touch the walls on either side of my bed it feels like I'm in a nest all of my own. And something in me thrills that it's just me in there. After all the years of sharing breathing space with so many strangers, the fact that I can sit there in isolation is special. I'll curl up on the ancient sofa in the lounge listening to the sounds of people outside and cherishing the quiet around me.

I'm pretty sure that Levi believes I'm scared of having a relationship after being alone and independent for so long, but the truth is that I'm just protective.

I'm protective of him and what we're building together. Moving too quickly might damage that. I see him clearly and so do other men. He's clever and funny and bloody gorgeous, but he's also mine and I don't want that ever to stop. He's the first thing in my life that's ever belonged just to me and I hoard that to myself. He's the first thing I've ever dared to ask for.

We see each other every day and usually end up in the same bed together, whether it's at his or mine. Let's face it, it's more often at his. I'm not stupid. His house is gorgeous and two people fit comfortably in his bed without risking suffocation. However, he seems to find my flat charming and I don't complain when we have to snuggle tight.

My group and I finally move off down the lane, the Minster a bright light ahead of us.

I pull up my collar against the cold wind which persists even though it's spring. It's amazing how much has changed in my life.

A year ago at the end of a tour, I would have been dreading the cold, thinking of the damp squat I was heading home to. My life was dreary and dark and filled with so much fear, but I only recognise that now because of its absence. Now, I'm learning to look forward to a future rather than living firmly in the present.

I've learnt that I like certain things about the cold weather. I like walking with Levi, one hand around his waist as his arm rests comfortingly over my shoulder. I like the fact that I've learnt to cook stews and how good they taste in a warm room that smells of apple from the log fire and wild fig from the candles he buys at a little shop around the corner.

But most of all, I like it because I know that at the end of the night I'll be able to curl up in bed with Levi. He'll let me put my cold feet on him, and we'll talk and laugh about the things that have happened in the day. He'll listen to me with those warm dark eyes of his intent on me as if I'm somehow fascinating to him. Then he'll draw me to him or I'll move over him and we'll fuck. It's so much more now, even though I'm still wary of naming it.

When we're spent, he'll fall asleep, and I'll curl myself around him, feeling his warmth seem to move into my body. I'll lay my head on his chest, listening to his heartbeat. And then I'll be able to identify what I'm feeling, even though I've never in my life felt it before.

I think it might be happiness.

*L*evi

It's lunchtime when I come down the stairs. Going into the kitchen, I whistle as I grab my keys and the sandwiches I made earlier. Then I pause. The kitchen is as neat and tidy and clean as an operating theatre, and I certainly didn't leave it that way this morning.

I bite my lip. "Erm, thank you," I say out loud, and if my voice is slightly high then at least my boyfriend isn't around to take the piss. "Thank you for clearing up, Rosalind," I say. "It was very good of you." I nod to emphasise my point.

There's no reply, and I still don't see her, but a light drift of lily of the valley swirls around me and the kitchen cools slightly—things that always happen when she's around.

Blue wasn't quite right in the cellar when he said everyone had gone. Rosalind never moved on. We've never heard from Alfred again. and Blue says that he never sees his last victim anymore. But somehow, and for some reason, Rosalind is still here. Maybe it's because she sees this as her house. Maybe she sees it as her due for what she went through. But here she stays.

I've never seen her, but Blue has. He says she seems content. I'd replied that surely it's a good mood for someone who once had a predilection for letting a cutthroat razor do her thinking for her, but he'd just laughed as if I was joking. News flash. I wasn't.

Instead of being landed with a traditional ghost that walks the corridors and endlessly drags dead bodies about, we've ended up with someone who seems rather particular about how the house is being kept. If we're messy, we soon know about it. Like the other night when the covers were pulled off us at two in the morning, and she banged the doors on the wardrobe until we got up and cleaned the bedroom.

It's rather like having a homicidal Kim Woodburn living with us, but as Blue thinks it's funny, I've learnt just to let go and accept it.

Still, I was brought up to be polite so, as I grab my coat and my sketchbook, I tip my head respectfully. "I'm just going out, Miss Rosalind. Be back soon."

The perfume swirls around me again and then it's gone as quickly as if it was sucked out by a vent.

I shake my head and let myself out of my house, pausing to look up at it affectionately. It has such a good feeling about it now that Alfred is gone. It feels warm and light and welcoming. Although some of that must come from me and Blue.

I'm so happy with him. He's utterly unlike anyone I ever went for before, but somehow he's everything I need. Friend, partner in crime, sounding board, and lover. I've never had all that in one person before, and it's why I love him.

We haven't said the words yet. I don't know whether he ever will. I don't even know whether he's realised that he loves me, but I know it. It's written over every inch of him in the way he looks after me, the way he strokes my chest at night and whispers secrets into my skin that I can't hear. I don't need the words, when I have him.

I look up at the house again. I do need him to live with me eventually, but not until he's ready, and that isn't now. Waving to Mrs Petersham who lives in the big house, I set off up the lane towards the Dean's Park.

Spring is in the air. Although it's still very cold, the tulips and daffodils are starting to poke their heads bravely above the ground, offering bright splashes of colour amongst the trees. A family is sitting on one of the benches watching their children run along the grass, and I can hear the familiar clattering and banging as the stonemasons work on the Minster. It's a cheerful and busy sound.

I settle on what we now think of as our bench which is next to the old war memorial. Stretching my legs out, I start to sketch while I wait for Blue. I quickly become absorbed, and although not much pulls me from my work while I'm in it, Blue still manages it ably. A short time later, I feel a tickle on my senses, and when I look up, he's coming towards me. Dressed in jeans, combat boots, and a forest-green jumper with a beanie covering his shock of dirty-blond hair, he looks a world away from the boy I first met.

He still has the same restless eyes that quite obviously see more than anyone else's do. But now he's happy and sleek and satisfied, his expression clear and content. He's filled out due to eating regular meals, but it's turned to muscle from when he runs with me or the yoga he's discovered that he loves. I love it too, mainly because he's now fantastically bendy like he's made of plasticine.

He smiles as he gets close and it does things to my stomach—happy things like how he looks at me. Warm and intimate as if, unseen by the world, we have our very own tightknit unit.

"Brought some fresh doughnuts for pudding," he says, holding up a paper bag from the bakery near the shop.

I smile. "We'll have to fit in a run tonight."

He bends to kiss me before sitting down. His lips are warm and soft and he sucks gently on my bottom lip before tangling his tongue with mine. I feel his lip ring against my mouth, the metal warmed from his lips. He pulls back, and I blink to clear my eyes. As is his custom now, he runs one finger gently down my face over the slight scar at my temple. It's the only physical memento we have from that horrible night.

"I don't need to run anywhere. I've been moving boxes all morning. Tom's had me hopping." His tone is affectionate.

I don't think I'll ever understand his and Tom's bond. It's born of things that I can never and will never understand. But I know how happy it makes Blue to have Tom in his corner advising him, and I've grown to love the cantankerous old man myself. I suppose I should. He's more than likely a harbinger of what Blue will become.

It's probably a good job he has Tom, because I can sense that Blue's abilities are growing along with his confidence. Sometimes I think his confidence has grown a little too fast, but I haven't said anything yet. I just watch and wait because something tells me that he'll need me again. Something will be waiting around the corner for Blue. It's inevitable, but all I can do is be here for him and protect him as best I can. And maybe that will be enough, because God knows I love him so.

"What are you drawing?" he asks.

I point at the gnarled old tree in front of me. "That. It looks like a demon is pulling its way out of the trunk. Like it's an exit from Hell."

He looks at it seriously. Anyone else would have laughed at the fanciful idea. Mason certainly would have. Blue, however, just looks thoughtful.

"I think it would have longer arms," he finally says judiciously. "If you were clawing your way out of Hell, you'd certainly look like it had been arm day at the gym." He nudges me. "I only want the best monsters for Blue, Psychic Detective, to fight."

I smile. I'd started drawing Blue as a whimsical gesture born of my fascination with him. Gradually I'd added monsters and spooks for him to fight and dreamed up cases he could investigate in York. When my agent saw it, she got very excited and promptly sold the concept to a newspaper. It became almost a cult thing overnight, and now every day my inbox is full of people wanting more Blue, to the extent that a publisher has commissioned a graphic novel. I haven't told Blue yet, but I will, and he'll celebrate with me as if it was his own triumph because he has the most generous nature of anyone I've ever met.

I draw busily for a few seconds. "Better?"

He nods. "Much. Now, let's eat while I tell you about what Tom said to a customer today."

So we eat and we talk and I laugh and watch his mobile, clever face with that wicked curling smile, and I hoard the images so I can draw them at some point. However, he seems almost edgy today even while he chatters brightly. Like his mind is far away, focusing on something only he can see.

"You alright?" I finally ask when he comes back from putting the rubbish in a bin.

"Of course," he says, shooting me a quick glance and scratching at a hole on his jeans, working his fingernails through the small tear.

I fold my arms. "What's the matter?" I ask. Normally, he isn't a huge fidgeter.

He bites his lip, and I'm suddenly worried.

"What is it, lovey?"

He looks up, startled, and I flush slightly. I know I love him, so the endearment came off my tongue easily, but it must seem strange to him. I watch as his eyes brighten, and he blows out a long breath.

"Blue?"

He says something quickly then. The words flood out and seem to merge into one, so what I hear is, *"Iloveyousomuchallthetimeloveyou."*

It takes me a long second to understand what he's said, but then my whole body seems to wash hot and cold. "What did you say?" I ask breathlessly.

He grimaces as if I'm torturing him. "Surely you heard?" he says snappily.

I smile. "I think I did, but it was the longest word known to man." I pause. "Unless the man is Welsh, in which case well done on the vowels."

"Twat," he says affectionately. He draws in a long breath. "I love you," he says as if steeling himself to make a speech on the guillotine. "So much," he adds forcefully as if I might be thinking that it's just a little bit. I open my mouth to speak, but he carries on fiercely. "I know I'm not Mason. I'm not educated and well dressed. My hair is messy, my clothes are the same, and although I read a lot, I'll never have school smarts like your ex. I'll never go to uni." I open my mouth again, but he shakes his head. "I don't need you to reassure me." He pats his chest. "I know all the reasons I should be wrong for you in here." He nods thoughtfully. "But I also know in here that I'm somehow just right for you. That I can make you happy, and you already do that for me. I've never had anything that was just mine before." He glares at me, and it's so adorable. "So, I just needed you to know, and let's not *ever* talk about it again."

He sits back and silence reigns for a few seconds. "Am I allowed to talk now?" I say slowly.

He gives a choked sound and waves his hand rather regally.

"I love you too," I say and feel the happiness unfold in me. "I can't believe you said it first. I thought you never would, but I was okay with that because I can say it often enough for both of us."

"You love me?" he says rather loudly and startles a pigeon. The bird gives him an indignant look and flies off, but his attention is on me. "Why?"

"Why do I love you?"

He nods.

"Well, because you're Blue. You're fierce and funny and kind and loyal. And although you're full of more prickles than a thistle, I sort of think of you as *my* thistle. Shit, that's so lame. I can think of much better things."

"Don't." He looks around and, seeing that the park is empty now, he scrambles onto my lap and kisses me fiercely. "You really love me?" he asks wonderingly.

I swallow the lump in my throat. "So much."

His forehead wrinkles and he plays with a strand of my hair. "Can I tell you a secret?"

I nod solemnly. "Always."

"It frightens me a bit how much I feel," he whispers. "I never wanted to love anyone, and I'm pretty positive I'm going to be shit at it."

I smile and tighten my grip. "It doesn't matter. As long as we treat each other right, there's room for error."

"I don't want to live together yet though," he says quickly, watching me closely for any sign of upset. "I want to go out and court or whatever the fuck Tom says we're doing. I don't want too much too soon because it frightens me how much I feel already. What if it goes wrong, and I lose you?"

"I don't know the future," I say slowly. "I can't see that any more than I can see Rosalind. But just as I know that she's there, I also know that it's going to be fine, and when it isn't, it'll still be okay, because we'll be together."

"How do you know that?" he asks curiously.

I want to tell him that it's in the way he's nestled close to me now despite his fears. The way he holds my hand, the soft way he kisses me last thing at night. Even in the way he tells me his problems openly and the way he tries to solve mine so fiercely. As if, at my birth, the fairies appointed a once-blue-haired and still wickedly smiling man as my guardian.

But I can't tell him that, so instead I pull him close on my lap in the empty park, and I inhale the scent of peaches and squeeze him for a moment.

"I just know," I say solemnly.

While another man might argue and worry, he doesn't. Instead, he curls into me with his customary slightly sceptical expression, and I tighten my grip around The Mysterious and Amazing Blue Billings.

Thank you for reading. If you'd like to be the first to know about my book releases and have access to extra content, you can sign up for my newsletter here

THANK YOU

My husband. Thank you for reading this story first and convincing me to show other people. If it wasn't for you, there wouldn't be a Blue and Levi. But that's appropriate because I wouldn't be writing at all if you hadn't persuaded me to give it a go and supported me so much.

My boys. I'm immensely proud of both of you and continually astonished that I had a small hand in you turning out so well.

Hailey. One of my best friends. Thank you for all your support and here's to London again. This time I'll wear trainers!

Edie. Thank you so much for doing an amazing proofreading job again and for being such a good friend.

Leslie, Courtney, and everyone at LesCourt Author Services. I couldn't do it without you.

The members of my Facebook readers' group, Lily's Snark Squad. I love my time spent in there.

To all the bloggers who spend their valuable time reading, reviewing and promoting the books. Also, the readers who liven up my day with their messages and photos and book recommendations. I love being a part of this community, so thank you.

Lastly thanks to you, for taking a chance on this book. I hope you enjoyed reading it as much as I enjoyed writing it.

I never knew until I wrote my first book how important reviews are. So if you have time, please consider leaving a review on Amazon or Goodreads or any other review sites. I can promise you that I value all of them.

CONTACT ME

Website: www.lilymortonauthor.com
This has lots of information and fun features, including some extra short stories.

If you fancy hearing the latest news and interacting with other readers do head over and join my Facebook group. It's a fun group and I share all the latest news about my books there as well as some exclusive short stories.
www.facebook.com/groups/SnarkSquad/

I'd love to hear from you, so if you want to say hello or have any questions, please contact me and I'll get back to you:
Email: lilymorton1@outlook.com

ALSO BY LILY MORTON

Mixed Messages Series

Rule Breaker

Deal Maker

Risk Taker

Finding Home Series

Oz

Milo

Gideon

Close Proximity Series

Best Man

Black & Blue Series

The Mysterious and Amazing Blue Billings

Other Books

The Summer of Us

Short Stories

3 Dates

Best Love

Made in the USA
Las Vegas, NV
18 November 2022

59752243R00163